380110 50 83466 5

KU-369-339

La faiblesse est le seul défaut que l'on ne saurait corriger.
(Weakness is the only fault we don't know how to correct.)
— François, duc de La Rochefoucauld, *Maximes*, No. 130.

HIGHLAND
LIBRARIES

WITHDRAWN

PRESENTED BY:

Cape Breton Regional
Library Service

FOR REFERENCE ONLY

Copyright © 2015 A. J. B. Johnston

This book is a work of fiction and as such contains deliberate or accidental historical or geographical inaccuracies. The characters, places and events depicted are either products of the author's imagination or are real historical figures but are used here in a fictional context. Any resemblance to living persons is purely coincidental.

All rights reserved. No part of this work may be reproduced or used in any form or by any means, electronic or mechanical, including photocopying, recording or any information storage or retrieval system, without the prior written permission of the publisher. Cape Breton University Press recognizes fair use exceptions. Responsibility for the opinions, research and the permissions obtained for this publication rest with the author.

Cape Breton University Press recognizes the support of the Canada Council for the Arts, Block Grant program, and the Province of Nova Scotia for our publishing program. We are pleased to work in partnership with these bodies to develop and promote our cultural resources.

Canada Council for the Arts   Conseil des Arts du Canada

NOVA SCOTIA

Cover by Cathy MacLean, Chéticamp, NS
Layout by Mike R. Hunter, Port Hawkesbury and Sydney, NS
Edited by Kate Kennedy, Halifax, NS

The font used in this manuscript is Garamond. It was familiar to all French readers in the 18th century. Claude Garamond created the typeface in the 1540s for the French king, François I. Over time, the Garamond fonts came to be used throughout Europe. The Garamond typeface uses less ink than many other fonts.

Also in the series: Thomas, A Sectret Life (2012), The Maze (2014)

Library and Archives Canada Cataloguing in Publication

Johnston, A. J. B., author
    Crossings : a Thomas Pichon novel / A.J.B. Johnston.

Issued in print and electronic formats.
ISBN 978-1-77206-020-1 (paperback).--ISBN 978-1-77206-021-8 (pdf).
--ISBN 978-1-77206-022-5 (epub).--ISBN 978-1-77206-023-2 (kindle)

    1. Pichon, Thomas, 1700-1781--Fiction. I. Title.

PS8619.O4843C76 2015   C813'.6   C2015-905227-0
                                               C2015-905228-9

Cape Breton University Press
P.O. Box 5300, Sydney, Nova Scotia B1P 6L2 CA
www.cbupress.ca

RECYCLED
Paper made from recycled material
FSC www.fsc.org FSC® C103567

CROSSINGS

A Thomas Pichon Novel

by A. J. B. Johnston

**CAPE BRETON
UNIVERSITY
·P·R·E·S·S·**

Third in the Thomas Pichon Novel Series

Thomas, A Secret Life
978-1-897009-74-1 (2012)

The Maze
978-1-897009-76-5 (2014)

For Mary, Kate and Mike,
without whom the Thomas
Pichon novels would not exist.

I
Outing

En route – November 1734

There comes a sudden drumming of hooves. It stirs Thomas
from his languorous state.

The rolling motion of the coach and the absence of conversation had induced something close to sleep. But the sound of
horses coming on fast brings him straight up in his seat. He rubs
a hand across his face and tilts his head.

No, the pounding hooves are definitely not coming from up
front, from the horses pulling the coach. The sound is coming up
from behind and fast.

Thomas glances down to the floor of the coach. In the middle, surrounded by four sets of feet, rests their hope. It is a small
wooden coffre. He bends and lifts its lid. Yes, everything is still
there: a half dozen small bottles and flasks containing ointments
for various diseases, diseases no one in the coach has. It is a cam-
ouflage of stink, for in the hollow compartment underneath,
Thomas and his companions have placed their coins.

"Cleland," Thomas whispers to his friend seated across.

"Cleland," he repeats, louder than before.

Still not enough. Thomas knows the man consumed too much
drink at the Windsor coach inn where they stayed last night. De-

1

spite Thomas's frequent warning looks, Cleland would not take the hint. He said he wanted to celebrate being so close to the royal castle, and would not stop filling his glass. This is the result. Thomas shakes his head.

The horses' hooves grow louder. Thomas lifts his right leg and with one of his new black leather shoes, with the buckles that look like real silver though they're only plate, taps his friend hard on the shin.

John Cleland's eyes shoot open. "What? What?"

Thomas puts a finger to his lips. He darts a glance at flaxen-haired Fanny, asleep with her mouth slightly agape. Her head is on Cleland's shoulder. There's a hint of a smile on her face. Next, Thomas nudges his own sleeping lover, the dark-haired Élisabeth Cauvin, at his side. Ah, she's waking on her own. A good Swiss is she, as punctual and smart as a clock.

Élisabeth blinks into consciousness. "Thomas, des chevaux. I hear horses."

Thomas nods and smiles to see that her eyes also go immediately down to the little coffre of ointments near her feet. It's surprising how alike they often are.

He turns back to Cleland. "It may just be riders. In a hurry. Mais—" Thomas waves at Fanny as if to say, just look at her. "We *all* need to be prepared."

John Cleland blinks his agreement. He turns in his seat and whispers, "Fanny. Fanny, it's time."

"Time?" The young woman's blue eyes stare unblinkingly into Cleland's face. "Bath so soon? How long was I asleep?"

"No, not Bath. Riders, Fanny. Riders. Listen."

Fanny sits up straight and tries to come to alert. She adjusts her straw yellow dress. Her hands go to her hair and cap.

"Stay calm," says Cleland. Glancing at the chest on the floorboards between them, there is concern on his face. "Like a lady."

Fanny gives Élisabeth a quizzical look. The latter nods.

"Come on, you two. Lively now," Thomas says.

"Yes, please," Cleland adds.

Fanny shrugs. She inserts a hand into the dark paisley sack beside her on the seat and pulls out a fox fur muff. She lays it on her lap. With a deep inhale she places her hands within, from both ends at the same time.

Thomas cannot take his eyes off Fanny, such is the show of concentration on her face. "That's right," he says. "Like we are London ladies and gentlemen. Not a souci in the world." He swings his attention Élisabeth's way. She already has her hands in a muff that appears to be made of the fur from a black bear. Does the Swiss not look lovely in her off-white cotton dress with slender stripes of pale blue?

"Prête," she says.

"It's wait and see," Thomas replies.

The sound of the horses is louder, advancing on both sides of the bouncing coach.

Thomas casts one more glance at his companions. Fanny's usual prettiness is gone, replaced with a tight-lipped severity. Cleland's expression is much the same, Élisabeth's too. He supposes his cannot be much different. He has a small hole burning inside his bowels and his lungs are being squeezed by a tightening rope.

With the hooves drumming alongside the coach, Élisabeth's thoughts are of the life she once knew and has long since lost. Her father claimed he never blamed her for having taken her mother's life as she came into the world. "You are my only child," he often said. How fortunate she was that he educated her as if she were a son. It made her an oddity in Geneva, but it was a separateness and an independence Élisabeth came to like.

She turns Thomas's way. Though he is trying to hide his worry about the riders, she sees it in his eyes. She gives him what she hopes is a reassuring smile. Élisabeth is more than a little pleased that he has taken a shine to her. Their relationship has come a long way since that first night in the room upstairs at the Shakespeare's Head. When he was the customer, and she the... the goods.

———

"Stay relaxed," Thomas says aloud to no one in particular. "Need our wits." He looks at each of his fellow travellers in turn. Cleland purses his lips. Fanny gives nervous agreement, after glancing at Élisabeth. The Swiss removes a hand from her muff and taps Thomas on the knee.

"Halt!" It's a deep-voiced shout from the left. "Halt, I say."

"Pull up! Stop, we say." That's a second voice, almost a tremolo, from the right side of the coach. Its owner is evidently younger and more nervous than the first.

Two horsemen ride up beside the coach, one on each side. Each has his nose and mouth covered by a black kerchief tied around the back of the neck. Combined with the tightly pulled-down tricornes and the rolled-up collars of their coats, there is almost nothing of their faces to be seen. The man on the left is dressed in greys. He has a coil of rope looped round his neck and across his chest. The man on the right is clothed in brown. Each is waving a pistol in one hand, the other gripping the pommel and the reins to their galloping horses.

Thomas sucks a breath as the highwayman on the far side extends his arm. The pistol slowly takes aim up high, at the top of the coach. He must be aiming at the driver.

A bang, a cloud of smoke.

The driver yells, but it sounds more like shock than pain. The old fellow must not have known there were two highwaymen riding alongside. It is apparently only a warning shot, a command to bring the horses to a stop.

"Whoa there, whoa. Whoa!"

The four passengers within the compartment jolt and sway as the coach jerks up and down and side to side as the horses strain to slow down. Thomas and Cleland half stand. They use their outstretched arms to steady the two women in their seats They don't want them tossed about. Fanny and Élisabeth withdraw their hands from their muffs. Each takes hold of her leather seat and the wooden frame of the coach.

Thomas nods approvingly. "Everyone all right?" He looks first at Élisabeth then at Fanny and Cleland.

Élisabeth and Cleland nod. Fanny blinks.

"Here he comes," says Cleland. "Say nothing. Understood?"

No one in the coach says another word, but four pairs of eyes rove to warn and implore each other in turn. Where before the coach smelled of the different sweet sprinklings each had applied to cover their various human aromas, the air now carries more than a hint of sweat.

"Hands! Hands up." It's the younger, wavery-voiced highwayman. The other rider, the commanding man in greys, is out of sight.

The pale blue eyes of the young highwayman peer through the window. With curled lips, he scowls at Thomas then Cleland. The two women seated on the far side do not appear to register in the young man's gaze at all. He extends his pistol more than a foot through the open window. The hand is trembling, but the young man tries to hide it by swinging the blue steel barrel back and forth. Thomas and Cleland both lift their arms up in the air.

Is it Thomas's imagination, or can he feel the chill from the barrel each time it points his way? He has a sudden metallic taste in his mouth.

He closes his eyes when the young man cocks the firing mechanism the next time the barrel comes his way.

"Bang!" the young man shouts.

Thomas opens his eyes.

"Saying your prayers, blue pants?"

There is much mockery in the highwayman's eyes, but at least now the pistol swings away, over to Cleland's side. What is wrong with the blueness of Thomas's new breeches? The tailor said the colour, queen's blue, would be appropriate for a trip to Bath. Guaranteed to impress.

The young man's gaze and gun come back to Thomas. Then he waves the pistol at the two women, who have disobeyed orders and returned their hands into their muffs.

"Youse two, skirts. Hands up."

Fanny steals a look at Cleland then at Élisabeth and Thomas.

"Not them in charge, pretty face," says the highwayman. "If *I* says hands up, hands up it is."

Élisabeth speaks up. "Here, look." She withdraws both hands from the black fur muff in her lap. Two empty hands dance in front of her face.

Fanny does the same.

"That's better." The young highwayman uses the tip of the barrel of his flintlock pistol to edge his hat up an inch. He seems to be assessing the two women, going back and forth between them.

In the silence Thomas hears the whinnies and snorts of the horses. A bird is calling cheerily from the woods.

The highwayman withdraws his attention and his gun from the inside of the coach. "Dick!" he shouts, then glances back inside. "Dick," he yells again. "We want them out, right?"

The four passengers crane to see where Dick might be. Thomas catches a glimpse. The man is off his horse and on the ground. He has the driver of the coach spread-eagled, a foot on the man's ass, a pistol aimed at the centre of his back.

"Chrissake, Petey," Dick shouts back. "Get it goin'."

"Hear that?" Petey asks those inside the coach. "Dick says it's out you get."

"Petey," the unseen Dick yells. "Get their shoes first. Look for coins."

"Right you are." Petey cocks his pistol again and points it at Thomas. "Hear that, blue boy? That's the famous Dick Turpin. That's right, my own Uncle Dick. 'E says off the shoes. Could be coins."

Four heads nod at once.

"So hurry up!" Petey's shout makes his horse neigh and twist. "Whoa, boy."

Thomas and Cleland lower their hands to unbuckle the metal clasps on their shoes. Toe to heel, the shoes come off. The women untie their lacings and help each other tug off their boots. One by one, Thomas hands the footwear to Petey astride the horse. He gives each a shake then tosses it over his shoulder, to the ground.

"Nothin', Unc."

"All right, get them out of the box," Dick says.

"You're not deaf. Get out."

"Might you open the door?" asks Cleland. "So we can do as he asks."

"As he asks?" Petey looks like he wants to spit in Cleland's face. "It's no ask."

No one within the coach moves or says a thing.

"Youse look like you're all about to shit!" Petey laughs. He dismounts, keeping his pistol trained on Cleland now. The young highwayman reaches out with his free hand to open the door. His horse wanders around.

"Now?" Thomas asks.

Petey says nothing but beckons with his pistol. Thomas stoops into the doorway.

"Well, look at you!" Petey's eyes light up above the mouchoir covering his nose and mouth. "Who-hoo. Dressed for the city, out on a country ride."

Petey suddenly reaches out and grabs Thomas by the hand. He yanks hard and Thomas comes sprawling into the air. He kicks at nothing then hits the ground, his legs taking the shock. He clasps his hands around the left knee, the one that hurts the most. Fleeting visions of another time, another place – a tumble in an underground tunnel in his youth – race through his mind.

Petey barks, "That's right, fancy pants. Now, face down, arms out."

Thomas feels the sharp pain where Petey kicks his ribs.

"Hey!" Thomas hears Cleland shout. "Can't do that."

Thomas twists to see Cleland's frame fill the doorway of the coach. Petey leaves Thomas where he is and goes to his friend. The muzzle of the pistol presses on Cleland's brow.

"Can't do? Can't do what?"

Even though he is a dozen feet away, Thomas sees the grin in Petey's eyes, above the mask.

Cleland waves a hand toward Thomas. "You can't—"

7

Petey lifts his gun up off Cleland's forehead and brings it back down hard, wooden handle first. Cleland recoils, hands to his brow. Thomas sees a trickle of blood.

"Fuckster," Cleland mutters. He makes a single threatening fist, keeping the other hand over his brow.

Petey puts on a show. "Oh my," he says, and dances a quick jig. Then, to the women inside the coach, behind John Cleland's frame, he says, "See, ladies, me and me uncle, we do what we want." Petey raises his pistol again, threatening to strike John Cleland once more.

Cleland holds up both hands in front of his head.

"Get down," Petey shouts.

Cleland twists through the doorway and climbs down the iron steps. He goes to lie down beside Thomas. Both men's noses hover just above the road's packed earth, their backs to the clouds.

"Dick," Petey sings out.

Thomas sees Dick glance up. He's just finishing tying up the driver, who is face down with his hands tied behind his back. "Hold on," Dick shouts back.

"Dick does the tying," Petey explains conversationally to Thomas and Cleland's backs. He gives Thomas's then Cleland's socked feet a kick. "Then it's pickin' time." Petey does another jig. "Better to give than receive. Is that not it?" Petey puts his hands on his hips and gyrates like he's having sex. "Youse give, and Dick and me receive."

Petey makes a clucking sound. Then, arms extended, he takes a bow before the thicket of blackberry brambles that runs along the road.

"Enough of that." It's Dick clapping Petey on the back. "Hurry. We just might get another one before day is done."

Thomas twists around to have a better look, as does John Cleland at his side. Their heads nearly strike. Dick Turpin has lowered his black kerchief to take a deep breath. The man looks to be well past thirty, his face grizzled with several days of beard. Petey lowers his mouchoir as well. Thomas spies the face of a choir boy, except for when he smiles. Then something alters and Petey becomes a brute.

Thomas and Cleland exchange a knowing look. They both know thieves don't want their faces seen. Each averts his gaze before he's caught.

"Here, take this," Thomas hears Dick say. The voice sounds slightly muffled, so Thomas risks a fresh glance. Sure enough, both highwaymen have pulled their mouchoirs back up.

Dick hands his nephew a length of rope. "Hold it taut," is the command. Dick cuts it with a long knife to make four lengths.

"See what you can do with him." He points at Thomas. "I'll do the tall one myself."

"And the skirts?" Petey shrugs toward the coach.

Thomas follows the shrug. Élisabeth and Fanny have come down out of the coach without being compelled and are standing on the ground. They look like soldiers at attention, except that they're in long pale dresses and have their hands inside their muffs, held tight to their waists.

"Not bad," Thomas hears Dick mutter.

"That they are." Petey gives his uncle a shifty look. "Hickory dickory dock? What do you say?"

Dick gives the boy's shoulder a hard push. "No, you keep it in your pants."

"Could be quick."

"I bet," says Dick, "but the answer is still no." Then he bows to the women, who curtsey in return.

Thomas rolls his eyes. He cannot believe how foolish the two women are being. First, they came out of the coach. Now they are presenting themselves to the highwaymen as if they are all in a salon. Tempting fate.

He hears Dick snort a laugh. He can hear what the man says to Petey behind a cupped hand. "We'll strip 'em to their shifts though. Those dresses'll fetch some coins."

"So why not a bit of hickory dickory?"

Dick shakes his head.

"Shame," says Petey. "Likes the blonde."

"Bet you do." Dick tucks his pistol behind his belt. "First things first." He bends down to begin tying Cleland's hands.

"You lookin' at?" Petey shouts at Thomas as he puts his own pistol behind his belt. He gives Thomas's socked feet a kick. "Turn round."

Élisabeth elbows Fanny. They share a glance, two sets of flickering eyes. Then with a sharp intake of conviction, Élisabeth tilts her head quickly forward to let Fanny know their moment has come. Fanny blinks, then nods.

The highwaymen are on their knees, their backs turned to the women as they tie up Thomas Tyrell and John Cleland.

Each woman casts her muff to the ground. Each lifts her feet as silently as she can and makes her swift advance.

"Up the hands!" Élisabeth shouts. Her little pistol, known as a Queen Anne, makes hard contact with Petey's back.

"Yes!" Fanny yells beside Dick Turpin's ear. Her Queen Anne lightly touches the man's back. "Your hands up, I mean."

Élisabeth sees Thomas and Cleland lift their heads up off the ground. They are twisting round to see what's going on. Their hands are partly tied but their feet are unbound.

"Up, full height," Élisabeth commands Petey. "Un mauvais tour and I'll put a hole in you." Élisabeth jabs Petey's back with her Queen Anne.

"That's right," Fanny says to the back of Dick Turpin's head. "You do wrong, I shoot."

The two highwaymen slowly turn their heads. Each scowls to see that the two women really do have guns. "God's arse," Dick spits out. "Didn't you check them for guns?"

Petey shrugs. He shakes his head.

"Stupid arse," Dick sputters to himself.

"We will shoot, we will," Élisabeth says as calmly as she can. It occurs to her that this must be what it's like to be a man, a soldier. The power is in your hand. She flashes a look Thomas's way. He and Cleland are getting up off the ground, their mouths agape. Her chest swells. So it was a good idea after all.

Thomas shakes his hands free from the unfinished knot. Cleland does the same.

"Did you—?" Cleland whispers.

"Not me. They must have—"

"They must."

The two men trade shrugs and grins.

"Well done, ladies," Cleland nearly shouts.

"En effet," Thomas says quietly, adding a salute.

Élisabeth and Fanny dart a glance, and flick nervous smiles, but both keep their attention and their tiny pistols pressed into the backs of the two highwaymen whose arms they have forced into the air.

Thomas hurries to grab first Dick's then Petey's pistols from their belts. A gun in each hand, he inhales deeply to slow his thumping heart. He takes aim at the two men's chests.

"Bang and bang," he says. He jerks his hands as if he has really fired the guns. He cannot help but smile.

"You wait." Petey's upraised arms come down.

"Up!" shouts Élisabeth. Petey winces, so Thomas figures she has jabbed his back. The boy's arms climb up into the air.

"That's right, Petey," Thomas says as quietly as he can. He wonders if anyone else can hear the pounding in his chest. "You are dead front and back."

"Curse yer blue arse."

"Shut it." Dick gives his nephew a scornful look.

"It seems our wheel has turned." John Cleland comes to stand shoulder to shoulder with Thomas. "And yours as well."

"Lickspittle." Petey lifts a saucy chin.

"My, my, what a large word." John Cleland thumbs his chin at Petey.

"Leave off, John," Thomas says. "Come."

He and Cleland sidestep in a circle round the highwaymen. They come to stand alongside Fanny and Élisabeth.

"We'll take over now, ladies," Thomas says. He hands Cleland one of the two confiscated pistols.

"Yes, Fanny," says Cleland, "give me your gun and you go untie the coachman."

Élisabeth and Fanny glance at each other. Then come two tiny smiles, as if in a mirror. Each woman shakes her head.

"Think not," Élisabeth says. "How about you give her your pistol, John, and *you* go untie the coachman."

"That's right." Fanny waves her Queen Anne like it might be a fan. "We like our guns."

Dick Turpin makes a snorting sound. "So it's the skirts with the balls?"

"Pussy boys." Petey smacks his lips.

Cleland holds up a hand as if he were a bishop. "And yet," he says, "who were the ones surprised by the women with their wee guns? Answer that."

"Stick up your arse," says Dick.

"Yeah," says Petey. "Up the shit hole and twist. Youse fuckholes." Petey spits over his shoulder. The gob lands on the road just short of Cleland's socked feet.

"Ill-bred nit," Cleland says.

"Suffit. Enough." Thomas rams the barrel of the pistol he still holds into Dick's back. "Not another word. Compris?"

"Does fuck off count?" Dick makes a face. "'Cause you sound fuckin' French to me."

Petey grins. "Fuck yer arses, we says."

Dick Turpin makes a sucking sound. Petey speaks. "You're a joke, blue pants."

Thomas's eyes widen in disbelief. He and his friends hold the guns, yet it's the outsmarted highwaymen spouting off. Thomas takes the muzzle of the pistol in his hand and grazes Dick Turpin's face. He pretends he's a barber-surgeon giving a shave. It makes Dick squint.

"Excuse me." Cleland taps Petey on the shoulder to get him to turn his way. Then he flips the pistol Thomas gave him into the air, catching it by the barrel. In one movement he clunks the back of Petey's head with the butt of the gun. It makes a loud thud.

"Hey!"

Cleland shrugs. "Maybe we should get out of here, before I do something I regret." He hands the pistol back to Thomas and takes a half step back. Then he launches a kick at Petey's arse.

"But so far, so good. Nothing yet I regret." Cleland widens his eyes at Thomas like he's just told a joke.

"De grâce, Élisabeth," Thomas says, "would you please untie the coachman? So we can roll again."

"I shall," replies Élisabeth, "since you ask so nicely. Here, Fanny, you take this." And she hands over the pistol.

"You more than surprised Cleland and me, Élisabeth ... you and Fanny," Thomas says. "I'm a little in awe."

"I like the sound of that." Élisabeth gives him a wink before she turns away.

———

"Do we take them to a judge?"

Thomas cannot tell if Fanny's voice is filled with hope or dread. Her focus is straight ahead, where she has the two pistols pointed at Dick Turpin's back.

"Cleland says we should not dally. We'll take their pistols and horses and sell them in Bath. Whatever they fetch, we'll divide five ways."

Fanny's head tilts back. Thomas can see her eyebrows are raised. "The coachman," he says. "Deserves a share, don't you think?"

Fanny nods.

"Alors, bien fait, let's go then." Thomas jabs Petey's back with the guns in his hands. "You and Uncle Dick. A bas. To the ground and arms stretched out."

As Dick and Petey lower themselves, Thomas glances to see what his companions are doing. Cleland is tying the robbers' horses to the back of the coach. Élisabeth is speaking with the coachman, who is shaking the crimps out of his arms after having been tied up a quarter hour. He is getting ready to climb back up on top and get the coach rolling again.

Fanny taps him on the arm, and gestures that she wants to back away toward the coach.

Thomas nods, and steps over to place himself halfway between the two highwaymen spread-eagled on the ground. He too begins to inch backward toward the coach.

Something rigid makes contact with Thomas's back. He leaps sideways like a cat. "Quoi?" He raises both pistols to fire.

It's Élisabeth, with two firm fingers as the pretend barrel of a pretend gun.

Thomas averts his eyes, away from her laughing face. He sees Cleland and Fanny, standing at the steps to the coach, hands across their mouths, trying to keep the mirth in.

Thomas scowls, then remembers. He spins back toward the highwaymen. Each is now up on his knees and elbows.

"A bloody finger!" Dick shouts. He makes a sucking sound.

"Shit the cookie, blue pants," Petey chimes in.

"Shit a cookie?" Thomas shakes his head. He takes two steps toward Dick and Petey. He aims the pistols at their chests. "Pas un mot," he warns.

"Sorry," Élisabeth whispers near his ear. "Désolée, mon cher."

Thomas glances her way. Though her voice is saying sorry, there is amusement in her eyes. He shows her his disappointment with a shake of his head.

"Oh, it *was* funny. How you jumped."

Thomas exhales, not taking his gaze off the two highwaymen crouched ten feet in front of him.

"Come on!" It's John Cleland's voice.

"Let's roll," another man yells. Thomas steals a look. It's the coachman. He is waving his whip. "We have to get to Bath."

Thomas comes back to Dick and Petey, now on the balls of their feet. They are creeping forward in a squatting position, but freeze when Thomas's eyes meet theirs. He notices their hands are in fists and there are signs of strain on their faces. They are ready to leap.

"Allez, Élisabeth," Thomas says over his shoulder. "To the coach." He takes aim at the faces of the highwaymen.

"Whoa." Dick shows two beseeching palms.

"Those guns, they …" Petey says.

"Careful now," Dick pleads, "they could – explode on you."

"Not an inch." Thomas sets his chin. He has never killed any-one, and he'd rather not start today. Though if he must, he must. Two quick squeezes are all it would take. What's more, no one would think ill of him. Highwaymen have no friends, save ballad singers. Thomas might even get a reward.

"Tyrell!"

Thomas hears panic in John Cleland's voice. Easy for him. He is safely inside the waiting coach. He does not have two lives in his hands.

"De grâce, Thomas. Venez, et venez vite."

Élisabeth. Thomas is pleased to hear the worry in her voice. Yet he will not turn her way. He does not dare. He has to hold robbers at bay. Or shoot them both. That is his choice.

He senses his gaze goes somewhere he does not control. It is a blur.

A stirring sharpens his focus. The highwaymen are moving.

"Your lives!" Thomas shouts. "In these barrels. Compris? You understand?"

Dick and Petey nod that they do.

"That's right." Thomas's voice has calmed down. "It's simple. You move, I shoot."

Their fists uncoil. The toes of their boots dig in.

"I can put balls in you from any range," Thomas lies. He's not fired a pistol in his life. He lifts a foot to the rear. Then he lifts the other. "Stay and you live."

"Presqu'ici," he hears Élisabeth say. "A few more steps. Bit to your left."

The two highwaymen stand to their full height. Thomas feels a numbing tension in his trigger fingers. The pistols have come to feel like they're embedded in his hands. He is holding steady. But what if he is squeezing more and more? At what point do the triggers go too far? He will say it was an accident.

Dick and Petey begin to step forward at the same slow pace as Thomas is moving backward toward the coach.

"One more," Élisabeth says.

With the small of his back Thomas makes contact with the coach.

"Beside you. The steps," says Élisabeth.

"Quickly. Climb up," Cleland's voice implores.

Thomas summons a deep breath. Dick and Petey have halted no more than a body length away. A leap is all they would need.

Thomas feels movement in his scalp. It must be sweat, because his armpits and the small of his back are soaked. His eyes burn into Dick Turpin's who he can see is not in the habit of backing down.

"Reculez," he says. He shakes the pistols to make them understand.

That brings a scornful curl to Petey's lips. Dick lifts his chin high. "This is England, not bloody France."

"Step back! Step back, I say."

Dick brings his hands together in front of him, a standing supplicant. Petey does the same. They look like pilgrims on their way to Rome or Rocamadour.

"Would be a mistake, Frenchie," Dick says, soft as butter. "You have to give us our property back. We're Englishmen."

Dick's hands shift from praying pilgrim to spread-open, showing the world he has nothing in his hands. Then he raises a foot to step forward.

Thomas lowers one of his pistols to aim at that foot. Dick shrugs, and puts his boot back down. "We want what's ours, nothing more. Our horses and pistols. Then you're free to go, Frenchie, you and your friends."

Thomas forces a laugh. It comes out like the cry of a crow.

"'Fraid so." Dick's head tips back. He places his hands on his hips, an impatient akimbo. "Law's on our side, not yours. You being a foreigner and all. Solemn word."

"Word," Petey shouts.

It occurs to Thomas that the stupid are likely braver than the smart. It is probably Petey he should be the more wary of.

Life really is simple. It is about predators and prey. Those who have power want to keep it. Those without – like these two highwaymen – they'll wheedle, coax, cheat and steal to get what they have not. It feels good, for once, to be higher on the ladder than someone else. A ruler of sorts. Yet what a sorry kingdom: a rogue and a simpleton on a tree-lined country road.

Thomas exhales. As ruler, he must decide. Squeeze the triggers and let the pistols do their work, or—

"Tyrell, come on. We have to go."

Cleland's voice makes Thomas twitch. His friend is right. Two bangs, two puffs of smoke. Then they'll be on their way. Thomas extends both arms, the steel barrels moving closer to the highwaymen's faces.

The two thieves' eyes go wide.

"Petit mot, Thomas."

"Parle vite." Thomas leans Élisabeth's way.

"You don't need to do it," she says in French. "Hand us the pistols, to me and John. We'll keep aim while you climb in. Do you hear me, mon Thomas?"

Thomas likes that she calls him *her* Thomas. No one, except maybe his mother, ever called him *hers*. Not even Hélène.

Thomas looks Dick Turpin in the eyes. "Your lucky day," he says.

He lifts the pistol in his left hand up to where John Cleland's hand waits. "Et voilà," he says, placing the other pistol into Élisabeth's outstretched hand. He hauls himself up the iron steps and into the coach. He wonders if his grin might split his cheeks.

"Rolling! We're rolling," the driver shouts. The coach moves with a jerk, then another, until there comes a steady roll.

II
Talk

For a long delicious moment, no one inside the swaying coach says a thing. All are content, Élisabeth Cauvin observes, to do nothing more than press their backs against the leather seats and fill their chests with air.

Élisabeth closes her eyes to thank her dead father for teaching her the need for ploys. He told her a female needed to use every advantage and trick she could to stay safe in the world. It is the best advice she has ever heard, and it has become her creed. The only sour note is that Thomas took such fright when with her fingers she jabbed his back. Did he think a third, previously invisible, highwayman had suddenly appeared? But then, what does she really know about the background of the man sitting beside her? Other than he is the most tender lover she has ever had – a velvet man. He loves her body as much as she does herself. For that, she gives Thomas Tyrell an appreciative glance and straightens the folds of her dress.

Did he perhaps have a sheltered, easy life, two parents always looking out for him? Maybe so. That might make a man jumpy if he's not known danger before. Perhaps a soft life engenders fright? Thomas certainly appeared rigid with those two pistols. Unless she is mistaken, he came close to pulling the triggers on those two highwaymen.

Or maybe it's the reverse. Maybe Thomas did not receive the love he needed as a child and as a result is not sure exactly who he is as a man. Élisabeth exhales. It is impossible to know what really goes on in anyone else's head.

She glances across to Fanny and her man, Thomas's friend John Cleland. Élisabeth is not sure what to think of him. There is no doubt he is clever, but clever is not everything, not by a long shot. She prefers Thomas, someone who keeps more of his thoughts to himself. Though....

Élisabeth turns again to the man beside her on the seat. He is looking wistful. The grin of escape is gone, the escape of either being killed or having to kill. She will let him be. Work it out.

But not forever. If Élisabeth is going to let Thomas lie with her, the greatest of intimacies, it is her right to find out as much about him as she can. This is the only life she has. She will not make any more false steps than the ones she has already made.

———

Thomas rolls his eyes to hear himself sigh. Yes, it was close. But in the end he didn't kill anyone. Had he done what he was tempted to do, he is certain the mood in the rolling coach would not be what it is. Oh, Cleland might be the same, silently beaming like he's just won the jackpot at a hand of cards. But Élisabeth and Fanny would not be so serene. Neither would have wanted to see the rogues shot, even if it's what was deserved. It's one of the traits that make most women better than most men. They feel what others feel. So, for that reason alone, Thomas chose correctly. He prefers Élisabeth and Fanny bright and cheery, not downcast.

"Did you see them?" John Cleland breaks the silence with a triumphant cry. "Punching the air and kicking the dirt as we drove off?"

That brings smiles all round.

Fanny places a hand to her chest. "My heart was racing when we were creeping up on them. I could scarcely breathe, fearing they might turn."

"It did not show." Élisabeth taps Fanny on the knees. "Not at all."

"Yes, you skirts, as the ill-bred louts called you, you did all right." Cleland pretends to study the back of his hand. "Not too, too bad."

"Not too bad?" Fanny's face is one of disbelief.

Thomas controls his smile.

"John is right." Élisabeth winks at Thomas. "Fanny and I might have done more." She holds up a hand for effect.

Fanny's blue eyes blink.

Élisabeth brings down the hand. "We might have … spanked them."

Cleland shows a grin.

"Spanked them?" says Fanny. Then she recognizes what is going on. The usual twinkle returns to her eyes. In a voice Thomas supposes is her impersonation of a London grande dame, she says, "Because one must show ruffians discipline." She points her nose high in the air. "Is that not right?"

Élisabeth claps, Cleland roars and Thomas shows his approval with several quick nods. He did not know that Cleland's willowy lover had a sense of humour as well as her other more obvious charms.

"Again," says Cleland. "Say more, my dear."

Thomas shares a knowing look with Élisabeth. It is good to see their travelling companions so smitten with each other. He wonders, however, if Élisabeth would be so pleased to know that Cleland is creating a fictional version of Fanny in a novel he has begun to write. Thomas read the opening chapter a while back. It kept him turning the pages, but the real question is how many of the erotic adventures Cleland writes about are truthfully based on this Fanny's real life. If only he could ask, which he knows he dare not.

Beaming at the response to her first small acting part, Fanny offers a fresh performance. This time she fixes Thomas in her gaze. "What say you there, my good man?" comes out in a deep voice.

Fanny casts a glance at Élisabeth, asking with her eyes if it's all right to speak in this manner to her man. Élisabeth waves her on.

"Pleased at your escape? I say, dear man—old chap—I—" Fanny loses the flow of words. She covers her face with both hands.

"You are truly a lady. Lady Fanny." Thomas offers a quarter bow from his seated position.

"A delight." Cleland looks at each of his companions in turn. "This is a true delight."

That brings a mix of smiles and shrugs.

"But," says Cleland with a sudden stern look, "we should acknowledge why and how we are here."

"Oh, the big question," says Élisabeth, leaning forward. "Do say, John, why are we here?"

"I mean on the road to Bath, my Swiss friend, no more than that."

"Ah, a much smaller question is that."

"Isn't it? In any case, my friends, I want to point out whose idea it was for us to come on this outing. Merçi, Thomas." The words come with an outstretched arm.

Fanny gives him a quick clap, which comes with a warm smile. Élisabeth looks like she actually is feeling something akin to pride. Thomas offers a humble shrug. "Remember, Bath is still a few hours away. Should we not—"

"True enough." Cleland purses his lips. "Let's wait. On the way back to London we'll know if it's thanks or curses we owe this man."

Thomas allows a sage shrug.

———

Thomas likes to gaze out at the stone walls, especially those topped by hawthorn hedges, as the coach rolls by. They seem the perfect boundary for the many fields of freshly turned furrows. The winged ones, birds large and small, mostly brown and black, are busy finding their food in the broken earth.

It was Jean Gallatin, Thomas's other good friend, who initially asked Thomas to join him on a trip to Bath. Well, not just *him* but *them*. Hélène, Gallatin's wife, would be coming too. Gallatin confided that she wanted to take the waters in the spa town in the hope that she would be able to conceive a child. "Six months," Gallatin said with a hushed voice, "and still no result."

"Seeking an heir for the throne?" Thomas quipped.

The grimace on Gallatin's face said he saw no wit in the remark. "Hélène is nearing her mid-thirties. She worries it might soon be too late. Bath's waters worked for the late Queen Anne, so she wants to give it a try."

Thomas pretended to consider the matter. The truth, of course, was that under no condition was he going to travel any such distance with Gallatin and Hélène.

"I thought as an old friend to the both of us, you might want to come along."

"Hmm," Thomas had replied.

Then he listened as the bookseller went on about how Bath's hot, sulphurous waters were once known to the Romans. Aquae Sulis they called the town, explained Gallatin, as if that were a clinching point.

"What dates?" Thomas asked.

"November. Fifth, sixth, seventh."

"Oh," Thomas sighed. "What a coincidence. I'll be in Bath at the same time."

"Really?" Gallatin's eyes narrowed at the news.

"Yes, with John Cleland and our lady friends."

How Gallatin's face fell at that. He detested Cleland, which Thomas well knew. The trick then was for Thomas to propose just such an outing to the others. As he expected they would be, Cleland, Élisabeth and Fanny were eager to see the place everyone was talking about. A town with a famous spa and the renowned Assembly Rooms. And topping it off, a place that was said to be writing new rules for how polite society should behave.

Later that evening, when Thomas had reached underneath Élisabeth's chemise as she got into bed with him, she grabbed his hand and said, "Are you sure the new rules allow that?"

Thomas took back his hand. "Pardon me."

She laughed. "In Bath. Do they not have rules to rein in that kind of thing? Are men and women even supposed to tumble there?"

"Good one," he said. "I doubt the rules venture into that area. But who knows?" Thomas held up his hand for Élisabeth to see. "May I, Madame?"

"If you must," she said, but with a wry smile.

"Merci."

"You know, Thomas, I think I'm going to like Bath. There are a lot of men in this world who could use some rules."

"Me?"

"No, you're not too bad."

"High praise."

"Enough talk."

———

"What's that little smile about?" Élisabeth asks in the bouncing coach.

Thomas swings back from the window to face her. "Nothing."

She can still see the trace of a particular smile, one she is guessing has something to do with their bed.

"Pray, leave the man alone, woman." Cleland is leaning forward. "The enigma does not wish to share what is on his mind. Surely, that's fair."

Élisabeth gives Cleland the compliant expression he wants.

"Imagine," he says, "if we all knew what we were secretly thinking. What a nasty world it would be."

"Speak for yourself," says Élisabeth.

"That's right," Fanny adds.

"I assure you, ma chère," says Thomas with a wink, "my thoughts were not nasty at all. Quite the opposite."

"Too bad." Élisabeth shows Thomas a fleeting pucker of the lips.

"Tell us again, what are we going to do once we get there?" Fanny's eyes are wide. "Please, Tom."

Élisabeth sees Thomas wince.

24

Cleland places a hand on Fanny's knee. "I don't think he likes the short version of his name."

"Oh. Sorry." Fanny twitches her nose. "But Tom is better than Tom-ass, is it not?" She covers her mouth.

"In French we say Tom-ah, not Tom-ass," Élisabeth says in what she hopes is a helpful voice.

"Whatever Fanny prefers." Thomas presents an amiable face. "Our inn is in the centre of town, on Staule Street. Comfortable and well appointed, I am told."

Three contented listeners settle back in their seats.

"We have two rooms."

"I should hope." Cleland makes his eyebrows dance. "Fanny and I don't want any impolite noises coming from your room. The Bathites will complain."

"Is that what they are called? Bathites?" Élisabeth wants to know.

"No idea," says Cleland.

"Shall I continue?" Thomas asks.

"If you must." Cleland rolls his eyes.

Fanny places a quieting hand across John Cleland's mouth. "Yes, please."

On his fingers Thomas counts off: "We take the waters. Sips, not full drinks. It is hot and sulphuric. Second, we visit the baths. Third, we promenade in the streets. And fourth—"

"Fourth," Cleland interrupts, "we make sport at the gaming tables. And in our beds."

Élisabeth watches Fanny pretend to be shocked. "And the Assembly Rooms?" Élisabeth asks.

"My apologies." Thomas turns her way. "Of course, we will go to the rooms. We have to show le tout Bath just how charming, clever, pretty, handsome, smart and witty we are."

Expectation lights up Fanny's face as she leans back against the seat. Élisabeth realizes she is doing the same thing, with anticipation on her face as well.

———

"From what I hear," Thomas says, glancing away from Élisabeth to take in the other two, "the spa town is like a London shop. Everyone is on display with everyone else. "

"Sounds like dreadful fun," intones Cleland, pretending to be glum.

"Tell me, Thomas," says Élisabeth, "will we be meeting up with Hélène and Monsieur Gallatin?"

Thomas is sure he does not show anything other than a cheery face. While he was pleased Gallatin had granted him the favour of hiring Élisabeth to work in his bookshop, he knew it carried risks. His current lover might befriend his former, Hélène, now Gallatin's wife. That would lead to talk, which sooner or later might be about him. Has it happened already?

"How could we not?" Thomas feigns a yawn and stretches his arms and legs. "Bath is a small town."

"Not good form, Tyrell," Cleland says. "To show the boredom one feels."

"I was just—"

"If you're not careful with your rudeness, people might start thinking—well, they'll think you're French."

Fanny's laugh is a bark. "But he is. French, I mean." A guilty look crosses her face. "Sorry, Tom, but you have to admit it. You are French."

"The secret's out?" Thomas casts a dark look Fanny's way. But then he sends a wink, which preserves the mirth in the bouncing, rolling coach.

———

Thomas hesitates to speak of it, but then decides he must. To begin he makes a show of testing the fabric of his coat's left sleeve. "Do you— do you think my coat and pants are— well, are they too blue?"

"Ah, the fancy pants," Cleland nearly shouts.

Élisabeth and Fanny sputter mirth.

"No, I just—"

"Oh, tell the truth, Tyrell. You're afraid highwaymen know more about fashion than you."

"No, I—"

"You know what I say, Tyrell?" Cleland raises his eyebrows.

Thomas does not like that all three faces are wearing grins, at his expense. "What is that?"

"Shit the cookie."

"Shit the cookie," Fanny and Élisabeth sing in chorus.

"You know," says Élisabeth, wiping a tear of laughter from one eye. "If you covered your face with a mouchoir, Thomas, you could join their gang."

Thomas decides he might as well join in the mockery being sent his way. With his right hand he covers his mouth and nose. "What do you think?"

"Mysterious," says Élisabeth. "What women want. Or so men think."

Thomas lowers his hand and pretends to blow her a kiss. "Remember, if I'm a thief, I answer to only myself. It will be a return to the state of nature."

"What does that mean?" Fanny asks. "A state of nature?"

Thomas, Cleland and Élisabeth trade glances. With their eyes, the men ask Élisabeth to reply.

"What I take it to mean, Fanny, is it was the time before civilization imposed its rules. Men were like the beasts."

"Doesn't sound good." Fanny looks genuinely troubled.

Cleland leans forward. "No, it likely wasn't. But people … well *some* people of our time," he shoots Thomas a knowing glance, "like to think it was. Freer. Unencumbered."

Fanny winces.

Thomas holds up a hand. "In any case, we will soon be in Bath. Which, from all we hear, is the opposite of nature's state. It is all rules. No base elements, no nature allowed."

"We shall see, won't we?" Cleland gives his chin a rub.

"What shall we see?" Thomas asks.

"Well, today is the fifth." Cleland puts his right hand up in the air. The voice that comes out is deep.

Remember, remember
The fifth of November.

Thomas and Élisabeth exchange puzzled looks.

"Pope Day," Cleland explains with disdain. He gestures at Fanny for support.

"It is. It's the Fifth." Fanny is all smiles. "But do you think they'll have a fire in Bath, John?" Her face shifts to balancing between expectation and doubt. "It's not the quality who come out, is it?"

"Well, shame on them."

"That's right." Fanny is stern.

Cleland puffs out his chest. "No popery and no foreigners in this green and fertile land!"

Fanny beams at Cleland, which causes Thomas to swing his focus round to Élisabeth. Together, they slyly raise their eyebrows.

"I see that!" Cleland calls out. He takes Élisabeth by the hand. "Fear not, Huguenot, you are all right. You, alas...." Cleland points an accusing finger at Thomas. "You are not, you half-hearted atheist."

"Vraiment, Cleland?" Thomas shakes his head. "That is what you think?"

Cleland smiles like he has just taken the last piece of cheese. He stretches his long legs. "Of course not. But I did have you going there, did I not?"

Thomas chooses not to reply.

"The thing is, Tyrell, where *I* might not burn you for your beliefs, or rather the lack thereof, there's more than a few who would."

Thomas looks out at the hedgerow bouncing by.

"Hey," says Cleland, calling him back. "Seriously, Tyrell, Pope Day is not to be missed. It's always a milling, mumbling, stinking crowd. Cheers, smoke, the smell of tar, the effigy lighting up."

"Even in Bath?" asks Élisabeth.

"We'll see. The great thing about the Fifth is it reminds us English of who we are. Well, more accurately, of who we are not."

"That's right," Fanny chimes in. "Who we are not." She sets her eyes and chin. "Remember, remember." Her finger ticks in the air.

Thomas and Élisabeth blink.

"Word of advice." Cleland leans forward, eyes on Thomas. "If there is a bonfire in Bath, don't go spouting French."

Thomas shrugs. "I'll be prudent."

"Prudent?" says Fanny with a wrinkled brow. "Prudent as in you will or will not join us in burning the Pope?"

Thomas extends his right hand like he's swearing an oath. "What I say is this: Down with everyone who is not with us."

Fanny crinkles her nose then turns to John Cleland, who is all smiles.

"Well put, Tyrell. You've summed up the very essence of the Fifth. Now if this damned coach would only get us to Bath, we might begin the fun."

III
Heat

The warmth swells up, much greater than Thomas had imagined it could be. It's like being right beside a fireplace, only he's nearly a hundred feet away from the bonfire. Yet he can feel sweat trickling in his armpits and inching across the small of his back. The near suffocation is made worse by the flaming torches held aloft on all sides of him. The men, women and children of the pressing crowd are straining to get as close as they can to the conflagration in the centre of the square.

Thomas looks with envy at Cleland and Fanny. He and Élisabeth chose to put on their warmest winter clothing, a cape for her and a cloak for him. They thought they would have to ward off a chill November night. After all, everyone's breath was producing puffs and trails by the time the coach rolled to a stop in front of The Bell. Yet here in the square, three-storey stone buildings pressing in on all four sides, the blazing mountain of branches and faggots is throwing out mid-summer heat.

"Just tough it out," Cleland says.

Apparently, to go back to the inn now would mean missing the highlight, quite literally. That is when the effigy will be brought into the square and set afire.

Thomas sees he is overdressed in a second way as well. He kept on his new outfit and added his best wig and tricorne. The idea was to show the spa town he knows how to dress for the upper circles of the world. Alas, virtually none of the type he was hoping to impress are here in the square. If they are, they came in disguise. The sole exception is an older man with a prune face standing up front, close to the fire. The fellow is wearing an oversized hat, and his expression says he disapproves of everything he sees. Thomas knows how he feels.

"Well, what do you think?" Cleland roars in his ear.

Thomas sees the excitement in his friend's eyes. It's there on Fanny's face as well. She's clutching Cleland's elbow like it's a lifeline.

"Interesting," Thomas says.

"Interesting?" Cleland leans back. "That's damned faint."

"It's better than that," says Fanny.

"Sorry, but—" Thomas bites his lip. He looks away from the two disappointed faces. Where is Élisabeth? The Swiss is nowhere to be found.

"What don't you like?" Cleland wants to know.

"Too English, I bet." Fanny shakes her head.

Thomas shakes his head in reply. He wonders if Élisabeth has gone back to The Bell. If so, he wishes he were with her, away from this heat.

"Well, if you must know," Thomas says looking Cleland in the eyes, "it's that—"

"Thomas! Thomas!"

He turns to the sound of his name pronounced the French way. A waving hand. An arm of light blue. Élisabeth. She's mouthing something he cannot catch. The roar of the crowd, combined with the bonfire's lick and spit, fills his ears instead.

"Excusez." Thomas nods at Cleland and Fanny as he spins around. He adjusts the shoulders of a wavering man with hot alcoholic breath who stands beside him before he is able to slip past.

"I bear no grudge," the fellow says in a slurred voice.

A few whispered apologies for stepped-on toes and elbowed bellies, and Thomas comes at length face to face with Élisabeth. He hopes she wants to slip away from this horde.

"Thomas, look who it is." Élisabeth stretches out her arm.

He shifts his gaze, and feels his head jerk back. It's Hélène with those terrible twinkling eyes. Thomas notices Élisabeth has lost her smile and is studying him. He composes. A stiff bow to Hélène is the best he can do in the pressing crowd.

"Madame Gallatin, comment allez-v—"

"Shhh." Élisabeth pinches his forearm. "In English."

"How good to see you, Mrs. Gallatin, this night." Thomas doffs his hat. "A surprise agree-able."

"Mister Tyrell." Hélène gives Thomas the slightest curtsey a woman can make, then leans forward. "Those words are usually reversed," she whispers.

"Oh, correct," Thomas mouths.

"Bath is wonderful," Hélène says in a loud voice, "is it not? As fine as all say it is."

"I suppose," is Thomas's reply. How sad that what was warm and passionate between them for so long is now cold and detached. Could she not give him more tender words? A kiss on the cheek, if not on the lips?

Instead, Thomas sees Hélène send a wink to Élisabeth. It confirms what he suspected. Now that the two women work together they are growing close. Soon, if not already, Hélène will be telling Élisabeth stories about him he wished she did not know. Oh well, what's done is done.

Thomas presents an amiable face. "And your husband, Mrs. Gallatin, is he not with you tonight?"

"Yes, John is here. Though where I cannot say." Hélène does not make the slightest attempt to scan the crowd. Her eyes stay on Thomas.

"There he is." Élisabeth is pointing toward the great bonfire with something like admiration in her voice. "Up front."

Thomas sees the bookseller among those milling about close to where the fire blazes so high. He can only imagine the heat.

Gallatin seems to be locked in an intense conversation with the same older man Thomas spied before, a well-dressed fellow with a prunish face. The man is wearing a shoulder-length periwig topped off by a large tricorne. Whoever he is, he's listening intently to Gallatin. The bookseller is gesturing, counting off points on the fingers of his upraised left hand. The sight brings a smile. Gallatin does not change. For him, earnestness will never be out of style.

"Come on, brighten up that long face." Cleland's hand claps Thomas solidly on the shoulder. Fanny is by his side. "The effigy will soon be here. Greetings, ladies." Cleland doffs his hat.

"John Cleland." Hélène's face is expressionless. She reflects her husband's dislike of the man.

"Hello again, John," says Élisabeth.

"Let's hope it lives up," says Cleland, raising his voice. He is trying to compete with the crowd, a million buzzing bees.

"There it is!" Fanny has taken hold of Cleland's upper arm, redirecting his attention.

"Aye." Cleland's rapt expression suggests he is witnessing a holy scene.

An immense roar lifts from the crowd. It reminds Thomas of events from his childhood. The procession of the young king through the streets of Paris, which his father took him and his sister to see from afar. The sound of the crowd at the public execution of a murderer one time he was in Rouen. But for a fire? The English are a curious bunch.

A larger-than-life-size effigy, a straw figure of a man with a tall pointed hat, is being held aloft on a long pole. It's moving slowly above the crowd, moving toward the fire. Who and how many might be holding up the pole Thomas cannot see. No matter. It's clearly the straw man who counts, with his mitre hat and crozier staff. Thomas knows that to this English crowd the figure represents the pope. He wonders what would happen if he were to shout that the straw-stuffed man was their own top Anglican churchman. Look, it's the Archbishop of Canterbury! What would they say to that?

"I detect a little smile." Cleland is leaning in from Thomas's right. "Knew you'd enjoy it." Then in a loud voice to the entire crowd, Cleland yells, "Curse Rome and its pope!"

All round, other voices call out. "Whore," "Scarlet" and "Babylon" are words Thomas hears repeated. He's astonished to see Hélène, standing beside him on his left, cross herself. She is giving herself away. He hopes for her sake that no one else has seen.

Bells begin to toll in the towers of the nearby abbey church. The ringing – rolling, joyous notes – remind Thomas of a wedding.

There is a sudden whoosh. A heartbeat later, fireworks burst overhead. Flares of yellow, orange and green light up the black sky. Thomas leans back to take it in.

"Makes you wish you were one of us, doesn't it?" Cleland's breath is warm in his ear.

Thomas gives a quick nod and keeps his eyes overhead. The last bright flare, a dazzling yellow white, slowly fades. Black ink reclaims the sky, with the stars seeming much duller than they were before. The bells, too, sound their last toll. The final peal echoes fainter and fainter until it's gone. The crowd goes silent, with only the crackle and roar of the bonfire and the lick of the torches held aloft all round.

"'E's gonna burn now, 'e is," a man shouts from behind.

Looking past and over a hundred heads, Thomas watches the straw man dance. He kicks and writhes atop his skinny pole. He sways and dips, coming ever closer to the flames. Just in the nick, the ragged pope dances away. He is only teasing the bonfire, playing with the swaying heads, who "ooh" and "ah" with every move. Sure enough, back comes the mitred man of straw. This time the crozier staff falls away. The man himself, however, dances on. Suddenly, teased enough, Thomas wants to see him burn. He wants—

His eyes go wide as he feels a hand cup his ass. It caresses his contours and one finger slides underneath. Then it stops. Thomas swivels toward Élisabeth, slightly behind him on the right. Her face is blank, her eyes revealing only the reflection of the bonfire's

35

blaze. He turns left, to Hélène. She too is staring straight ahead. No grin, no wink.

"What is it?" Hélène's expression is bafflement.

Thomas shakes his head. He twists completely around to see who is standing directly behind him.

"You lookin' at?" demands a scowling, red-faced man.

Thomas raises his hands. "Nothing."

"That's right," the man nearly spits.

There's a tug on Thomas's sleeve.

"Penny for the Guy?" asks a boy dressed in rags, no more than five. He holds out a doll, stuffing sticking out where a head should be.

Cleland reaches past Élisabeth and taps Thomas on the shoulder. "A penny will suffice. A tradition, it is."

Thomas nods. He digs in the pocket of his coat to find a penny. The boy takes it without a word and pushes on, working through the crowd. Could it be the boy who was feeling Thomas's ass? Thomas shakes his head. But if not Élisabeth or Hélène, then who?

"Huzzah! Huzzah!" comes from all round. The entire square resounds. Thomas's eyes turn. The straw pope is in full flame, a licking shape that squirms and twists as he goes from bright yellow to bright grey smoke. Thomas sighs. He missed the moment when the effigy went ablaze. Oh well, maybe now he can get away from this place and its crowd.

There is a tap on his wrist. It's Hélène, leaning his way. Her mouth is close enough he can taste its warmth. There is a hint of cinnamon on her breath.

"Must go," she says above the murmur of the crowd. "Find Jean. See you again, I hope, Mister Tyrell." Then she leans closer still, her cheek rubbing his. Her voice drops to a whisper only he hears. "Miss you."

Thomas leans back and looks at her, those dark, shining eyes. Did he hear right? She misses him? He can feel a stirring at the touch of his former lover's skin. "Of course," he says in a firm voice anyone might hear. "Give Jean my regards."

As he watches Hélène wend her way slowly through the crowd, toward where Gallatin is still in conversation with the prune-faced man, Thomas plucks at the front of his breeches. Is Hélène having second thoughts about having married Gallatin? Thomas starts to take in a deep breath, but it is spoiled by the thick tang of smoke. It makes him cough.

"Where is she off to?" Élisabeth presses close.

"She? Oh, Hélène?" Thomas shrugs. "She … she was right here." A tightness in his chest tells him he is overdoing it. "She said she's joining Gallatin. Her husband."

Élisabeth gives Thomas a narrowed look. "Her husband? I work with them, you know."

"Of course. They are wed, well wed."

Élisabeth's eyes widen. "You must be tired. Listen, I'm heading back to The Bell. I have more than enough smoke on my hair and clothes. Tell Fanny and Cleland where I have gone, will you?"

"No." Thomas casts a quick look Hélène's way.

"No? Are you all right? You don't—"

"I mean I'd rather come with you."

"You would? I thought maybe you would—"

Thomas offers a bow. "With you, Milady." He holds up a hand.

An instant smile sweeps across Élisabeth's face. "Kind sir." She takes his hand.

———

Down to her cream-coloured stockings and fine linen chemise, the shift she purchased especially for this trip, Élisabeth glances over to the four-poster. Thomas is already beneath the bedclothes. But where he always likes to watch her unlace and peel away the layers, his gaze tonight is not on her. Hands behind his head, he's staring at the overhanging panel of green serge. Élisabeth might as well not even be in the room.

Élisabeth takes a seat upon the upholstered ottoman. Off comes the first stocking, rolled down then gently pulled. She folds it carefully to make sure the edges are square before placing it beside her on the stool. She sets it down as if it might come apart if she is any less careful.

She turns toward the bed and sees her lover still lost in another world. Where and with whom? She swings back around and a long ago conversation rises up, unbidden, from somewhere deep. Élisabeth yanks the remaining stocking and balls it up in her hand then casts it to the floor. She feels a surge in her chest. She swivels to face Thomas again. Yes, he's still there, still under the covers staring up above his head. Complicit by his silence, complicit by his absent gaze. She feels the weight of her head, how badly it wants fall forward. How did she not see this – nay, *hear* this before? The evidence was there from the start.

Thomas senses movement to his left. It interrupts his imagining of what Bath's famous Assembly Room will be like. Rooms, that is, for there are two, in rival parts of town. He has been rehearsing various witty things he might say about the place – a miniature London in some ways – should he get a chance to impress someone who matters. Appearance and wit are the crucial first steps.

He has also been mulling over his fleeting encounter with Hélène. Thomas rolls onto his side. What should he, what can he—? There's a white shape standing next to him. Élisabeth. Stiff as a sentry and staring hard.

"What's wrong?"

A serious-faced woman shakes her head. Disapproval, if ever he saw it, directed his way. Thomas does not recall ever having seen such a cast on the Swiss's usually good-natured face.

"Here." He lifts the covers to invite her into bed. "Come. I'll warm you up."

Élisabeth keeps her bare feet planted where they are. She turns her head toward the room's only door. Thomas watches as she curls her toes. He watches her shoulders hunch. He sees that her hands seem to wring the air.

"Can't be so bad as that." He tries a light-hearted tone. "Whatever it is."

Élisabeth swings back to face him. Her expression is still troubled, but this time she nods. She steps on the stool and climbs onto the bed. Thomas casts the covers over her as she stretches out. His right hand makes wary contact with her right hip.

"You're cold."

"I know."

"What— Has something happened? You look so ... I don't know. Are you sad?"

"Just warm me up."

Thomas pulls her close then rolls her so that her back is to him. Her entire body is chilled. The cold is even in the linen chemise itself. His first instinct is to get right down to business, starting with little kisses on her neck and soft touches on her breasts. But no, he thinks not. At least not yet. He keeps his hands on her back, making long, caressing strokes.

Élisabeth has to think this through. Almost certain is not certain, is it? No, it is suspicion, not proof. Nothing more than that. So she has to proceed in a way that is both careful and just. One thing at a time. She owes Thomas Tyrell that.

The sometimes secretive man has been good to her. It is because of him that she now works with her brain and not just her body. True, it is only a job in a bookshop. But it's a lot better than emptying out chamber pots, cleaning rooms and occasionally letting men fondle and rut. More than that, Thomas brings affection along with his lust. In fact, she thought she detected a genuine attachment deepening on his part. Not from anything he has said, but rather in the way he sometimes looks at her, with appreciation and trust. Still, it's hard to tell with a man who mostly keeps his thoughts and feelings to himself. Where she shared her life story with him, a true tale of which she's proud, what he told her in return could best be described as a thin sketch. That he grew up in Normandy and moved to Paris as a lad. When asked how he came to be in London, he shrugged the question off with

"It's complicated." In any case, Élisabeth wants to be fair to him, like Justice with her scale.

On the negative side of the ledger, she needs to remember that she continues to repay Thomas for what he has given her. She contributes to the betterment of *his* life. Not just by allowing him to know her intimately, but by holding her own in discussions of books, ideas and the rest. He is never bored, nor does she let him get too cocky for his own good. She gives him attentive ears when he tells her about the various writing projects he intends to undertake, a sympathetic face when he goes on about how tricky it is to find subjects the world wants to hear about. She still does not fully understand why he is so convinced he deserves better than what fate sends his way, but she does not make fun of him.

But this, this deceit – or apparent deceit, for it is not confirmed – she is astounded she missed. It makes her feel taken in. Yet she must not let disappointment bring her down. She has dealt with worse than this.

She was seventeen. She and her father had plans to cross the great Atlantic to faraway South Carolina. That was where, others in Geneva assured them, Huguenots were beginning their lives anew. But six weeks before they were to travel to Le Havre for their ocean trip, everything came undone. One moment her father was in the salon reading a book, the next he was dead. His concealed debts came quickly to light, and Élisabeth had no choice. She fled. To London, where her father had often told her she had an uncle in the merchant trade. Yet when Élisabeth showed up at his address, Uncle Léo's eyes narrowed to slits. He said he didn't recognize a single Cauvin family feature in her face. He wouldn't even let her inside the house to warm up. With only pennies to her name and a single sack of clothes, Élisabeth found a position as a parlour maid. To make ends meet sometimes she did the other thing.

"Hello, dark eyes," a thin stranger had whispered in her ear one night at The Swan. "Men would pay to be with you." That was how she met Billy Bing. It was never more than an occasional resort, one that allowed her to buy things no parlour maid could afford, including books. And one such night it presented Thomas. And now, she's here with him as he warms her back.

———

Thomas can tell his hands are having a good effect. Where Élisabeth was cold and tense, now she is warm and soft. She rolls over to face him. Eye contact, however, is fleeting. She buries her face into his neck. Thomas has not seen her like this. She's usually direct, clever and independent.

Women are insightful creatures, so very complex. Yet their very complexity sometimes makes them hard to understand. Thomas cannot fathom what might have happened to turn his lover into something like an upset child.

"Thomas?" His name arises from his neck.

"Yes?" He leans back to look at her, but it's not far enough. He takes Élisabeth by the shoulders and shifts her half an arm's length farther away. He wants to look into her eyes.

"That first night—" she says, so quietly he almost can't hear.

"You have to speak up." Thomas feels a tiny smile. "Which first night is that? We've had our share."

"The *first* first. Upstairs at the Shakespeare's Head."

"Oh." Thomas feels the smile disappear from his lips. He props himself up on an elbow. He prefers to be looking down into her questioning eyes.

"When I was sent to you. By Billy Bing."

Thomas exhales and makes a face. "You know that's over. I paid him off. You're safely away."

"I know, and I thank you again."

Thomas says nothing. He waits. Élisabeth glances away. He sees her take a quick breath in through her nose then hold it in.

"Well?" Thomas says at last. He takes her chin between his thumb and index finger. He brings her face toward him.

"I don't know why," she says, "but there is something I did not earlier recall."

"What is that?"

"What Billy told me … he said the one and only thing you wanted was a French woman, a woman called—"

Thomas places a hand over her mouth. He briefly closes his eyes. He wills her to do the same. Eyes back open, he sees that she has not done as he wished. Her eyes, with reddish-orange hues showing in the brown, are staring at him. She looks startled, maybe even frightened.

He removes his hand and fills his chest with air. He swings his gaze to the ottoman, then over to the writing desk in the window between the drapes. He sees the thin stack of folio pages he brought with him from London. And there's the inkwell with several quills, his knife and the small container of sand. He thought it unlikely he would write anything on this trip, but had brought everything along just in case. In case the change of scene sparked something.

The candle in the brass holder on the desk has burned low. He wouldn't mind if it just guttered out. Darkness in the room might bring an end to needless talk.

"Thomas?"

He brings his focus back to the voice. "Sorry."

"Where were you?"

He shakes his head. "Nowhere. So you're thinking back to Billy Bing. Are you reflecting … regretting you used to be a whore?"

"You know I prefer that word used as a verb, not a noun. But no, that is not it."

Thomas lifts his elbow and lowers himself so they lie shoulder to shoulder. Like her, he is now staring straight up at the canopy overhead. "Do we have to talk about this?"

"We do."

"But no one knows us in this town. We are as high and well-born as we dare. This is our chance. Forget what's past."

Élisabeth merely exhales. She does not say a thing.

So that's how it's going to be. Thomas pushes himself to sit all the way up in the bed. He pulls down his chemise to cover his knees down to his mid-calves. "All right, what then?"

Élisabeth does as he has done. She sits up and adjusts her chemise to down below her knees. Then she reaches out to take hold of Thomas's chemise.

"I'm not going anywhere," he says. "You don't have to do that."

"No?"

"No."

"Maybe not." Élisabeth lets go. She tilts her head the way she often does, then ventures a half smile.

"Is that an apology?" Thomas asks.

Élisabeth's eyes go wide. "An apology?" She blinks repeatedly.

"I guess not. Listen, just say what is on your mind."

"Billy Bing said you wanted a French woman."

"I don't recall."

"A French woman called Hélène."

Thomas's vision blurs an instant.

"Hélène, Thomas. Hélène."

"I hear you."

"You honestly don't recall?"

"I guess not."

Why in the name of all things holy is she asking all this? The speckles of red and orange he'd seen in her eyes before are nowhere to be seen. Only fierce dark brown. He wonders if those eyes of hers can calculate the difference between what is literally true and what might be a harmless twist to save them both.

"That's always your preference, isn't it?" Her tone is disappointment itself, like a parent with a child. "To keep everything to yourself."

Thomas offers a humble smile. "Discretion, I suppose."

"Discretion? Discretion has nothing to do with it. You fear the truth." Élisabeth's eyes are a taunt. "What to do with you?" Thomas hears her mumble as she puts a hand to her brow.

He reaches out to place a hand on her shoulder. She does not bat or shrug it away. Instead, Élisabeth tilts her head to rub her cheek upon his hand. The fierceness in the eyes is gone. What an expressive face she has. And what a great mouth. Thomas would like to kiss those lips and pull off her chemise. He'd like to be with her, the two as one.

"You're not listening to me, are you?"

Thomas blinks. Élisabeth's head is no longer inclined. Her cheek no longer touching his hand. Did he imagine that?

"Of course I am. Listening."

Élisabeth rolls her eyes up to the green serge panel overhead. When her gaze comes back down, she lifts his hand off her shoulder as if it might be something soiled, and lets it drop.

Thomas sighs. He supposes she must have noticed something about how he reacted when he saw Hélène at the bonfire. But she cannot have heard what his old lover whispered in his ear.

"This is about Hélène, isn't it?" Thomas says.

Élisabeth's mouth falls open. "Is that not what I said?"

"Yes, yes, all right, maybe I did ask Billy for Hélène. But it was *an* Hélène not *the* Hélène."

Élisabeth's head swivels left and right, like a teacher with an errant child. The smile on her lips is not one of happy amusement. It is one of triumph. "There it is," she says, "*the* Hélène."

"It's a name I like," he tries, adding a shrug. "That's all, my beautiful Swiss."

"Really, my French?" she asks with mocking lips. "I want the truth. Were you and Hélène lovers? No, I can see that. So the question is, was it before or after she chose Jean Gallatin?"

Thomas feels his eyes go wide. "I— I can't get into this."

"You can and you will."

"It would take too long."

Élisabeth glances over to the table, which is providing the room's only light. "There's another candle in the drawer."

Thomas fills his chest with air. "From the beginning?"

"That's why it's called what it is."

Thomas smiles, then reaches out with both hands to cup and caress Élisabeth's breasts.

"Not now."

"Later?"

"Tell me first about you and Hélène. Later looks after itself."

IV
Discovery

Bath – November 1734

Thomas's legs do not feel right. Nor his chest, nor his eyes. Everything is out of sorts. He'll have to be careful on the cobbles until he shakes off this fatigue. He would like to have stayed in bed, but he simply could not remain any longer in the room with Élisabeth.

Hearing himself sigh, Thomas picks up the pace. Once more he will look to his legs to put him right.

The dark shine on the cobbles says it rained overnight. But no, that's not right. He can see from the rooftops still in shadow that the sheen on the stones in front of him is a thin frost that has melted away. It's simply a slow November morn. The sun is taking its time climbing the sky.

Most people still have their shutters closed. As Thomas makes the turn at the corner he reaches out to touch the line of mortar between the sunlit stones of the two-storey house. He hears someone a floor above opening the faded blue shutters. How could they not? The light this morning is the colour of butter and so filled with promise.

To shake off the torpor Thomas decides to follow the streets of Bath on a gradual upward tack, taking in some of the sights. It was dark when the coach arrived and then they had had to hurry, but only as far as the square. With the sun on its climb, and feeling restless, he will walk about.

Walking along the narrow streets with the houses yawning upwards, Thomas is reminded of the town where he was born. Vire too is a town resting upon a hill with a river running through the bottom of the vale. It too has gates and is surrounded by walls, as are all the old towns built across Europe in long ago and darker times. So how is it this place is supposed to be *new*, which is what Gallatin and many others boast? Where is its innovative, striking architecture? All Thomas has so far seen of Bath looks old.

The stone and half-timber construction on this street rises to about the same three-storey height and the same twelve or so pieds across one finds in all small towns. The gate the coach passed under last night looked ancient, though Thomas has to admit the statues adorning it were interesting. The innkeeper says there are four gates in total, linked by connecting walls, which follow an old Roman trace. By that account, Bath is simply one more old, outdated place. Yet that is not what everyone is saying, so Thomas is keen to discover what it is they are all talking about. There must be another, newer Bath somewhere away from this confining street.

The air has taklen on a sooty grit, which makes Thomas look up. Yes, people are beginning to warm their hearths as they start their day. Alas, as in London, he can taste that Bath burns coal. How much Thomas would prefer to take in a whiff of wood smoke instead of the sulphurous bite that comes from coal. He hopes that as he moves to higher ground he will leave the haze and smoke behind. As well as fresher air, the prospect of the town and its river should be pleasant from the hills above.

"Well, look who it is."

Thomas feels the clasp of a hand on his shoulder and spins round.

"Gallatin. You caught me by surprise."

"So I see. Sorry, friend. I too am out for an early stroll."

"It seems we have the streets to ourselves." Thomas points at a grey cat slinking along the edge of the street. "Or near enough."

Gallatin smiles. "Too early in the day to wear your new royal blue?"

Thomas gives him a narrowed look. "You saw me at the fire last night?"

"No, but I bumped into Cleland in the square. I asked where you were, and he said you had scampered off. Then he told me to tease you about your new blue clothes. According to him, you are sensitive about the hue."

Thomas hunches his shoulders. "Not really."

"Good to hear it, Pichon. I wondered if Cleland was putting me on."

"Remember Jean, in England I'm Tyrell. Pichon was for France."

Gallatin's eyes roll. "You know, Thomas, you're not that— Oh, never mind."

"Not that important?" Thomas halts and reaches out to stop Gallatin from taking another step.

"I didn't say that ... but it is the truth. You're a tutor and a seller of cloth. No one cares what name you use."

"Am I not good enough to walk beside a bookseller and an inkie?"

Thomas locks onto Gallatin's gaze as if he is cross. But then he is not sure which of them smiles first. Laughter spreads from their eyes across their cheeks.

"Oh, Jean, I am more than a little tired. I did not have a good night." Because I was kept awake answering endless questions about my previous relationship with your wife, he does not say.

"I'm going up into the hills to stretch my legs. Take in the prospect of the town. Will you come along?"

"An ambitious climb. No, Hélène and I are going to take the waters. She wants to get there between six and seven, before the full crowd descends."

Thomas gives his friend an understanding face. "Hot and sulphurous, I hear. Like what the priests used to warn us about Hell."

"That's true, isn't it? Oh well, it's all the rage. Bath's waters simply must be taken. We're hoping that for Hélène it does what's needed."

"Well, good luck." Thomas examines the earnestness on his friend's face and recalls what Hélène whispered in his ear. No, he decides, he does not wish to take her away from this man. Their lives, as they are, are complicated enough. "I mean that. Good luck to you both."

"Thank you, my friend."

Have Jean's eyes become wet? Thomas looks away. He spins round, arms out. "I don't know exactly where the Roman bath is located, but I imagine you're looking forward to dipping in the same pool the ancients used."

"I am, you know." Gallatin looks embarrassed to admit it. "Aquae Sulis."

"I recall."

"Look, Thomas, I still have a bit of time. I could show you the new Bath if you like."

"I do like."

"It's called Queen Square. After the late Queen Anne, who—"

"Yes, I know. Lead on, Cicero."

Gallatin gives Thomas a broad smile. "I was there last evening and saw it under torchlight. Beau Nash took a few of us on a tour and—"

"Was that the famous man himself speaking to you beside the fire last night? Large hat, equally large wrinkled face?"

Gallatin winces. "Nash is transforming the place, you know."

"The man with all the rules. Politeness reigns."

"Mock if you wish, but his rules are having their effect. Polite society is— Well, it's becoming just that."

"Who knew it was so easy to change the world?"

"Listen, rules are what people need. Some among us are not by our nature good. A society needs controls. They lift us up."

Thomas keeps from smiling, but he knows his eyes are aglow. "Does that mean there is a role for religion too?"

Gallatin raises his gaze momentarily to the sky. "I know what I *used* to say. I was young. Some faiths, it turns out, are not all bad. Truth be told, a few do good."

Thomas's smile can no longer be contained.

"All right, I've mellowed, I admit. Blame it on Hélène, if you want. She is an influence."

Thomas turns away as he clenches his lips. Is that not succinct? Thomas knows first-hand how influential Hélène can be. Yet to turn the anti-religionist Gallatin into an apologist for churches – that is no mean accomplishment even for her.

"We're in prime Bath season, did you know?" Gallatin gives Thomas a quizzical look.

"I did not."

"From October until June."

"I'll have to write that down."

Gallatin does not react to Thomas's sarcasm. Instead, he waves a hand up the hill. "Queen Square is up ahead." His eyes are as cheerful as his voice. "They're doing quite a job with this town, aren't they?"

"So everyone says. Who might *they* be?" Thomas asks.

"Nash, of course, and on the building side, John Wood and Ralph Allen."

"I don't know the latter names."

"The architect and the builder of the new projects."

Thomas cranes to take in the buildings as they walk past. The look of the buildings on the street where Gallatin is taking him is nothing like the old medieval structures where The Bell is situated. The houses are newly built and all of stone, a golden-coloured stone that seems to glow in the morning light. How much more appealing Thomas finds it than the older part of town, or for that matter the bricks that are used in construction all over London.

"Run-down, sooty, dowdy, that's how Bath was before," Gallatin continues on. "Hélène was very impressed last night."

"Was she?" Thomas is careful not to smirk.

All at once he finds himself not thinking about what his friend is imparting about the spa town and how people are choosing to finish their interiors, but rather on how much he gave away last night to Élisabeth about his previous relationship with Hélène.

"Trim Street this one's called, the first to be redone. Hard to believe, but before the turn of the century the area hereabouts was very mean. Elegance was not a description anyone—"

As an interrogator the Swiss was good. Her questions wore Thomas down. No first response was ever good enough. She ferreted out a lot. If Élisabeth Cauvin were a man, she'd make as good a lawyer as any he ever saw in Paris.

"Just look." Gallatin's right arm sweeps out as far as it can go. "This is it. Queen Square. A place for the people of the city to assemble together."

Thomas makes sure he nods.

"Beau is thinking an obelisk in the centre would complete it."

"It would, wouldn't it?" Thomas smiles at Gallatin's enthusiasm.

"Does not the completed side bespeak elegance and class? Palladian, of course."

Thomas is impressed.

"Ralph Allen is a genius of both business and the building arts. He came up with a tramway that runs along the Avon to bring the cut stone from the quarries, which are not far away. It is much more efficient than the roads or a barge. And just look at the stone, is it not beautiful, the fairest you've ever seen?"

"It is," Thomas replies.

When Élisabeth's questioning was finally done, without so much as a beguiling look, she tugged off her chemise. "All right," she said, "you've kept your side. Have me."

"Would you not swear that it's a single house?"

Thomas blinks in the direction Gallatin is pointing. "I would."

"Well, wait until you see the backside."

Thomas follows as he must, and recalls with a shudder the act itself. It was no good. Élisabeth might as well have been a whore in a Paris stall. She barely participated.

Gallatin comes to a halt and his arm goes out. "There. Just look. Here in the rear of what is built we see the truth. The single grand front is just that, a front. The reality is seven townhouses united only by the uniform facade."

Thomas can still hear the sound the two of them made. The sound the English use to describe the act itself. Fuck. Direct from their ancient Anglo-Saxon tongue, no doubt. The sound of a hand clapping mud.

"Muck."

"Muck?" Gallatin's face is aghast. "Oh no, Thomas, this is a clever and fine design. By the architect I told you about, John Wood. A true achievement."

Thomas offers a sheepish face. "Sorry."

"You weren't even listening, were you?"

"Yes. No. Look, I was. I am impressed, I really am."

"It doesn't look like you are."

"No, I am. I just— Well, I *was* thinking of something else. I need to clear my head."

Gallatin does not remove the disappointment from his face. "Yes, maybe you do. Well, I must leave you here anyway. It's time. Hélène wants me to escort her to the bath."

Thomas nods.

"Perhaps we'll see each other later. Hélène and me, you and Élisabeth?"

"I don't know. Maybe."

"All right, no it is."

"Écoutez, Jean, I'm sorry," Thomas calls out to his friend as he heads back the way they've come.

Shoulders slumped, Gallatin does not turn round. He does, however, raise an arm in something like a backward goodbye wave.

Thomas leaves behind the last of the stone houses and heads to the gap in the hedgerow. Up over the wooden stile he goes. A few moments later, maybe fifty strides up the hillside, he slows his pace. He's well into a field of turf and tufts, and his shoes and socks are quickly wet in the long grass. He does not mind, for he expected as much and has worn old clothes for this walk. Yet he finds the rising hill behind Bath is putting new muscles to the test. It's been years since he's been scampering up hills. It feels good, but still a test. He has to grab a few deep breaths.

It is now a slower climb and is suddenly especially slippery. Thomas lifts his shoe. Yes, he has stepped in a mound of freshly dropped pellets. He looks around. There they are – a small herd of guilty sheep is farther up the hill.

Thomas scrapes the bottom his shoe on a tuft and continues the climb. Here and there he sees evidence that cows also use the field. Their dried-up patties the size of pies.

A few more careful paces and he comes to a full stop. He cannot do what he came for, take in the view, when his eyes are constantly studying the ground. He finds a place where he is sure there is no shit, plants his feet and stands erect. He inhales the fresh morning air. He fills his lungs. There is no smoke up here.

What a fine valley the spa town is in. Its buildings form a near circle, while the rising ground on both sides of the river are open fields. Thomas supposes the other fields are like the one he's in, tufted ground where sheep and cattle graze all day. It is especially pleasing the way the fields are defined by either hedgerows or lines of trees. In this morning light, which warms and flatters everything, it is almost as if the scene before him is one some painter might conceive. A wonderful prospect in all directions. And speaking of painters, do not the clouds hang as if put there by an artist's shaky hand? They are swirls of grey and white, loosely brushed across the pale blue sky. The rising sun emphasizes the clouds' canescent glow. It is truly a November morn.

There is a solid patch of blue sky over the distant hills. It seems to widen as he studies it. Yes, the clouds are indeed slowly moving westward. If that keeps up, it may turn out to be a bright day.

As for the little city itself, it offers an arresting scene. Some rooftops – they must be slate – glint brightly in the sun. Here and there the upper reaches of a few yellow stone buildings shine like pearls. From this angle and at this hour, Bath might be a box of jewels.

Thomas's gaze goes to what has to be the abbey. He walked past it last evening on his way to the bonfire and was struck by how large it is. From up here he can see that it is more than large. It is an enormous cruciform shape for such a small town. Its mass and towers dominate everything else. Cleland told him that on its western front there are angels carved in stone, on a ladder going up to Heaven. The thing is, one of the little buggers is coming back down. Cleland said that's because the contrary-minded angel does not like what Heaven offers. He is choosing Earthly pleasures instead. Thomas could not make out the angels' ladder in the shadow, but he intends to do so before he leaves town. He always admires the effects stone carvers achieve. They can be jesters second to none.

He notes a few other towers and spires in Bath, but none capture his interest. What does intrigue him is the veil of haze that has formed over the rooftops of the town. It is coming from the chimneys as people warm their houses and shops. The plumes lighten their hue as they rise and mingle with the clouds above. Thomas is glad he is where he is, up where the air is clear. He fills his lungs. If the town below is to expand as its renown grows, attracting those with money in their pockets to visit its streets, hot baths and assembly rooms, the builders would be wise to put their new construction up on this hill. Yes, that is what Thomas would do. He would put up more eye-pleasing, golden-coloured stone symmetry, such as Gallatin showed him at Queen Square, away from the older town below.

Thomas has stood still long enough. He sees a track that looks to be free of animal droppings. At a sauntering pace he will follow where it leads, while still taking in the view.

He selects the River Avon as his focus as he strolls, and follows it as it threads like a ribbon through the town below. Everywhere he's ever lived there's been a river coursing along. Only the scale of the city or village has varied. It is unlikely he will ever come to live in Bath, but its river must delight those who do live here.

Something is moving far below, along the river to the south. It gives off a plume of smoke. He decides it must be the tramway Gallatin was talking about, the one the builder uses to move his stone from the quarries into Bath. Their day starts early it seems.

Thomas sucks in another deep draught. He should soon start back down. Eventually he has to face Élisabeth. He hopes he did no irreparable harm with his behaviour last night. Neither his confessions about Hélène nor the loveless fuck.

A clutter and thrum from a copse higher up the hill makes him look that way. A covey of partridges bursts out and takes flight. The skirr of their wings fills the air. Thomas watches as the partridges disappear into the dense woods still farther up the hill. From some dark corner up there comes a raven's call. It is a cruel laugh. The great dark bird gives its location away when it skips from the top of one tree to another nearby. Thomas is mightily pleased. He'd like to see more winged ones. Pheasants with their bright red necks. He counts to twelve, waiting patiently, but no more birds take flight.

Thomas spies a different footpath than the one he used to climb the hill. It loops up and over the crest of the next gentle rise, then descends to a different opening in the hedgerow that defines the edge of Bath. He will follow that beaten earth track as it twists back toward the spa town.

He is not even a dozen loping paces along the track when he spies the bouncing tip of a white parasol. It rises and dips above the top of the next hill. Then there is the top of a second, a lemon-coloured parasol. Thomas wants to laugh. Women? Women of leisure up in the hills? He would have assumed all such women were either asleep at this hour or preparing for the day. Or like Hélène, heading to the thermal baths. His curiosity is piqued. He picks up the pace of his advance.

He sees the rest of the parasols, then the gloved hands holding them. Finally, the top halves of the two women themselves. One in a dress the colour of fresh mint. The other in light and dark shades of rose. They are dressed for a salon, not for a country path.

The women startle to see Thomas coming at them along the path. He smiles to see them jump and to make their expressions as funeral-worthy as they can. With the gesture of a gallant he steps off the track and gives a courtier's bow. Then he raises a hand in what Gallatin has told him is a Roman salute.

"Good morning, ladies." They are pretty and young, maybe even as young as Élisabeth. Their cheeks are charmingly rosy from their early morning walk.

"Bonjour, Monsieur." The one in mint lowers her eyes.

"Et bonne journée." The one in rose takes the other by the hand. They hurry past.

Thomas puts his hands on his hips. "Alors, mesdames, vous êtes Françaises?" He admires their curvaceous forms as they stride away. A force within him stirs.

The ladies slow their pace then come to a full stop. They look to exchange words. The one dressed in red is the first to peek over her shoulder back at the man whose path she has just crossed. The one in mint does the same. Neither offers him a further word or wave, but their look lingers longer than Thomas thought they might. At last they show him their backs and continue their slow climb.

"A plus tard, peut-être!" Thomas calls out.

———

As the three sisters from Bristol slowly drift away from where they've been gabbing for far too long, Élisabeth finally has a chance to extend her arms. She knows it's an opportunity that won't last long. Other waiting bathers are pacing under the stone arches. Everyone, it seems, wants to immerse themselves in the hot sulphurous water of the King's Bath. Before lunch, that is, and before the clear blue sky overhead fills again with clouds and a cold November drizzle might begin. Not that any chill from above would affect the steaming water so very green. Such a downpour would, however, ruin hair, caps and make-up.

Though she's been in the water well past long enough – her fingers are already pruned – Élisabeth will stay another bit. She's been waiting for some room to swish her arms. She reaches out both ways. Like a conductor, she swings her hands through the green water, fingers splayed. It feels good. Better than when she had to keep her arms to herself and endure endless talk – which wall finishing and which wheeled conveyance the three Bristol ladies wished their husbands would purchase, if and when they move permanently to Bath. Élisabeth sighs to see the chatty sisters reach the far wall. As they step out, the water streams off the canvas covers that the Master of the Bath insists all women wear. Their jaws are still at it, not pausing for a moment to take a breath.

Élisabeth pushes farther away from the wall. The canvas clothing makes it difficult to float. She gives a few tiny kicks lying on her back and swirls her arms. She is keen to see how buoyant the hot sulphurous water is.

"Hello there."

Élisabeth sees a red-faced man with what looks like a floppy maid's cap atop his balding head. He is peering at her. She slaps her hand atop the water to send spray his way.

"Feisty," he says. His smile reveals yellowed teeth.

"No." Élisabeth swishes through the water, her feet touching bottom. She grabs hold the closest brass ring.

"Trying to be friendly is all," says the man in a raised voice.

Élisabeth does not so much as glance his way. The niches at the other end catch her eye. They're of a different stone than the rest of the King's Bath. Earlier construction it appears. In one niche there's a couple— Oh. Élisabeth averts her gaze. They are snuggling close. She cranes up and away, around the gallery of fully-dressed men and women at street level above; most are staring down. Beyond the stone balustrade where they stand are the houses that overlook the thermal bath. A few buildings have their windows up to welcome the day. Her father would approve. Regardless of the temperature, he always insisted their house bring in fresh air.

Her gaze pans back to the balustrade. She'd like to think she's not looking for Thomas, but she is. She's not seen him – well, not heard him – since he crept out of their room thinking she was still asleep. She dressed not long after and spent the morning exploring the town. Her unescorted walk drew some disapproving glances, from women, alas, even more than men. Well,

Élisabeth does not care. She'll be back to London soon enough, and if it's over with Thomas, because of all her questioning, well, she's not sure what comes next. Surely, he wouldn't have Gallatin fire her just because he wants to go his separate way. Would he? She doesn't know.

Her eyes go the ring she has grasped with her right hand. She detects an inscription. *THANKS TO GOD.* That makes her eyes go wide. She sees another ring six feet farther on. She strides through the water to examine it. It has a coat of arms as well as words. *BY GODS MERCY AND PUMPING HERE AYDED.*

It seems these rings are offering proof, or at least belief, that some who have stepped into these waters have been truly cured. Élisabeth hopes for Hélène's sake that coming to Bath will give her what she seeks, the ability to conceive a child.

Élisabeth closes her eyes and sinks. She lowers herself until her shoulders are covered. If this hot, smelly water really can change someone's life, what would she want that change to be for her?

She submerges more, to bring the water to the bottom of her chin. Then to just below her lips. Far enough. The other bathers are not standing still. She does not want to take into her mouth any of their chop. God alone knows what might be washing off them. She hopes that the sulphurous vapours are enough to neutralize what is foul.

Élisabeth opens her eyes just far enough to keep the world around her a blurry swirl. The nattering of others sounds faraway when she does this, which allows her to stay within her own thoughts.

All right then, what does she want the hot water to bestow on her? Security? Yes, first of all. Affection? Yes. Truth? Maybe. But which truth?

Thomas assured her last night that what once was hot between him and Hélène has since grown cold. Élisabeth would like to know if she can really count on that. She fears, alas, that Thomas is the scorpion in Aesop's tale. No matter what he promises, he cannot change. His true nature is fixed. If so, does that not make Élisabeth the frog in the river, doomed to her fate?

Élisabeth opens her eyes all the way and glances across the surface of the steaming water. A canvas-covered woman wearing one of the large hats not meant for the bath is heading directly her way. Élisabeth lowers her gaze and pretends to study her outstretched hands. She does not need any more conversation or acquaintances.

"Oh my, so far away."

The spoken words come with a soft touch on her shoulder. Élisabeth's eyes scramble to focus. It's a woman's face beneath a broad-brimmed hat. She is dark-eyed.

"Hé ... Hélène?"

"Not the greeting I was hoping for."

"I am the one who is sorry, sorry for giving you a start."

Yet it is not merely surprise that Hélène reads on Élisabeth's face. There's a nervousness in her eyes and in her voice. Or is it embarrassment? No, it looks like guilt. This is curious.

"This likely doesn't help." Hélène removes the large hat and places it on the stone ledge, revealing the small white cap she wears beneath. "It's not for in here, I know that. But I'm going to be pumped on in a bit. I'll need it then."

Élisabeth blinks. "The pump is even hotter, I hear. Practically a punishment."

"No, no, not so bad as that." Hélène makes a deliberate smile. "It's in a private room and ... well, I endured it early this morning, up to fifty times, and here I am back again. The hat protects the head. You wear flannel and open yourself up to the pump."

"I don't think I could." Élisabeth waves a hand in front of her face. "This is hot enough. You're brave, Hélène."

"That's a first, someone thinking me brave. But surely you recall why I'm here, in Bath. A means to an end, our men might say."

Confusion flickers in Élisabeth's eyes. "Our men? Oh, you mean Thomas and Jean, don't you?"

"I do."

Élisabeth reaches out to tap Hélène's canvas cover. "I hope you know that I wish the very best for you. You're a friend. I would never do anything to hurt you. He will be a good father, your husband, Monsieur Gallatin, will."

———

Sweet, deliciously sweet. Thomas savours the morsel taken in with his first bite. The innkeeper said his buns were good, and Thomas has to agree. Much as he deplores people who eat while they walk, he makes an exception for himself on this day. All his rambling over the past few hours – first in the hills and then up and down the spa town's twisting streets – have given him an appetite. The bun is half gone by the time he stands in front of the Abbey Church. Yes, there's the ladder up to Heaven that Cleland told him about. Thomas smiles to the see the angel coming back down to Earth. Well done, little one. Fortunate is he who discovers what he prefers.

There's only a small portion of the bun left by the time Thomas comes alongside the stone balustrade that overlooks the King's Bath. When he was by earlier, there was a horde of bathers down below. The steam rising off the water was a comfort looking on, though the sulphur stink was not. He pops the last bit of the bun into his mouth. The baker called it a Sally Lunn, but it's a variation on a brioche, is it not? Sometimes he does miss France.

"Twice in the same day. Hello, Tyrell."

It's Gallatin. He has his back against the stone rail.

"Halloo," Thomas intones, pretending to be an Englishman.

"Halloo, you." Gallatin reluctantly gives up a smile.

"I apologize again for this morning, Jean. I had a lot on my mind."

"Never mind." Gallatin looks to be himself again.

"I've tramped miles today," Thomas says. "How about you?"

"Not as many, I'm sure, but I have explored the town a bit. And now I'm at the bath again. Hélène immersed and did the pump first thing, as I told you. I stay up here. There she is." Gallatin extends an arm. "With your Élisabeth."

"Élisabeth?" Thomas lowers his voice and switches to French. "In the bath? With Hélène?"

Gallatin replies in French. "Such a worried face. Come see."

———

"It's hard to accept …" Hélène glances toward the old niches at the far end of the bath, "to accept that this hot, smelly water is going to …" She swings her gaze back to meet the waiting eyes of Élisabeth.

Élisabeth nods and stays with English. "It really is. But then …."

"It must help to believe," Hélène says and makes the sign of the cross.

"I suppose it must."

"But you still have to—" Hélène stops when she realizes two women coming through the churning water are near enough to overhear. She leans closer to Élisabeth and switches again to French. "I mean, none of us is the Blessed Virgin, are we now?"

Élisabeth's eyes laugh at that. "Well, this place worked for Queen Anne, so…." She holds up two uncomprehending hands.

"Except Anne didn't come here."

"But everyone says so. That it was Bath that—"

"Yes, Bath, but not this hot spring."

"There's another?"

"There is. The Cross Bath, which is also where the queen of James II went. She had a baby nine months later."

"Really? So why are you not in that one?"

"It's under repair. Or something. Anyway, it's closed. Though there's only a rope. I ducked under to look around."

"Is there water?"

"None."

"Well, surely this is as good." Élisabeth lifts two handfuls of water. "The stinky water must all come from the same source."

"That's what I tell myself."

Élisabeth shrugs. "It'll do the trick."

"A trick, yes, that is what I need."

"I'm sorry, Hélène, I should have been more careful in my choice of words."

Hélène leans forward. "It's all right. Men have their uses, though I prefer a bed. To this." She adds a wink.

Élisabeth does not smile, which surprises Hélène. Is something wrong? As innocently as a child, she asks, "And Thomas? Where is your man today?"

"He … he's on a walk."

"And taking the waters?"

"Thomas?"

Hélène nods.

"I cannot say."

"You cannot say. I see. Well then."

"What about Jean?" Élisabeth asks.

"Oh, he is here." Hélène turns round to point. "There, at the rail."

"The rail?" Élisabeth leans back.

Hélène watches as the Swiss looks for and finds Gallatin at the rail above. The two of them exchange waves. Then there comes a less enthusiastic second wave from the man standing alongside. He removes his hat and makes a stiff bow. Hélène is more than a little surprised to recognize that it is Thomas at Gallatin's side.

"Two good friends, are they not?" Hélène hears Élisabeth say.

"They are, that they are. As are we, my dear Élisabeth."

———

"Wonderful, are they not?" Gallatin glances at Thomas.

"Hélène and Élisabeth? Yes, I guess, though those are not the most fetching clothes, those canvas things. They look more like bales ready to be shipped."

"True enough, but I mean who they are. Beautiful and smart. I like seeing them together, talking as friends."

Thomas knows he is supposed to agree, but words do not arrive. He forces a smile instead. The truth is, Hélène still unsettles him. He'd prefer it if she would not get too close to Élisabeth, or at least not talk about him.

"Thomas, I have to tell you I am so happy you came to London with Hélène. She is perfect for me. And," Gallatin leans closer, "if you don't mind me saying so, Élisabeth is a good match for you."

"You're especially earnest today, Jean, even for you. So close to midday that you're feeling faint?"

"Jest is always your escape, isn't it? But listen, opportunities for happiness are rare. And our lives do not last as long as we might like. You could do much worse than your Swiss."

Thomas studies Gallatin's face. A few signs of aging, creases round the eyes and a few brown spots on the skin, but other than that Jean is still Jean. Where once he was passionately anti-clerical, now he is passionate about other things. Everything is a lesson to pass on or an example to avoid.

"Is that the best a person can aspire to, to not do worse than everyone else?" says Thomas. He looks again down into the bath. Hélène and Élisabeth are no longer looking up.

"You know I do not mean it like that." Gallatin sounds miffed. "Listen, if you do not want to speak plainly of the nature of your attachment to Élisabeth, that's fair enough."

"It's still early days."

"If you say so, then I suppose it is. Tell me, Thomas, what do you think of women?"

"You mean in general?"

"Yes."

"Well, I don't think anything. The general does not exist. Neither for women nor for men. Nor for anything else."

"Yes, of course, you're right. Yet, still, do you not think there is something special about women, something they all share?"

Thomas stops himself from rolling his eyes. "And what would that be?"

Gallatin looks around to make sure no one is too close to listen in. "Don't laugh, but lately I keep having this thought."

Thomas holds out a hand. "And …"

"That they're eternal. Women."

"Eternal?" Thomas winces. Then the two women with parasols he met up on the hillside path come to mind. The recollection makes him smile. "Maybe you're right, but you must be careful. A woman might think you are saying she's old."

"No, not old."

Thomas dares not shift his gaze away from the intensity of his friend's eyes until he has explained.

"What I mean is they are closer to nature. Without them—nothing." Gallatin shrugs. "They are so different." His voice becomes a mumble, but it sounds to Thomas like he says, "More important than us."

Thomas turns to the sound of a cart rolling by. It carries a full load of furniture heading to or from someone's house. The faces of the two men pushing the cart are streaming sweat. They must wish they had a horse. Thomas swivels back to Gallatin.

"True, the female form *is* the subject of countless paintings and poems."

"Of course it is. It's where life begins and is succoured." Gallatin claps Thomas on the back. "I hoped you'd agree."

Thomas decides it does not matter if he does or does not agree. There is never any point splitting hairs with Gallatin. The man's intensity cannot be matched. "So," Thomas says, "if women are eternal, what are we?"

"Men?"

Thomas nods.

Gallatin wrinkles his brow. "I ... I don't know. We're stronger and we govern. We fight the wars."

"Which means women have to be careful. More observant. Smarter."

Gallatin gives Thomas a firm nod. "That's the truth, is it not?" His friend sends out two beseeching hands.

"We the men, on the other hand," Thomas announces, "we are ephemeral."

Gallatin's eyes go wide. "We are, aren't we just? Well said, my friend."

Thomas shrugs and looks away. The cartful of furniture is nearly out of sight. He's not sure why he said what he just did. Except that ephemeral is exactly what he personally has become.

He wallows in insignificance. He has had not a single accomplishment since coming to England. Unless you count toiling at selling bolts of fabric and teaching French, history and geography to aristocratic boys with thick skulls, which Thomas does not. His advance is not merely checked, he's completely fallen off the ladder he was once on. And despite his aspirations as a writer, he still has nothing in print for anyone to read. Ephemeral.

He breathes in the steam that rises in smoky coils. He hopes its vapours are giving his nostrils a good cleanse. If only they could refresh his humours as well.

Hélène and Élisabeth are still locked in conversation, though there are signs it could be nearing an end. He doubts either woman sees herself as eternal. Each is far too practical for any foolish talk like that. One is racing the clock to be with child while the other ... the other.... Thomas peers down into the steaming pool. He has no idea what Élisabeth thinks or wants as it concerns a baby. Does she, like Hélène, want a child? Is he the father she would choose?

"I should go," Thomas announces.

Gallatin blinks at him. "Go? But Élisabeth—"

"No, the legs must move."

"Later at the Assembly Rooms? Hélène and I are going to the lower of the two. We would like to see you there, you and Élisabeth."

Thomas is not sure if he smiles or not, but he sends Gallatin a nod. Is it not striking that all those who are married want everyone else to be as well? Is that to raise others up, or to bring them down?

As he swings away and picks up the pace, Thomas's thoughts are about his Swiss. Élisabeth Cauvin is a good match, yes she is. Yet he resents Gallatin trying manoeuvre him into a marriage with her. Such a step has many angles to consider, which requires time. For the time being, he prefers being answerable to only himself.

———

"What it is to be a man, I suppose." Hélène places her large hat upon her head. She folds up the brim so she can see Élisabeth. "Are you and Thomas coming to the Rooms this evening?"

"I think so, but we are travelling with John Cleland and Fanny, you know."

Hélène cannot stop the frown. "Jean does not warm to Monsieur Cleland, I'm afraid."

"Yes." Élisabeth exhales. "I have heard."

"Well, the less said. I have to go. The pump awaits."

"You are an example, Hélène, you really are."

"First brave, now an example. You'll turn my head."

Élisabeth leans forward to meet Hélène half-way. The embrace is quickly done. "I hope you get the result you want," says Élisabeth.

Hélène looks into her friend's hazel eyes. The worry that was there before is gone, replaced by sincerity. "You're very kind, Élisabeth."

As Hélène climbs the steps of the slip, heading for the small room where she will sit with the hottest water streaming down, she turns back to wave one more time at the woman she works with, the woman who works for her and Jean. The Swiss, however, has her eyes closed. She is back down in the water up to her chin, as she was when Hélène came upon her a while ago. The sight of an unseeing Élisabeth brings a flicker of something pulsing behind Hélène's eyes. Whatever it is does not take shape. It does not come into words.

She pads lightly toward the small, subterranean room. It's time to put on the slippers and the flannel garment with the great sleeves. The pump awaits. Through the doorway into the small room she goes. There is the rack where the large-sleeved garments hang, the slippers placed in pairs on the stone floor below. It is reassuring that there is an order to things. Hélène slides her feet into the slippers and puts on the flannel shift.

Yes, an order to things. Things wanted and things obtained. Though a child is hardly a thing. It's a gift, a precious gift her husband wants more than anything. She has ingested red raspberry and red clover for months, and even paid for a packet of chaste-berries the herbalist assured her could not fail. Though fail they did. She insists Gallatin do his duty on the days she is supposed to be most fertile, but still, there is no result. Her monthlies keep coming without fail. So, she wonders as she waits for her turn beneath the hot flow, maybe it should be Gallatin, not her, going under the burning pump?

V

Favour

Bath – November 1734

Thomas and John Cleland exchange grins. No sooner have Élisabeth and Fanny entered the outer portion of the Assembly Rooms, in the building overlooking the Parade Gardens, but their excited chatter comes to a halt. Their footsteps too. It is the sight through the wide-open double doors of men and women sauntering in and out, dressed to the hilt and presenting expressions that suggest the eyes of the world deserve to be on them. It can only be the ballroom.

"What say you, that we forget about this?" Cleland sends Thomas a wink.

"You are right. We have seen it now. We do not *have* to go in," Thomas says, not far from Élisabeth's ear.

Fanny sends each man a daggered look. Élisabeth purses her lips. "Only trying to get our goat, Fanny. Ignore them."

"Well then." Thomas places a gentle hand underneath Élisabeth's elbow. "If we are indeed to go in, would you do me the honour, Madame?"

Élisabeth raises her chin to look off nobly to some imagined distance. "We shall."

"That's the spirit." Cleland turns to Fanny and holds up a crooked arm. "And I should like the honour of entering with the prettiest of all. You'll be the one to bring me luck."

Fanny takes the proffered arm, and bestows on Cleland a radiant smile.

The flicker of candles makes the ballroom tremble with burnished light. The wavering glow comes not only from the four large chandeliers overhead but also from the sconces on the walls. Then the mirrors join in. The gilded light quivers to the rise and fall of the music, and to the hum of what must be a hundred excited conversations.

Élisabeth glances at the pocket of musicians in the near corner. The four men playing the stringed instruments are working their bows like there is nothing else of importance in the world. Their eyes do not leave their music sheets while their bow hands sweep back and forth. The harpsichordist, however, he who is providing the deep continuo for the rest, is looking anywhere but at the keys. He finds Élisabeth looking his way and gives her a conspiratorial wink. She returns a smile, but then realizes what she has done. She quickly shifts her gaze. Over to the man she entered the ballroom with a quarter hour ago. Thomas is slowly making his way around the perimeter.

He is easy to find in his queen's blue coat and matching breeches. It's funny that a man who prefers secrecy to almost anything else should chose such a colour for this trip. He must be hoping to be seen, to be noticed by someone who might have the power to change the course of his life. Because Thomas is clearly not content with being a shop clerk, nor a part-time tutor. The higher rungs of the ladder call out to him. She knows him.

She has to smile at the blank expression Thomas puts upon his face as he strolls around the ballroom. It is his way of pretending he is not paying attention to what he hears as he strolls by, when that's exactly what he is about.

Leaving Thomas to his game, Élisabeth scans the rest of the room. Beside the talk and above the music – no, that would be beneath, not above – she distinguishes the tap, slide and scuff of the few dozen pairs of shoes out on the central portion of the ballroom floor. Prancing and weaving, precision in their movements, the dancers move like kings and queens. From two long lines they separate into couples with raised hands. Once around in a pirouette then each peels off, until he or she finds the other again, this time for the promenade. None on the dance floor gives anything away by their facial expressions. No, there are a few couples exchanging sweet words when they come fleetingly into each other's grasp. Or else they trade knowing glances with smiles upon their lips. Would that she had someone like that with whom she could share a bond.

To the floor her gaze drops. She cannot imagine Thomas Tyrell, as good as he has been to her, ever taking her out onto this or any other dance floor. Nor ever whispering something in her ear to make her laugh or smile. It is not his way.

Thomas does not think he has ever seen so much contentment in one room. Everyone standing or moving around the grand hall and the small rooms off it carries a self-satisfied face. It's as if the Assembly Rooms exist not just as a place to display one's finest clothes, comportment and gait, which is obvious, but also to show how pleased one is. Keen to be exactly where and who they are. Can it be that the new rules for polite society, for which Gallatin has announced his approval, really do banish anger, disappointment and envy from the world?

Thomas feels his chest tighten at that. Yes, he wishes the world could be so easily improved, but he has his doubts. Surfaces are just that; faces can be masks. So he feels obligated to take on the task of wandering around the room and listening in. Surely not everyone is as delighted as they pretend to be, watching the contented chat and the dancers go through routine steps.

"Yes, you're right, it is my third mill," says a stocky man with a ruddy face.

There is great pride in his voice. He's speaking with a thin chap who is leaning in to catch every word. Thomas supposes it's envy he sees in the listener's eyes. Thomas pretends he has to adjust his wig, and halts to catch what comes next in this conversation.

"Blockley, this time, and no, I can't complain. The profits allow me to buy whatever I choose. I'm looking for a place here in Bath, as a matter of fact. To spend at least a part of the season here."

Thomas cannot hear what the thin man says, but there's no mistaking the stocky man's reply: "Yes, I have earned it, you're right."

Thomas begins to move again. What wealthy man does not think exactly that, that he has earned his standing in the world, just as the poor are supposed to grudgingly accept their lot? There is a relationship between the two. For the few to be rich, a great many must be poor. It's the equation of life. Inequality is nature's way. Predators and prey.

"I'd prefer something simpler, wouldn't you?" Thomas hears an elderly lady whisper to a young woman, clearly her servant. The latter has an arm round the matron to help her stay upright. "There's too much sound, too much noise in the way they play. It runs together in my ears."

The young one curtsies but does not let go. "Yes, Ma'am," she says.

Thomas nods approvingly. Though he likes the music, especially how its pattern of notes climb and fall then climb again, he understands the old lady's complaint. The old of this world are bewildered by too much sight and sound. His wife, Marguerite, had touches of that. He supposes it will happen to him one day, should he live long enough. Long enough? How long is that? Is it not the way of things to want more, especially months and years? He admits he does. He's had thirty-four so far, and he hopes for a like number to come. Only with more standing, comfort and ease than he's had so far.

Thomas veers toward two men whose fierce expressions, now that he spies them, stand out. They are so very serious when everyone else is light.

"A damnable thing," says the man dressed in brown.

Thomas sees it is a coat of finely napped wool. The man is speaking to a fellow who is wearing a less expensive grey coat. The latter has worry lines engraved upon his brow.

"But clever, just the same."

"Clever? What does clever have to do with it? It's ruining the way things work. There's not a weaver in Colchester who wants it. Nor any spinner. We've petitioned the King to stop Kay from making them. Not that that'll do any good."

The fly-shuttle is Thomas's guess. He's heard about it. Yes, the man is right. Change is not welcome, not if you're on the losing side.

He glances up ahead, back to where his tour of the room began. He sees John Cleland and Fanny are no longer standing with Élisabeth. She is still there, studying those out on the dance floor, but where the other two might have gone he will not guess. He only hopes Cleland isn't doing anything that will tarnish his own name because of his association with the Englishman. Thomas is beginning to think Gallatin is right. Cleland has a shady side – maybe slippery is the better word. He needs to be careful about that.

It is remarkable that Élisabeth can be sufficiently pleased to simply stand and watch the dancers on the floor. Wait. There is no woman anywhere who prefers to watch rather than dance herself. It's how they're built. Young or old, thick or thin, they love to measure their steps to the music's beat. And so, on occasion, does he. Sometimes Marguerite would hum a tune in the salon, and they would prance around as if they were somewhere grand. They'd laugh when the servants came into the salon and caught them dancing, not a musician in sight.

Thomas's gaze swings to three girls dressed in pastel shades. They are giggling at something seen or heard. He cannot recall ever being like that, not even when he was a lad.

Back his regard goes to Élisabeth. She does look very pretty tonight, and it's not just her clothes. It is the intelligence in her eyes and the lovely features of her face. Maybe Gallatin is right. Maybe Thomas should lock things up with her. She is good for him, good in every way save one. A marriage to her would not bring him any more elevated standing in the world.

Thomas sways slightly where he stands. He dare not be precipitous. He'll have to think on this awhile. But in the meantime, Élisabeth deserves better than he has shown her so far this evening. She should be out on the dance floor. He will ask her to join him for the next set.

"There you are."

Thomas swings round. It's Cleland. He has a frazzled look and is in a state of undress. No, not undressed, but his coat, it is inside out. Fanny is in tow, both hands clutching John's elbow, a pleading expression on her face.

"Cleland," Thomas whispers, "why are you … like that?" He points at the coat.

The Englishman looks down at his chest and sleeves. "Oh, that," he says with a shrug.

"It's reversed for good luck," Fanny says. Her expression asks how Thomas could not know that.

Thomas looks Cleland up and down. "The card room?" He shakes his head.

Cleland takes hold of Thomas's elbow. "Things have not begun well, true enough. But—"

"But they will," Fanny interrupts. Her eyes dare Thomas to say otherwise. "There was a pasty man who brought bad luck. Smelled like a turnip. But he just left."

Thomas controls his breathing. He does not think he shows his weary sigh. "Alors? How much?"

Cleland increases the pressure on his elbow. "Enough to keep me going until there's a turn in the tide."

"A turn in the tide," Fanny echoes.

"You understand we have yet another day here," Thomas says. He does not regret the disapproval he is likely showing on his tightened lips.

"Rest easy, Tyrell. I shall bring back double whatever you give me." Cleland's hand is out.

Thomas hears the air issue from his nose. "It is a loan, not a gift." He makes sure John Cleland sees the seriousness in his eyes. Only then does he reach inside his bright blue coat and pull out his leather pouch.

Élisabeth watches the exchange with Cleland, but turns away before Thomas might be inclined to glance her way. When Thomas comes to stand by her side a moment later she pretends she is surprised. "Oh, you're back. How was your stroll around the room?"

"Don't ask."

She cannot resist. "Someone asked for money perchance?"

Thomas squints at her then snorts. "You saw him?"

"I did."

Thomas shrugs. Élisabeth does the same, miming him in an attempt to draw a laugh.

Thomas does yield a smile. "Listen," he begins, "I was wondering if—" He takes her hand in his.

"Je t'écoute." Élisabeth was not expecting this. Is he about to ask her to dance?

Whatever words Thomas had in mind seem to be suddenly lost to him. His conversation and his attention loft elsewhere. Élisabeth pivots to see what it can be. Two women across the way. One wears a rose-coloured dress and the other a gentle green. Pretty, yes, and with the poise and posture of those comfortably at ease. Élisabeth swings back to study Thomas's face. He is clearly intrigued by those two, whoever they are.

"Friends of yours?"

Thomas returns to meet her gaze. "Those two? No, no. Well, they were up on the hillside this morning." His eyes go again to the unknown women. His voice becomes a mumble. "Don't know who …" Back to Élisabeth he swivels. "They spoke to me in French," he says with bright eyes.

"Incroyable," she says with a straight face.

Thomas blinks. Then it sinks in and he shows her an embarrassed shrug. Élisabeth accepts it as an apology of sorts. She will not mime him this time.

While Élisabeth waits for Thomas's thoughts to gather again – and go back to where they were when it looked like he was about to ask her to dance – she glances toward the entrance to the ballroom. People are still squeezing in, every shape and size. What was Cleland's quip? Something about "the vulgar and the great" being side by side. Well, she knows on which side of that equation she belongs, in the eyes of the aristocrats. Nonetheless, church mouse though she is, she is enjoying herself. And part of it is seeing the many dresses, shoes and jewels she will never be able to afford or even try on.

She cannot help but wonder how long it will be before the ballroom begins to stink, no matter that all the scents people have used to douse their skin and clothes. Were everyone in front of her dressed in rags, like the poor, the ballroom would be said to contain a mob. But with everyone in finery, no shouts or fists, no anger in any eyes, it's called an assembly of quality. It makes her shake her head.

Women seem to outnumber men, but that's only because their dresses shimmer and tremble to catch the eye. The men's outfits take up less volume and cover a smaller spectrum of the colour band. Besides, all that matters to most men – all except her beloved father – is that the world take notice of their success, nothing more than that. They dress more to impress than to enjoy.

Most women in the room appear to be wives, or aspiring to join that privileged club. A few, of course, a lucky few, could be widows. But you have to go through a marriage to get to that blissful state. Some women are clearly mothers. Well, maybe not. Perhaps they are chaperones with their girls in tow, girls they are eager – it shows on their faces – to present. Do the girls not look wonderful, so nervously expectant in their pastel stripes and flower designs?

"Still here?" Thomas's eyes are much amused.

Élisabeth feels her cheeks go warm. "De grâce, Monsieur." She curtseys to the man.

"Tiens, are you not sweet?" Thomas says. "The sweetest in this vast, crowded room."

"I doubt that," Élisabeth sighs. "For you know not what I truly think."

"No, of course, but I—"

Before Thomas can find another word he glances at a large woman passing behind Élisabeth. She commands attention because of her billowing, flame-coloured gown. Then, over her shoulder, thirty feet away and coming toward them, is Hélène, with Gallatin trailing behind. Hélène has a most determined look on her face.

"What's wrong?" Élisabeth asks.

"Nothing," Thomas says, but he knows he says it wrong. He apologizes with his eyes then raises a pointing hand. "Here come your bookshop friends."

Hélène slows her advance, waits for Gallatin to catch up. She wants him by her side as is correct. She had worried Thomas and Élisabeth might have gone to the other Assembly Room, the one higher up on the hill. But no, here they are, standing together like friends or lovers beneath a flickering candelabra.

"Hello and bonsoir." She embraces Élisabeth.

"You must be tired." Élisabeth's eyes display concern. "Such a long day you've had. The hot water will have worn you down."

Hélène waves that concern away. "Thank you. You are kind, but it's all done. I'll not go again."

"No?" asks Gallatin, surprised.

Hélène shows him a quick shake of her head, then turns to acknowledge Thomas with a shallow curtsey, nothing more than that. Then it's back to Élisabeth.

"We are here for gaiety, are we not? And look at you, my good friend, you are very pretty in lime and cream."

"Do you think?" asks Élisabeth. She looks down skeptically at what she has on.

"To be sure," reassures Hélène, though the truth is the Swiss's dress is only linen after all, and not a perfect fit. And her stomacher has no embroidery on it.

And so conversation begins. The two couples take turns smiling at wit or kind words, or else looking grave when there is a remark that merits such attentiveness. Hélène enjoys bantering with Élisabeth – about the ballroom, the many gowns and the overall circus before their eyes – but she is disappointed she cannot at the same time catch what it is Gallatin and Thomas are talking about. All she can take in is the rhythm of the male voices as they interrupt each other with teasing and the occasional laugh. Rarely do the two separate conversations overlap, though every once in a while, Hélène makes passing eye contact with the men, just to remind them that she is nearby.

A surge of joy suddenly fills Élisabeth's chest as she hears the music rise to match the swell of conversation circling round her head. She can only blink and smile. It must be how the religious feel when they experience what they call rapture. She supposes it comes to them in prayer, while for her all it took was to stand and talk with friends. It feels so very good. Where a moment ago she was half wishing herself a widow, now she is filled with the lightness and warmth that comes from having friends.

"We should dance," Élisabeth blurts out.

Three sets of eyes turn her way.

Hélène places a finger to her lips. "Hmm, dance?" she says, but there is something like laughter in her eyes.

Élisabeth grins at her. Thomas looks bemused and Gallatin covers his mouth with his hand. Clearly, he has not heard or seen a better joke than the one his wife is acting out.

Hélène releases a broad grin. "Yes, of course we dance."

"Let's," says Thomas, taking Élisabeth by the hand.

It's a hand she gladly accepts. But then it occurs to her that she pushed Thomas to the limit the other night questioning him about his past relationship with Hélène. It is history, and so time to move on. Élisabeth lets go of Thomas's hand and directs him toward Hélène. "You two, you start us off," she says.

Thomas's expression is stunned surprise. "Hélène et moi?"

"Yes. If you show you can dance well enough with Hélène *then* you get to dance with me."

Thomas's eyes go wider still.

"A joke." Élisabeth gives his sleeve a tender tug.

"So it shall be." Hélène reaches out and takes Thomas's hand. "Come on, sir, let's see if you measure up." She jerks a joking thumb toward Élisabeth. "And Jean," she commands Gallatin, "the Swiss will teach you a few steps."

Hélène winks at Élisabeth. "We have our work cut out, do we not? Hurry, let's join the fresh set."

Hélène knows crossing herself would be too much, especially in a crowd of Protestants. So she merely glances up to the candelabra burning bright. Thank you, God. She had wanted a quiet word with Thomas, but was uncertain how that could be done. Yet here is her opportunity, a gift from none other than Élisabeth. The woman's suspicions have clearly passed. It has to be a sign that what Hélène is going to say to Thomas is Heaven-blessed.

Thomas does not try to figure out how it is that he is out on the ballroom floor with Hélène and not Élisabeth. There are some things women do that defy the logic that is inside his head. It is what makes them so intriguing.

As he begins to follow the routine steps, with Hélène's up-raised right hand held lightly in his left, he makes a point to try and catch swirling Élisabeth's gaze. She is partnered with Gallatin in the adjacent circle of dancers. She is not, however, looking his way. All he can see is the flash of her smile as she promenades and twirls.

And so Thomas turns to face Hélène. Their hands go up, their hands go down, all in concert with the music and the movements of everyone else. As stately as can be, they move through the steps, coming together only fleetingly. The first encounter comes and goes. Hélène says not a word, yet it seems to Thomas that she is holding something back. Not until the promenade does she speak.

"Thomas."

"Yes."

"I need a favour."

"A favour?"

"That's right."

Then the steps of the dance send each of them in a different direction. They make and hold eye contact as they move around the circle. If he is not mistaken, there is apprehension in her eyes. Why would that be? There is no favour he can give. He has no money to lend, nor any position to grant. He is in need of both for himself.

As the next promenade begins Thomas is sure he picks up a ginger scent. It must be a fragrance Hélène is wearing, wafting to him as she leans close.

He does not catch what she whispers this time. "Say again," he says.

"Cross Bath," she says, barely louder than before.

"Cross Bath?"

"Shhh."

His ears fill with the movement and music, the scuff and tap of feet. Whatever does she mean? He does know where it is. He walked by it earlier in the day. But does she not know that it is closed?

The next promenade he seeks to know what she is talking about. "Hélène, I—"

"Tomorrow."

"Tomorrow what?"

"At the peep." Her look is threatening, her *do you not understand?*

Thomas wants to stand and demand, yet he cannot. He has to move along. There is the rest of the dance. All he can do is nod that he has heard and understood: Hélène wants him at the Cross Bath at the break of day.

The bouquet with the ginger notes is strong. If that is a new perfume, Thomas likes it very much.

As the music dies he and the visibly tight-lipped Hélène drop hands. Evidently she does not want to say another word. Side by side they shuffle silently through a delighted, mumbling crowd to rejoin Élisabeth and Gallatin. Thomas feels a tug on his sleeve.

"Remember, not a word," comes through Hélène's teeth.

Thomas is tempted to laugh. When has he ever told anything to anyone when he had a chance to keep it to himself?

———

Thomas mutters oaths under his breath. He has barely slept a wink. Afraid he might fall into a deep sleep and miss the early-morning meeting with Hélène, he has done nothing but toss and turn. One shoulder, then the other, then on his back. All night long he has not found a position that felt good. It was only when Élisabeth gave him a hard shove – "What are you doing?" – that he forced himself to lie still. He thought it important that she be asleep when he slips away. He does not want questions he cannot answer.

Judging by the lightening he is seeing around the edges of the shutters, the break of day is near. Good luck is with him. The Swiss is in a deep sleep.

Élisabeth tosses back the bedclothes the moment she hears the click of the closing the door. She doesn't know what it is, but something is up. Thomas was not himself in bed. It was a constant thrashing about. And now he's up and away, creeping like a thief before the sun is fully up.

Over top of her chemise she pulls on her travelling dress with its pale blue stripes. It'll have to do as it is. She has no one to tie it up in the back. But she does throw a dark blue wool cloak round her shoulders and puts on a cap. Into her shoes she steps. She has to hurry if she's going to see what Thomas is about. If she loses sight of him after he exits the inn, she won't know which way to turn.

———

Thomas pads the damp cobbles through the lifting gloom. The little city is still asleep. He does not pick up even a hint of coal smoke in the air. The cooing of an unseen dove is the only sound.

But are those footsteps? Is someone following behind?

Only a cart halted along the side of the street Thomas has just come down. It's loaded with barrels and bales. The horse is staring back at him. The master must be somewhere in a nearby yard.

Back to his descent down the hill, he makes sure to avoid the droppings where they lie. If he ever meets Beau Nash in person, he will suggest that the Master of Ceremonies get the horseshit off the street before people stir each day. That would be a *polite* way to make Bath differ from every other city in the world.

Thomas reaches out to touch a street corner as he goes by. If he remembers correctly, it's not much farther to the Cross Bath.

———

Cloaked in her hooded cape of dark green, Hélène paces in front of the stone arches along the inner wall, the ones closest to the street entrance. Back and forth, nearly on tiptoe. She is thankful the entrance has no door, just a rope braided twice across. Ducking under does no one any harm. On the contrary, it gives her a place to rendezvous with Thomas, so long as he shows up.

As she strides, Hélène sniffs the air. Though the Cross Bath has not been a working spa for months, you can still smell sulphur. Its sharp scent has apparently permeated the entire place, the very stones as well as the curtains that front the arches. Those arches, according to what the innkeeper said, are for ladies. The curtains are to give privacy while they soak. Gentlemen stay in the centre near the carved stone cross that gives the place its name. A proper protocol, Hélène thinks. Better than the King's Bath, men and women milling like fish in a barrel.

Back to the entrance she paces. She can see the sky is adding just a hint of palest yellow to the grey. Will Thomas let her down? True, all he heard from her was a vague appeal, that there was a favour he could do for her. Would she answer such a call? Not likely. But then, he's not her. She'll not give up on him for another while yet.

She hears footsteps out on the street.

"There you are."

She beckons Thomas to come quickly under the rope. His expression is that of a child startled by a wolf who has popped up in a puppet show.

"Hurry. Come in here."

"Listen, I—"

"Shhh— Don't talk."

"Don't talk?" Thomas leans back. He makes a stern face. Then he notices that Hélène has on only a chemise beneath her dark green cape. "Why—"

She tugs him away from the entrance, over to where a sun-faded scarlet curtain covers the entrance to a stone arch. She pulls back the curtain and gestures for him to step in. Thomas tries to read her face. He cannot. There is only fierceness.

"In," she says.

Hélène pulls the curtain back across. It is nearly pitch black.

"What are you …?"

"Quick," she says.

"Quick? What—"

She takes hold of the waist of his breeches. Her fingers go to his buttons.

"What? No!"

"Thomas," Hélène pulls him toward her and whispers close to his lips, "I need this."

"Are you crazy?"

"I am not."

Her hands are having trouble with a button.

"No, Hélène. This *is* crazy."

She says not a word. Her eyes lock on his while her fingers struggle.

"Think of Jean," he says.

"Not right now."

Thomas snorts. "I can see that."

She nods. "That's right." She gives his breeches a tug. They drop to his ankles.

Thomas reaches down to retrieve his pants but Hélène steps on them. She pins them underfoot.

He stands erect. "No, Hélène."

"Shhh." She touches her lips lightly on his. "That's right." She takes him into her hands. Against his will, he responds. Her grip feels good.

"But Jean."

"Shhh."

She burrows her forehead in the warmth of his neck.

Thomas finds it hard to talk. All he knows is that her hand is persuasive. His thoughts are taking flight. It's getting close to the point of no turning back.

"He must not know," he finally says.

"He will not know," she whispers in his ear.

Thomas sees only her dark eyes. They are huge, so close to his.

"Our secret then," he says. His hand goes to her private place.

"That's right," she says, soft as breath.

There is nothing more to say, only the doing of it.

———

Élisabeth does not need to see what she can hear. Coming down the street she glimpsed Hélène a hundred feet ahead waving Thomas to duck under the rope at the entrance to the Cross Bath. A moment later, having gone in herself, her ears led her to the curtained arch. First whispers and now this, breathing and moans.

She stiffens her wobbly legs. Much as she is tempted, she knows there is no point in pulling the curtain back. You cannot shame these two. Thomas thinks the truth can be cloaked by words while for Hélène friendship is just a facade, like make-up on a face.

Élisabeth pushes off from the wall, away from its hateful sounds. Enough. That's enough. She does not want to be around when they finish, recover their breath and pull the curtain back. It would be too much to see their embarrassed faces and for them to see hers.

She slides away from the curtained arch, silently lifting her feet. Back out under the rope barrier Élisabeth Cauvin goes, out again to the street. She lifts her dress and begins to run.

VI

Obligation

London – August 1736

Thomas twists his neck to assess the crick. He cannot move his head back or to the left. It's something that happens from time to time, which he blames on the bolster where he lays his head each night. There is only one cure he knows. It's the same cure he uses for everything that goes wrong with his frame. He gets out and takes a long walk. His legs always put him right.

As it turns out, he has to stretch his legs in any case. Two birds, as the saying goes. He has an obligation he would prefer to avoid but fears he cannot. He's expected at the house in Spitalfields where he once lived. It makes him sigh, although he does not scuff his feet. He's not twelve anymore. He has learned that half of life is disappointment and the other half things that must be done, regardless of whether you want to or not. This is just another of the latter. It is a rare day when he is able to do what he really wants. He has neither the position nor the wealth. Once he had a bit of both, when he was still in France and married to Marguerite. Not anymore, alas. He still does not know if his old kindly wife is alive or dead. Maybe he'll write to someone who would know, his old patron, the magistrate judge. He will write as Pichon, of course, but he can ask the judge to reply to him care of Thomas Tyrell.

Sometimes he wonders if he should simply return to the land of his birth. Trade the kingdom of George II for that of Louis XV again. If things do not look up soon, he surely will. Would it not be wonderful if the magistrate judge would take him back? Thomas still has the letter of recommendation the jurist signed, its seal unbroken because in England it is no help. What about returning to Pichon again and giving up Tyrell? What is it gamblers say? It's best to cut one's losses? Well, he has lost enough on this London gambit.

He turns right off Saint Martin's Lane onto New Street. It's not too many steps before he'll be cutting across the Covent Garden. The prospect lifts his spirits. The market square is always a spectacle, a circus of humanity. He tests his neck again. Yes, it might already be a little better than it was.

"Save your clothes. Get your props and pins."

Thomas takes in the tall, thin fellow crossing his path. The man is selling everything to do with clotheslines. That strikes Thomas as humorous. The fellow would be wise to clip on a few pins to attach the clothes on his back to the very lines he sells. A good wind might blow the hawker himself away. Thomas lightly shakes his head to show the man he is not interested. The hawker nods to show his appreciation to Thomas for not pretending he doesn't exist.

His thoughts go back again to what he is walking toward. It will be the first time in twelve months he has made a pilgrimage to the house round the corner from the All Saints Church in Spitalfields. As was the case a year ago, he is responding to an invitation. Invitation? Insistence would be a better term. That first time, three days after the baby was born, Gallatin laid it on the line.

"Thomas, you're my oldest friend and we're listing you as the *parrain*. The boy will be named after you. We want you to come and sign the register."

Now, twelve months later, Gallatin insists again. "Your godson, our little Tommy, he's turning one."

Not to go would be the equivalent of saying adieu to Gallatin and their well-travelled friendship. They have both invested too much in their closeness to let it wither away now.

Thomas looks up to watch two carpenters putting up a scaffold at the end of King Street. He wonders if they, and all who toil in the building trades, take pride in what they put up, or if it is simply how they put bread on their table. More likely the latter. Back when he was a clerk in a law office, it would be difficult to say he took pride in all the copy work he was obligated to do.

Obligations. The way of the world, are they not?

A racket fills his ears. The hundred stalls of Covent Garden are starting to surround him with their roar. Everywhere are hawkers' cries and buyers' chatter. Usually an annoyance, right now Thomas thinks it sounds good. It helps distract him from recollections he wants to dim and fade.

"Oranges sweet," sings out a girl in tattered clothes.

Thomas steps back to let her pass. Not far away, a short, round man grins between his shouts about his tray of fresh baked buns. On the next aisle a matron dressed in bright red says her strawberries deserve to be savoured and with cream. Another woman farther back, big as a barge, has both a tray and a backpack of wicker. Sticking out from both are toys to amuse a child.

"Pinwheels, toy boats and swords!" she cries.

Of course, Thomas thinks. Gallatin and H. will be expecting him to bring a gift, a gift for this boy child of theirs. H. Yes, it is better, as if she were someone other than the Hélène he used to know. H. Gallatin's H.

But where was he? Oh yes, a wooden sword. He had one as a boy back in Vire. His godson may be too small to wield it now, being only one, but he will learn in time. A weapon, even as a toy, comes in handy in this world.

As he goes round the fruit and vegetable sellers' stalls with their dark green awnings, en route to reach the seller with the wooden toys, he recalls another woman who was once in his life, now gone. Élisabeth Cauvin was not at The Bell when he went looking for her, and the innkeeper said he'd seen her march out the front door with her things in the early hours. It was only last week that Thomas heard from Cleland, who'd heard from Fanny, that Élisabeth had taken herself to Bristol for a time, before moving back to the continent, to Amsterdam. More than a few times, Thomas has thought of going to the Dutch port to see if he might find her there.

"What might have been," he mumbles aloud.

"Sorry, sir." It is the large woman with the wooden toys.

"Might I have a look at the sword?" Thomas holds out his right hand.

"For a boy, sir?"

"It is."

"The perfect gift, the absolute perfect gift."

"He is only one."

"No matter, sir, they grow into it. They do. Mark my words."

Thomas inclines his head. Isn't that exactly what he was saying to himself, only a moment ago?

———

Accompanied by Monique de Vins, her dearest London confidante, Jeanne-Marie Barbe Le Prince, the happily annulled and then widowed Madame de Beaumont, is on her way to visit an aged friend in his confinement. A welcome ritual it is. For Jeanne-Marie believes with all her heart that the world depends on such kindnesses. The poor man, a fellow Norman and an écuyer no less, is approaching eighty and finds himself in the Fleet Street prison, near St. Paul's. His crime was that of being weak, in his case for making promises at gambling tables he could not keep. Jeanne-Marie insists on helping him, by depositing a few coins in the man's outstretched hand through the window grille on the Farringdon Street side every Sunday. Her reward is the man's nobly expressed gratitude, nothing more than that. Thankfully, Monique no longer quibbles about her charity. Her good friend has slowly but surely come to share Jeanne-Marie's point of view. All it took, it proves yet again, was an example worthy of emulation.

Coming into the Covent Garden market Jeanne-Marie is struck by the thick bank of billowing clouds looming above the buildings on the other side of the square. Perfectly flat on the bottom and inky dark most of the way up. Only the puffy tips are shining white. How far up the great bank reaches. A veritable mountain in the sky. She doubts any painter could capture the sky exactly as it has painted itself. It is majestic.

"Oh, look at those clouds," says Monique de Vins. "We are going to get caught. We should turn round, Jeanne-Marie."

"No, no," Madame reassures. "They will blow over. Or at least wait until after we have made our visit. You'll see."

"I ... I'm not so sure. They are very dark."

Madame does not reply too quickly. She wants to show she is taking into account what her friend has said. So she pauses to look around the bustling market square. It is, as usual, as noisy as a barnyard at feeding time. She nods at a short, wide man who is yelling about his fresh baked buns. And Jeanne-Marie sends a smile to a tall, thin woman with a display of bright-coloured auriculas. The stand with three levels of the happy flowers in clay pots makes a gay theatre. Farther still Jeanne-Marie pretends to consider the hawker's claim that her strawberries are the best in England, deserving of the best cream.

At length Madame de Beaumont turns back to Monique. "No, I think Monsieur would be very sad if we did not come. It is Sunday, and he is expecting us."

"He will understand when he sees the rain. Besides, no one always gets what they want, do they?"

Madame de Beaumont gives her friend an understanding smile. It is the same she presents to any of her students who do not grasp an explanation the first time. "Monique, the poor fellow has no one else who visits him. If there's a shower, we do have our parasols."

Madame de Beaumont sees her friend turn a suspicious eye to the sky above.

"If that opens up," Monique says with a grim expression, "our parasols will not shelter us. They are for shade."

Jeanne-Marie clasps Monqiue by the hand. "A little faith, de grâce."

"Faith will not keep us dry."

"We'll see."

Madame de Beaumont hears a rolling rumble of thunder, and has no choice but to look up. The clouds are even thicker and darker than they were a few moments ago. Monique might be right. It does look like it will rain.

"Hear that?" taunts her friend.

"Let's hurry. It's only another quarter hour to the prison. Shorter if we hurry. We need not stay long." Her gaze is straight ahead to the narrow lane that leads to Tavistock Street.

"Jeanne-Marie?"

"Yes, Monique." She does not let her impatience show. "What is it?"

"That man," Monique says, voice down. She makes Jeanne-Marie come close to hear what she has to say.

"What man is that?" Jeanne-Marie indulges her friend.

"Dark brown coat. Child's wooden sword in hand."

Jeanne-Marie takes in the man as Monique suggests. It is amusing to see a grown man with a child's toy dangling in his hand. "A father, I suppose. What of him?"

"He is familiar. Remember the handsome man we met on the hill paths of Bath. Do you recall? He spoke to us in French."

"The man we later saw in the Assembly Room, studying everyone?"

"The same."

"You may be right. There is something familiar about how he carries himself."

"Let's see if we are correct." Monique lengthens her stride, picking up her pace.

"Monique! I do not think this—"

"Shhh. Come on."

———

Thomas's eyes go to the bottom of the blade. It's a scratched design of some sort. He brings it close. It looks like – could it be – yes, it is. A tiny fleur-de-lys. Some Frenchman must have made this toy. Not impossible, of course, for certain parts of London virtually swim with French. But they're mostly Huguenots and he cannot imagine any of them scratching such a symbol, not after being either slaughtered or exiled by the Catholic king for their attachment to the wrong faith. The wrong faith! As if there could be a right one. Faith by its nature means something not able to be either seen or proved.

"Bonjour, Monsieur."

The singsong voice sounds like it's directed at him. Thomas stops and turns round. He finds not one but two comely faces. The closer of the two is smiling, the other keeping back. Thomas feels the challenge. He tenders a smile to warm the farther one, then he makes eye contact with each in turn.

"Mesdames." Thomas begins to bow, but stops when he realizes he has a child's wooden sword in his right hand. A wry smile is his explanation. Women will understand it is a gift for a child.

"We bring no harm," says the closer of the two in heavily-accented English. She has a grin on her face. "No need for use of épée over us. On us. With us."

"De grâce, mesdames." Thomas switches the conversation to French. "Or do I misspeak. Am I addressing two desmoiselles?"

"Mademoiselle de Vins," says the one at ease. A curtsey comes with her smile.

She is coquettish, which is fine by him. He admires the cut and quality of the fabrics she has on. Her jewellery is discrete and her cheeks nicely rouged, not too much.

"And you, Mademoiselle?" Thomas rolls the hand without the toy sword toward the shyer one, she who is studying him. Her eyes are darting up and down, back and forth the way a woman's often do. She is as pretty as the other, but still showing much reserve.

"It is Madame. Madame de Beaumont." She neither curtseys nor smiles.

90

"But," adds Mademoiselle de Vins quickly, "her marriage that was, is no more. It was annulled."

"Monique!"

"It's all right, Jeanne-Marie. He should know." Mademoiselle de Vins turns to Thomas. "He who was her husband, he is dead in any case. You are not a scandalmonger, are you, Monsieur?"

"I am not. Discretion is … my command." Thomas mock brandishes the wooden sword.

"Admirable," says the one whose marriage was annulled and whose former husband later died, "but would not a knightly gentleman reveal himself?"

There is a sparkle in her eyes that was not there before. Thomas likes her bearing, accent and choice of words.

"Madame de Beaumont," Thomas replies, "I'm not sure I understand."

"No?" she says. "Would not a gentleman have told us his name?"

"Ah, yes, of course. I apologize. I am … Tyrell, Thomas Tyrell."

"You're sure?"

"Madame?"

"The hesitation. You seemed perhaps unsure as to your name."

"No, Madame, I am very sure. And as Thomas Tyrell, I stand before you as a man who recognizes ladies of true beauty and grace when he meets them for the first time."

The two women exchange a look, which gives birth to two tiny smiles.

"You think this is the first time we meet?" Mademoiselle de Vins gives him a cheeky look.

"Why yes, and it is entirely my pleasure." Thomas bows again.

"You do not recall another time?"

Thomas goes back and forth between two much amused expressions. Neither shows mockery, yet they are clearly laughing at him in a gentle way. "I did in fact think there might be a certain familiarity, a resemblance to—"

"Too late." Mademoiselle de Vins is shaking her head, pretending she is at the funeral of a close friend. "Too, too late."

"It was in Bath, Monsieur," says Madame de Beaumont. She places her folded-up pale blue fan against her chin. She apparently thinks she has given clue enough.

"Bath," Thomas says softly to himself. Memories swirl back. Of him and Hélène thrusting in the Cross Bath. The futile search for Élisabeth. The bonfire the first night. The climb up into …

"The hills?" he asks. "The footpaths? In dresses rose and green." Thomas looks down. He grins and points at their parasols. "The very same, are they not?"

"Voilà," says the one called Monique.

"Bravo," adds Madame, whose first names Thomas recalls now: Jeanne-Marie. "We were also in the Assembly Room as you— well, you were undertaking a study of some sort." Madame de Beaumont flexes her eyebrows.

"A study? I think not."

"No? Was it not an exploration of a faraway land, Assemblia Rooma and all creatures therein?"

Thomas stares at this Madame de Beaumont. They are barely introduced and she is already making fun of him. That she speaks the truth about his listening in on other people around the ballroom in Bath is beside the point. It is rude. Though she does describe it in a droll way, does she not? She is not just a pretty face and a shapely form. She is smart and wary at the same time. Whatever happened in her marriage that caused it to be annulled? Too bad he cannot simply ask.

"Well played, Madame," Thomas says. "You caught me out. I was a spy in the kingdom of His Self-Appointed Majesty of Rules, Mister Beau Nash."

Jeanne-Marie sputters a laugh. Mademoiselle de Vins looks confused, until she too gets the joke.

Thomas takes a half-step closer to the two women, pretending he is getting out of the way of a couple with full baskets passing behind. Without the ladies knowing it – he hopes – he secretly inhales their fragrances. Flowers and fruits distilled, with a hint of musk that seems to be coming from the more forward of the two, Mademoiselle de Vins.

"I would like to get to know you ladies better, if you would grant me that wish. I think we could become good friends. Tolerable at least."

Mademoiselle de Vins answers not with words, but with a coy smile. Madame de Beaumont at first looks far away then returns her gaze to fix it firmly on Thomas. There is much liveliness there. Her eyes have many shades of green, and he thinks he sees tenderness and vulnerability combined.

"We'll see," Madame says at last.

Thomas had hoped for no more than that. An encounter such as this is an audition, nothing else. He inclines his head slightly as he steps back then bows to take them in, head to toe. What a pleasure of discovery it would be to touch and kiss the warmth and softness of their skin. What a delightful mystery each woman is. And what an impression he made on them, he thought.

There is a flash overhead, followed by a crack of thunder. All three duck at the same time, along with everyone else in the market square. The hum of conversation stops. Then it begins anew with raised voices. The rain comes down at once, pelting hard and fast.

"I have to go," Thomas waves the sword in his right hand as he rolls up his collar with his left. "I am expected elsewhere. I have … an obligation."

He hopes his tricorne will give him a bit of protection from the downpour for at least a few blocks en route to pay homage to the child Gallatin and Hélène have brought into the world.

"As do we," says Madame, hurrying to open her parasol. "We have a friend we visit on Sundays."

"Alas," Thomas thinks he hears Mademoiselle mumble. She already has her parasol open above her head.

The women look ridiculous standing there, feet planted, under their already dripping, thin-fabric parasols. They are soon to be drenched. And judging by the look of fading hope on their glum faces, each knows that all too well.

"Au revoir," says Thomas, eager to flee.

"Oui, au revoir."

"Until next time." Mademoiselle's hand rises in a weak salute.

Thomas takes that as his cue. He is off. First at a rapid walk, then a skipping trot, finally a full-out run. He does not care how he looks. Besides, he is far from the only one running away from the market square. No one is standing still. All those who do not have tables and stalls to guard are fleeing like him.

Sodden as he is becoming, Thomas feels his spirits lift. It is the pleasure of the two women. He will do all he can to see them again, together for conversation or with good fortune separately to get closer still. He has not had a lover, meaning someone he likes to be with and whose conversation he enjoys, since Élisabeth took off from Bath. Sex, yes, for he has not become a monk. But he fights his urges more often than he gives in. It disheartens him to make the required purchase on the bridge or in the parks. Yet what choice does he have? He is not going to bring one of the purchase ladies into his own rooms, nor is he ever going to go to theirs. There is too much risk in that. A lurking billy boy could knock him and steal his purse.

And so it's off to play godfather in Spitalfields. It really is a joke. If ever there were someone ill-suited for such a church-based role, it is him. No matter. Gallatin will be glad to see him, as he will be pleased to see his old friend. H. of course will give him a chilly shoulder and he will reciprocate. That is simply how it is, or was a year ago the last time he saw her and her child at Church Street. Truth be told, it does sadden him. Once he would have done anything for her and to be with her. That affection has withered, as has hers for him, alas.

But there is the boy, the one whose birthday it is. Little Tommy, Gallatin's pride and joy. Thomas is curious to see how much he has grown. Since he is only one, there can be no real conversation. All a child that age can accomplish is to crawl about or maybe take a few staggered steps. Thomas shakes his head. The child will have to become a lad, to have attained the age of reason, before Thomas will be able to be the guiding godfather Gallatin wants him to be.

Thomas slows to avoid a giant puddle in front of an apothecary shop. In so doing he has to smile. Soaked as he already is from the heavy rain, what would it matter if he were to splash right through the pool? His shoes and socks could not get any wetter than they are. So Thomas stomps at the corner of the puddle, sending up a wave upon both ankles.

Ahead, through the thick slant of rain, Thomas can now see Christ Church Spitalfields. It looks good, the area he once called home. Gallatin will surely have a fire in the grate, a roaring one at that. And maybe his friend will loan him some clothes while he spreads out his to dry close to the hearth? Surely, his old friend will do that as well.

Yet H., the angry Hélène, what will she say when Thomas comes dripping water onto the floors of her home? He sighs. Maybe the year that has elapsed since they last saw each other will have done some good. Thomas would like that. He and she could be friends. But really, could they? *Friends* is not exactly what they ever were. Can a man and a woman who used to breathe in each other's breath – can they forget all that and be merely friends? Thomas does not know.

In the meantime, with the door to No. 5 only a few strides away, Thomas's thoughts spin back to the fresh encounter he had in the Covent Garden a short while ago. He can easily imagine himself getting close to one or the other of those two women. Something tells him he might have a chance with them, either the forward Mademoiselle de Vins or the hesitant yet obviously quick Madame de Beaumont. He would dearly love to have again the warm affection that he has several times had in his life yet always lost. He would not be so careless again.

VII
Amour

London – December 1736 to February 1739

Jeanne-Marie goes to her favourite window, the one on the right. Though now forlorn, with a thin dusting of snow, what lies outside on the ledge still draws her from time to time. For what is there is what led her last spring to choose this apartment on Woodstock Street, instead of an arguably better set of rooms she had viewed earlier that day. It brings a wry smile to recall it now, but when she first spied the nest on the ledge, with its solitary egg – that delightful shade of blue – she instantly wondered if it might be a sign. When a moment later a robin landed on the ledge and hopped into the nest to drop a second egg, her inclination was confirmed. Despite the apartment's dowdy furnishings and battered floors, these Woodstock Street rooms would be her new lodgings. The desire to see the eggs hatch and the mother take care of her young was too strong to resist.

Madame de Beaumont unlatches the window and reaches out. The abandoned nest is so very light in her hand. Just sticks, mud, dried leaves, a few threads and what looks like a lock of a girl's red hair. It is a marvel what birds are able to engineer, and how they give and protect life.

Through a curtain of gauze she put up right away, Jeanne-Marie followed what happened on the ledge last spring. There were four eggs. The mother warmed and rotated them, with the father dropping in from time to time. Sometimes he took her place; more often he brought the female something to eat. Once the eggs hatched they were both busy round the clock. Bugs and worms to quiet the crying brood. One morning Jeanne-Marie saw there was one less baby in the nest. It was too early for it to have fledged. That meant it had either been shouldered out by its siblings or prised away by an enemy bird.

How she could relate to that. Her father and step-mother, and a willing priest, had allowed, nay encouraged her, to marry young. She came out of a convent, not yet having taken her vows, and gave herself in holy matrimony to a man who turned out to be debauched. Diseased loins. Her intimate relations were a horror. She fended off Monsieur de Beaumont as often as she could, but total chastity was impossible. For months, once or twice a week, she endured what had to be endured. Finally she spoke to a different priest. It took a while but eventually the Church found a way to annul the union. Though released from her awful fate, the year and a half had taken its toll. And not only on her heart and soul. Jeanne-Marie fears she no longer has the capacity to bear children, should she marry again.

If she could make but one suggestion to God, it would be this: Immorality should show up on people's faces. Sinfulness should be a blot you cannot miss. If that were so, her parents and the priest would never have been so fooled. But since that is not the way of the world, in her classes to wide-eyed English girls about the French language and literature Madame de Beaumont passes on all the advice she can to help other girls avoid the fate she had.

Madame de Beaumont returns the nest to its place and latches the window shut. She hopes another pair of robins, or any other bird, will bring the nest to life again next spring.

Picking up her cap and cloak, Jeanne-Marie readies to go out. She has some time before her tutoring to visit what has become her favourite bookshop, near St. Paul's. This time, instead of looking for some novel for her own pleasure, she wants to see what there is on the moral education of children, for those old enough to read. If the field is as scant as she believes, she has an idea that she could write her own book. *The Triumph of Verity* is the title she has in mind.

Out on the cobbles she has a fresh thought. What if she were to create a monthly compendium of stories that children could read? It would be a literary magazine, only for the young. The formula works for adults so why not for those not yet fully formed? The right stories would help them on their way. Jeanne-Marie has already had a few stories published here and there. She could have more impact with a journal whose sole focus is the young.

She lowers her eyes to where her feet need help. There are horse droppings across much of this section of the street. Skirt lifted, she tiptoes safely past.

It occurs to her as she picks up her pace coming out of Hanover Square that she should also ask at the bookshop what is newly arrived from France. The man who has entered her life over the past few months strives to stay abreast of the latest Paris tomes. He aspires someday to see his own name in print, as she has now seen hers. Yet he is reluctant to send anything off for consideration, neither to the literary journals nor to the publishers of books. Jeanne-Marie wonders if, somewhere deep down, he does not have the confidence that he pretends to have. She knows from her own experience, nothing ventured, nothing gained. It is better to take the risk than not to try at all.

Oh, that makes her wince. It sounds like behind his back she is criticizing a weakness in the man. A silent reprimand. But that is not it, not at all. She merely wishes Thomas Tyrell could find the success he desires. And that is to be not only someone who writes, but someone who is read. That requires submitting his pages to an editor or a publisher, which he steadfastly refuses to do. It is as if he is afraid of finding out his words do not measure up.

That frustration aside, Jeanne-Marie is blessed to have found someone so unlike Beaumont as a new friend. Her Thomas is a good and learned man. If only his ambition would leave him alone.

The tiny shoots and blossoms are out, shimmering green and pink and white. Wherever they are, the springtime bursts, they bring life to the brick and wooden city. It has been a long winter with more than enough chilling rain. So what a relief to come out the other side, with longer days and new growth providing a feast for the eyes.

Thomas sucks in a deep breath. He can smell the tiny blossoms on the trees, a few fragrant snowflakes of which are gently tumbling down. It is life itself, all around him in the present tense.

He will take his time heading for his rendezvous with Jeanne-Marie in Green Park. Not because he is reluctant to see her, but simply because this is a spring day he wants to savour as much as he can.

The leaves have long since lost their deepest greens. Some now show the inevitable fading and here and there even hints of yellow. The end of the warm days cannot be too far ahead. The nights are already turning cool. Thomas saw his breath last evening, coming back from the shop en route to his rooms. Even now, just past midday, returning from a pleasant hour with Madame de Beaumont in Hyde Park, he can feel a change in the air. The smell is not of freshness and growth, but of impending decay.

It will not be long before they will have to add blankets if they want to keep having their conversations and side-by-side readings of separate books on the benches of the royal parks. That prospect makes him shudder. Thomas is only thirty-six. He always thought one had to be at least fifty before taking shelter beneath a blanket. Of course, La Beaumont, as he likes to call her, is eleven years his junior. Perhaps that age difference explains why she does not seem to mind the growing chill as much as he does.

What should happen, though he hesitates to bring it up, is that they should take their budding friendship indoors. He would like to see them include not just talk and books, but another kind of intimacy. Thomas thinks she is ready too, but one never knows until one asks.

Into his building and up the stairs, he pulls out the key from the inner pocket of his veston. The tumbler clicks and he's in. "Oh my," he says aloud. He is picturing his first room as a stran-ger might see it. Perhaps it would not be wise to invite La Beaumont up here after all, not in the state it is. There is more than a hint of dust. And the shabby confusion would undermine the restrained gentility and cultured dignity he has worked hard to display to her over the past few months. Jeanne-Marie is a keen reader, yet she is a woman. No woman Thomas has ever met is impressed by teetering piles of books. Nor by wooden boxes stuffed with folio sheets, his many not-quite-yet-finished essays and ideas for different books.

Nor by a floor dotted with heaps of letters, each pile grouped according to the kingdom or republic its writer lives in, as indicated by the colour of the ribbon Thomas has tied round them. Blue for Scotland, white for France, red for Switzerland, green for the Italian cities and black for the Dutch ones. True, Jeanne-Marie would be impressed by the insightfulness of his various correspondents. They keep him informed about what is happening in Edinburgh, Paris, Geneva, Genoa, Rome, Antwerp and Amsterdam, while he passes on what he sees and hears in London. Impressed by the information – maybe. Yet Madame de Beaumont would not smile at what would likely strike her as untidiness.

Thomas glances down at the letter he began last night, which is still on his writing table. It is a reply to Giovanni Codignola. The recently added correspondent in Genoa wanted to know about London's public squares, how many there were and if any had been added in recent centuries. Thomas shuffles the pages to refresh his memory as to where he left off last evening when he blew the candle out.

As for London's public spaces which you Inquired about, I can give you the Dates for the Creation or Establishment of Each in order of its appearance in London and Westminster. I am told that this information is absolutely Reliable. It might interest you to know that my Source is a Huguenot whose parents fled to England from France.

His name is John Rocque, and he is held in high repute as a Surveyor and a Cartographer. Rocque has in mind a project to create a new and detailed Map of this City, such as has not been carried out before. Or if such did exist, it is now outdated. There has been much recent Growth. London is now an oblong shape, expanding in several directions at once. Here is what Surveyor Rocque imparted to me.

1631—Covent Garden, 1630s—Lincoln's Inn fields, 1665— Bloomsbury Square, 1667—St. James's Square, 1671—Leicester Square, 1681—King's Square, 1688—Golden Square, 1695— Grosvenor Square, 1698—Red Lion Square, 1713—Hanover Square, 1717—Cavendish Square

You see at once what remarkable Construction has gone on over the most recent century. This English capital is a place that does not stand still. Of course, the Great Fire of 1666 provided a great opportunity, consuming as it did over Thirteen Thousand homes and nearly One Hundred Churches. Only ten died, yet One Hundred Thousand were left homeless.

Thomas must finish off the letter and commit it to the post, because he has two other letters to compose, one to Jacques Notter in Paris and another to Gallatin's old roommate Johnson, who is now in Edinburgh.

Thomas places the page back with the first two sheets, beside the blue and white faience inkwell he has had since he was a boy writing poetry in the cold grenier of his family home in Vire.

He gives his salon another good long look. No, he cannot invite La Beaumont here, not the way it is. But could they not go to her place? If it is anything like her, it will be pretty, pleasant and respectable. He will hint about it the next time they meet. If she is agreeable, well then who can say what happens next. All he knows is what he would like. For she is a woman and he a man. He thinks it well past time that they do more than just read. That brings a firm nod.

Thomas turns back to his writing table. This time not to the unfinished letter to Codignola but to the blank sheets up in the right corner beside the containers of ink and sand and the adjacent upstanding quills. It is obvious, is it not? He will approach Madame with his plume. He will compose a letter that raises the topic carefully. He has to be ever so careful, for Jeanne-Marie's ghastly experience with her marriage must loom large for her when it comes to the subject of erotic love. Nonetheless, he must not let his knowledge of what happened with that other man tie him in knots. He has seen La Beaumont look into his eyes longer than need required. That, he believes, is a sign that Venus stirs in her, just as Eros stirs in him. Thomas needs only find a way to release those old Greek gods who reside in them. A letter composed of carefully selected words can work the magic an uncontrolled conversation cannot.

Thomas goes at once to the writing table. He selects the quill with the best nib then flattens a fresh sheet. He makes his first dip into the ink and writes the date. He halts. The opening line is important. It must have the right approach, the right tone. There can be no rushing her. Yet at the same time the woman has to see what it is that he is asking of her. He hears the words, and refreshes his nib.

My Dear Madame,

We wish You to know that your Esteem is Precious to us. There is a Nobility in your character that cannot be denied. It deserves this written Tribute, for it is the Radiance of your Fine Qualities that prompts this Letter. Yes it does. You are, Dear Madame, the object of our Ambition. We are speaking of the Ambition of Affection, which is the best and truest Sense of that Word.

He needs more ink. More importantly, before he dips, is he being too bold, to say that it is his ambition to win her esteem? No, it is not. He will continue with his original thought.

It is the Kindness you have shown that Inspires us with a desire, a longing deep, to Receive from you the Expression of your precious Good Will. We trust you will agree that you have given me such En-

couragement. We hope and trust We are not being overly bold in set-
ting our Feelings in ink. Rather, it is our respectful Gratitude and

Oh my, so very wordy. Still, in for a penny, in for a pound. He'll wait until he has written the whole thing, then he'll be able to judge if it will do or if he'll have to start over again. He takes another dip into the well.

Ardour that bids us to take up the quill. What a Torment to my Sensibility it would be to lose your favour if we have misjudged how you feel. To be in Honourable Possession of your affection for us means the very world. We ask of you, Dear Madame, to give us your Consid- eration, and permit us to pursue the means to bring about a felicitous future for both.

He reads over what he has composed. Though excessive in ob- sequiousness, it is likely what is needed. It is the way a letter to someone important to you, a woman for her favours or a man for a position, must be composed. So, it's not a bad start as pre- ambles go. Now, however, it's time to hint at the gist of what it is he would like to have from Madame de Beaumont. That is, that he wants "to know her." How she will reply, in person when next they meet or in a return letter, will decide everything.

———

The letter in her hands brings a quiet smile. Jeanne-Marie cups her chin with her hand. How strange it is that a man can feel there are words he can write that he would not dare to say to us aloud. She nods her assent, and grins to hear herself use the same conceit Thomas did, that they are both *nous* when in fact they are but *je* and *moi*. She understands the effect. It is not just formality, it is the implied majesty. It is why kings and queens speak as they do, not just for themselves but on behalf of their realms. Well, she and Thomas are monarchs too – of their own hearts and souls. So the use of *nous* is right.

She rereads the letter, more slowly this time, studying it as a writer. She separates what Thomas said or was aiming to say – the underlying sentiment – from the words he selected to express those feelings and ideas. The first thing she would say is that Thomas really could have used a bit more time to compose his words. What was it the great Pascal wrote? That he would have made his letter shorter if only he had had more time? Well, that seems to be the case for this epistle from Thomas Tyrell as well. He would have been wise to set his letter aside and come back to it and eliminate the excessive wordiness. The best expression takes time. It is not a sudden outpouring.

Jeanne-Marie purses her lips then puts a hand to her brow. What is she doing? She is being so very unkind. Thomas has written to her of his affection, his admiration of her, and she is examining his words as if they are in some text she might take apart for her students. She is kinder and better than that.

Back to the letter she goes, skipping over the flattery with which it begins. It is mere puffery Thomas has used, a convention, nothing more than that. The heart of the letter, two pages in, that's a different matter. She reads it over, mumbling the words aloud this time.

Our mutual respect is the basis of our Friendship. It is deep and abiding, as is our Affection. Yet our Affection could be deeper still. This I believe with all My Heart.

Jeanne-Marie notes that Thomas has dropped the *nous* and gone with the *je* and *mon*. Was this a slip? No, she thinks not. Because the line that comes next reveals to her that Thomas was no longer composing at all. He was letting his quill spill the honest, simple truth.

We could have the ne plus ultra of Amour, and we should. That is when a man and a woman come to know each other as fully as Nature allows.

Jeanne-Marie rises from her chair and paces the floor. By habit, it is to the window she goes. The little nest on the ledge has a dusting of snow. She nods at the chilly scene. Or, she wonders, is she nodding at something else?

That makes her take in a great breath. Yes, it is true, she does want that to which the man alludes. The *ne plus ultra* that Nature has designed for women and for men. She imagines it will be … good. Platonic love may be the most admirable of all loves, but she is not there yet. Though once deceived and betrayed – by a foul husband who spent her dowry at gaming tables and died in a duel over his unpaid debts – her memory of him has happily gone dim. More importantly, this new man, sweet Thomas, is nothing like Beaumont was.

Jeanne-Marie does another circle of the room, takes yet another glance at the empty robin's nest. It is simple, is it not? She feels something in her heart and that is enough. What are feelings but longings revealed? The answer is obvious. Yes, yes, she would like to know this man.

———

By its light weight, Thomas can tell that the return letter from Madame de Beaumont is brief. Seal broken, he finds only a few lines.

Mon Cher Thomas,
  Your letter was Bold. For that I Confess I was glad. For I too see that there is a time to talk and times to read and write. And yes, you are right. There are the other times when Nature should be heeded.
  I invite you to my Apartment on Woodstock Street this Sunday, two hours after noon.
  Until then …

  Jeanne-Marie Barbe
    Le Prince de Beaumont

———

"Until then …" Thomas reads aloud to the empty room. He has to glance up at the beams above. He wants to laugh. Is that not good? This woman can entice and intrigue. And in this case it's not the words but the beckoning ellipsis at the end. It's up to him, the lone reader, to fill in what comes next.

That he does, in his imagination, and with relish. What an encumbrance, that he has to wait until Sunday to see if the real story unfolds as well as the one in his head.

––––

It is not her first sack back dress, but it is the finest she has ever owned. She turns round and cranes over her shoulder to see how its long, wonderful pleats look in the mirror. She loves the fabric of brocaded silk. How dark and luxuriant is the pink. The contrast with the floral motif, made from silver metal thread, is sharp. And so it should be. The dress cost Jeanne-Marie two months' wages from her hours of teaching children French, but every penny was well spent.

Though she would prefer to have a special event to attend to show it off, the first time anyone will see her in it will be tomorrow afternoon, when she expects Thomas Tyrell to pay her a visit.

Jeanne-Marie's gaze goes again to the mirror, this time face on. She likes how the edges of the bodice come close together yet do not meet. The open robe style allows the petticoat to offset the colour and pattern of the dress. When she puts on the pearls, not one but four strands round her neck, she hopes they will add to the look. Though there will still be her hair to solve. And to be sure, she has to decide which shoes to wear.

There is a knock on the door.

Jeanne-Marie turns to the mirror. A worried face stares back. Is this a mistake? What if he only wants to take advantage of her?

––––

This is good, as good as Thomas has felt in a long while. He has not a souci in the world. He is warm and soft. Delightfully spent.

"Thomas," comes a whisper.

He shifts onto his shoulder to find a focus on La Beaumont's twinkling eyes. Her face is flushed. There is perspiration on her brow and upon her throat. Thomas glances at her full breasts but resists the urge to touch. He is content to lie beside her, still for a while.

"Was it ... acceptable?" she asks.

"Acceptable?" Thomas wants to laugh. With a terribly grave face he says, "No, that is not the word I would use."

Her face is aghast.

"Heavens, woman, it was delicious. So very good."

Her eyes and lips are relieved.

"And you?"

"And me what?"

"What do you say about—" Thomas waves his hand above their two intertwined naked bodies. "About *it*?"

"Please, Monsieur, a woman does not talk about *it*."

"Why not?" Thomas urges her on with his eyes. Then he reaches with the fingers of his left hand to fluff her thin triangle of curly hairs.

"No, don't." She shakes her head so he withdraws his hand. She pulls the blanket across the lower half of her nakedness. "It was the first—" She hunches her bare shoulders and looks across the room. Thomas follows her gaze and sees that she is looking at the two folded piles that are their clothes. Her dark pink sack dress and his justaucorps and breeches are laid across a table and upon the arms of a chair. Then there are the other articles, in a heap on the floor where they landed after they peeled each other's layers away not long after Thomas came through the door. He hopes La Beaumont is not having regrets, because he has none.

"I'd rather you didn't call me Madame. I prefer Jeanne-Marie, or Jeanne-Marie Barbe if you want to use all three Christian names." She presses close. "Le Prince was my maiden name before I became Beaumont."

"Well, Jeanne-Marie Barbe ..." Thomas finds he cannot quite lean back far enough to see her whole face, pressed as she is against his chest. "Will you at least tell me if you found pleasure in our ... exchange?"

"Exchange? Yes, I suppose that's what it is. Better than some other terms. But, no, I will not say more. Shhh, I need a nap."

No, Jeanne-Marie does not want to talk about the physical, sweaty side of love. Yet to herself she confesses it was good. No, better than good. It was exactly what Thomas put in his letter a few days ago. It was the *ne plus ultra*. In fact, she felt the ultra not once but twice. That ultra must be what is making her so very tired.

———

And so it goes. Thomas and Jeanne-Marie meet in her apartment for months, usually once a week. The sequence in which things develop varies, but not the essentials. There is always conversation, if not before then after what they call the close touch. The talk always centres on what each has just written or read, or is about to read or write.

To Thomas's ongoing bewilderment, Jeanne-Marie has the jump on him in getting ink on the page. He cannot understand how she keeps up with her everyday life, meaning her work as a governess, and is still able to write as much as she does. She writes ten pages to every single one he completes. It baffles him. It would be one thing for La Beaumont to have good ideas for stories to write, which she does. But she also succeeds in putting them down. As Thomas sees it, and this he has shared with her several times, one particular tale of hers has the potential to be widely read. It's her tale of a beauty and a beast. It is good enough to be mistaken for an ancient fairy tale, honed over time, such a story of impossible love. Yet it is not old at all. It is entirely hers and comes from nowhere other than her clever mind, out through her quill onto the page.

Thomas, on the other hand, sometimes curses his own muses under his breath. Is poetry only given to the young? Is it that the older one gets, the verses dry up? Thomas feels that is how it is. He has now given up on Euterpe, she who when he was young used to whisper poems in his ear. She must have gone back to Olympus and left him on his own.

Clio does speak, at least once in a while. Thomas has been cobbling together pages of facts and observations with a hundred details about London. It's a lot of history, but so far they are nothing but disconnected paragraphs. What he lacks is something to unify all the bits. Details are not enough by themselves; they need a frame or path. One does not just wear lace, it needs a garment underneath.

Thomas is starting to wonder if writing might for him be nothing more than a pastime. It is something he keeps to himself, and so still puts ink on paper to prove to himself that his fear is wrong. At the moment he has put the history aside and is trying his hand at short essays. As far as he knows, the ancient Greeks had no muse for that. It is a modern form. His latest essay is about ambition, longing and betrayal. Or rather, that is his aim. Thus far it is a dishevelled mess. Yet Thomas knows in his bones that there is an inherent connection among the three, like the stages of a moth. The trick is to find the words that put what he feels onto the page. He is not there yet, and he does not want to ask La Beaumont for advice. She would think less of him for that, and he will not do anything to undermine what he has built. So Thomas will have to figure out how ambition, longing and betrayal are intertwined all by himself.

———

Not a day goes by that Jeanne-Marie does not tell herself that she is happy with this man. She likes listening to him talk about everything, or nearly so. Like when he tells her of the different letters he sends and receives from correspondents across Europe. It is a remarkable network of information he is part of. Or when he speaks about faraway wars in the colonies of France, Britain and Spain of which she had not previously heard. Or the enormous fortunes that come to the merchant families who trade in misery, by which Thomas means the trade in slaves. Out of Africa they bring the human traffic in numbers too great to comprehend, overseas to all of the Americas. "Their trade should be a source of guilt, not wealth," he said to her the other day.

Madame de Beaumont even enjoys the more mundane conversations they have. Such as the time when he came back with the details of an exchange he had had an hour before in a bakery two streets over. Thomas recognized the King's favourite composer, a German by the name of Handel, standing in line for pastries. Her man went right up to the musician to trade pleasantries. Or when Thomas tells her about the latest book he has read and what he judges to be its strengths and weaknesses. Though sometimes, Jeanne-Marie notices, he forgets that it was she who purchased the book for him as a gift, at the bookshop she likes so much down by St. Paul's.

The only time she feels like wincing when Thomas talks – which she hopes does not show – is when he tells her about the boys he tutors. He often says their heads are thick as planks. She has hinted more than once that he should adopt an attitude that is more positive. Children give back what a teacher sends out. Low expectations are almost always met.

Truth be told, Jeanne-Marie does not think her lover should be a teacher at all. What he *is* meant to be is not clear, but it would have to be a profession where his deductive insight and ability to analyze, as well as his quiet discretion, are what is required.

———

Thomas leans back in the chair at his writing table. It occurs to him that his intimacy with La Beaumont is nearing a mark. A most agreeable six months it has been.

He sets his quill into the well, and pushes aside the sheet on which he was to begin a letter to his correspondent in Genoa. Codignola wants information on London's pleasure gardens, and Thomas was about to grant his wish. He will get back to that later.

Yes, he and Madame have come to know each other well. Thomas feels he can fairly predict what she will say on nearly every subject under the sun, or just as importantly, the topics she would prefer they ignore. He has no doubt that she knows him equally well. No, they do not finish each other's sentences, but they likely could. And maybe one day in the future they will. That would not be bad, he thinks. Companionship is a foundation on which deep affection is built.

When it comes to playing Eros and Venus, what Madame prefers to call making love, Thomas was initially surprised by how much she took to the act. It was not what he expected at all, given her reserved demeanour when she is clothed. Yet that first time she treated it like it was a meal and she'd not eaten in a week. Which Thomas supposes is how it was for her, given how long she had gone without. In any case, that first time set the tone that has continued on. That Jeanne-Marie believes there is no risk of pregnancy, because of the misfortune of her previous marriage, must be another factor in why she shows such enthusiastic abandon.

Thomas fills his lungs as he reaches up. It is good.

He glances down at one of the notes he has made over the past few days. It is part of the information he has assembled to compose his letter to Codignola.

Sadler's Wells, Clerkenwell. Healing waters. Since 17th c. Escape and idyll. Curing of illnesses.

Vauxhall—New Spring Gardens, 1732, 12 acres. From pretty contrived plantation to a park of architectural delights. Musick too. Only a shilling. Lords and dukes side by side with commoners.

NB: Find the names of a few more

Magnificent country scenery in the city. Like going to a great estate, without having the title!

It is certainly not enough to compose a full letter, but it is enough to start. Provided Thomas comes up with an opening line, which as of yet he has not. So rather than waste his time waiting for words to arrive, he decides to go pay a surprise visit to La Beaumont. His musings about her has put him in a certain mood.

———

The smile on her face as she answers his knock is exactly what Thomas was hoping for.

"Good morning, Madame. I trust I am not disrupting your day?" Thomas offers her a fine reverence, as if they are not much more than strangers meeting in a public setting.

Madame plays along. She gives a curtsey. "That you are not, good sir." Then: "This is a pleasant surprise, Thomas. Your timing is good. I have something to show you, mon amour."

Down the hall they quickly step, Jeanne-Marie beaming and Thomas puzzled as to what she has to present. "There," she says, arm outstretched across the salon.

Thomas's eyes go wide as his neck snaps back. "You jest?"

"Jest?" La Beaumont strides across the room to rest her hand on the edge of the wooden tub. "Do not tell me that you are one of *those*. Please, Thomas, are you?"

He knows he grimaces, but he cannot do otherwise. "I do not know what you mean by *those*, but surely you know there are risks to sit in water. Everyone says the chills are—"

"Everyone says! Seriously, Thomas, I never expected to hear that from your lips. You are smarter than that."

Thomas can only look at her.

"It is to cleanse. To wash away what sme— what should not be there. I propose we immerse ourselves once every week for ten minutes, taking turns. One in and the other adding heated water from the hearth. As needed. Not too hot, but warm enough to keep us from getting any chill."

Thomas knows he should say something, but nothing comes to mind. He has never had a bath, nor ever swum for that matter. He likes to think he keeps very clean in the usual way.

"Are you suggesting that I ... that to your nose, I ... I give off a repellant smell?"

"No, no," Jeanne-Marie says, placing a kind hand on his sleeve, "you cover yourself well with a lovely scent. Most of the time. But ... but this will be better, I am convinced. We will not have the sulphur water they have in Bath, but it will be much better than a damp cloth from a basin."

"And this is something upon which you insist?"

"Insist? Well, I had hoped you would see the merit. Do you not?" Jeanne-Marie shows him a hopeful smile.

"As you wish, Madame," Thomas says, lowering his gaze and making a subservient bow.

"Enough of that," she says. "Here, you take the other side. I want to move it closer to the hearth. And then I say we strike a fire and warm some water."

"Should I go to the well up the street with your two buckets?"

"Would you?"

"I would and I will."

"I suppose it will take a few trips. I am sorry for that, but I do believe the immersion will be something we enjoy. A pleasure we look forward to."

Thomas attempts a smile. Does she know how many trips with full, heavy buckets that will be? And then afterwards he'll have to carry the soiled water away to spill in the street.

"I'll be back as soon as I can," he says.

"I am content that you are happy about the tub, Thomas."

"Yes," he says.

———

Sure enough, as she predicted, Thomas does look forward to sitting in the steaming water for his allotted time, with the flames in the nearby hearth warming the air as well as the next bucket to be put in. More than once he has recalled how often over the years Gallatin preached the merits of such a full ablution, citing the Romans, of course. Thomas wishes now he had listened to his friend way back when. It really is a pleasure to soak in a bath. Additionally, it kills some of their ticks and lice. He itches less now that he immerses in hot water, and Jeanne-Marie says the same.

"Don't forget to give your underarms a scrub," La Beaumont says.

Thomas gives her a look. "I will get to that."

"Of course, I apologize. Continue on." Jeanne-Marie glances at the small clock on the mantle. "You have another three minutes."

––––

"Thomas?" La Beaumont asks one warm, sunny Sunday afternoon. They have finished soaking in the tub and are sitting naked, cross-legged on the Persian rug, drying slowly in the air.

Thomas twists so he can have eye contact. "Yes, Madame."

He glances over at the nearby tub. After they finish their love-making, which should be coming up, he will have to carry two buckets at a time down the stairs to empty them in the street. It is usually half a dozen trips.

"I think today maybe we should go for a walk instead."

"I do not understand."

"A walk, instead of … you know."

"Instead of skin on skin?"

"That's right." There comes a nervous smile to her face, followed by an exhale of relief.

"Why would we do that?" Thomas asks.

"It's … I'm not sure." Jeanne-Marie shivers like she has suddenly been caught in a north wind. She reaches for the nearby red blanket and wraps it round her shoulders, pulling it to cover her front.

"What is wrong?" Thomas asks. He cannot tell what his lover intends by this unforeseen conversation. It does not look to be a joke.

La Beaumont hunches her shoulders then fixes him with her gaze. "What we do is not right."

Thomas knows he goes wide-eyed. "What we do? Our closeness? The … oh, please, Madame, you know it is good. I see your face and hear you moan and—"

"Thomas, we cannot pretend that there is a likely prospect of me ever being with child."

But is that not a relief? Thomas thinks. He knows Madame is sensitive, nay disappointed on that score.

"I don't understand, I do not." He slows his speech, picking his words carefully. "Jeanne-Marie, how could a pleasure we both enjoy not be good? And therefore right?"

"The Church." Exasperation fills her voice. "The teaching is that the reason men and women come together – the sole purpose – is to have a child."

Thomas does not groan or shake his head. He is able to control that. Yet he fears she can read his expression. The Church! He has to close his eyes, then slowly, like he is considering her point of view, he looks at her gravely and nods his head.

"Do not treat me as if I am a child," says Jeanne-Marie, a flash of anger in her eyes. "I see your mask."

The blanket falls off as she reaches toward the nearby wooden chair, where her folded chemise has been waiting for her. She pulls it on.

"Though *you* have fallen away, I have not," she says to him with a challenge in her eyes. "You were raised in the faith, Thomas Tyrell. It must still be within you somewhere."

Thomas still does not say a word. Instead, like Madame, he reaches for his own fresh chemise, resting upon the floor. Modesty, it seems, is suddenly required. On goes the chemise.

"You know," Thomas ventures, "what you say is true." He aims to keep any fierceness out of his voice. "What priests inculcated in me as a boy is still inside me, it is. And yes, there are times when I do wonder, despite the implausibility of it all, if I might not end up in the fiery cauldron of Hell." He hunches his shoulders and waits for her reply.

"Oh, Thomas." Jeanne-Marie clasps his hands and her eyes glisten. "That is what I thought. It need not be like that for you."

"I know." He frees his hands so he can stretch out both arms. With his right hand he taps the top of his head "But Reason has to triumph over ... over old ideas." He is pleased he has avoided the word foolishness.

Jeanne-Marie shakes her head. Up she stands. Thomas smothers a sigh. It is now certain there will be no intimacy today. He too gets to his feet.

La Beaumont is staring at him. "I'm afraid," she says, "you have it upside down. Yes, Reason is a tool, an important one, but it is no foundation. The only base is the religion that is true."

There is a hardness in her eyes. Softly, he says, "There are those who disagree."

"And you are one, is that it?"

"I am."

Thomas watches Jeanne-Marie inhale. It is deep and long, in through her nose, with the release long delayed. When it comes, it escapes through pursed lips.

"I do not want to give up on you," she says.

"I hope not, Madame, for we are ... close. We are both friends and lovers."

"You think me weak, don't you?"

"Not I." Thomas snaps to attention. He makes sure his lips and eyes are grim. "I do not. I understand the hold a religion can have."

"It is not *a* religion, Thomas. It is *the* ... well, it is *my* faith."

"I have an open mind."

Jeanne-Marie studies him. Her eyes do not blink. "Do you, Thomas? Do you really?"

"I do. Of course I do."

He steps toward her and takes her in his arms. He feels her embrace him back, her hands pulling with force upon his waist. "I hope so," he hears. It's a muffled whisper spoken against his chest.

"Is there anything I could do?" Thomas asks, softly, close to her ear. "To make things better, between us, my dear Beaumont?"

Jeanne-Marie releases her grip and steps back. She takes him in, head to toe. What was a forlorn face becomes a hopeful one before his gaze. While Thomas waits for her to speak, he hears the mantle's ticking clock. From somewhere out on Woodstock Street, below the open window, there are shouting voices and a barking dog.

La Beaumont is swaying slightly. Her eyes are wet.

"Tell me," Thomas says, taking hold of both her hands. "Just let me know what it is I can do."

"I...." She bites her lip.

"De grâce, go on."

"I ... I have to be married."

———

That evening, pacing round his sober apartment after the long trudge home, Thomas finds he is still mumbling to himself. His relationship with Madame has taken an unexpected turn. So it's marriage she wants. Why did he not see that coming before she said the words? He must have a blind spot about these things, because that's how it turned out with Hélène as well, which he found out too late, after she'd opted for Gallatin instead. Thomas wonders if that is also not what Élisabeth desired. He never got to have such a conversation with the Swiss, not before she disappeared. What complicates the matter is that he recalls all too well the one marriage he has had. The union with well-placed Marguerite had much to recommend it. Well, in the beginning at least. Not much after it was underway, and then it slowly petered out.

True enough, a marriage with Jeanne-Marie would not be with someone overly aged, as was the case with Marguerite. In fact, La Beaumont is younger than him and will outlive him in all likelihood. Moreover, she is a person with whom he truly does like to spend his time. They share a bond, a deep affection. It must be what women call love. He enjoys all they have in common, and yes, the physical dimension too. But still? Does he want to be tied, in an official document, to a single woman? Is not marriage by its very nature an entanglement, a fancy word for a trap?

———

"But where?" he asks.

Jeanne-Marie can see that he does not like to be in the dark. No matter, it is good for him. He will be pleased once they arrive. It is her treat to him, a week late, but a birthday gift nonetheless.

"You know, Thomas, I am beginning to think you want always to be in control."

"That's ridiculous."

"Is it? Well, I am heartened to hear that."

Thomas shrugs, as if to forgive her for her wrongful allegation.

"So then?" she says, offering him an outstretched arm. It appears to be with some reluctance that he takes her hand.

"So then what?" he asks, immediately letting go.

"You will just have to come along," she says. "It will be a surprise."

Jeanne-Marie hears a mumble from Monsieur as they turn the corner. It makes her want to laugh. She supposes a grudging acquiescence is better than a refusal to go along.

The route is familiar, but then what part of London is not well known to him? Over the years he has come to explore just about every square, street, passage and dead end in the city, and a fair part of Westminster as well. Where La Beaumont is leading him Thomas has no idea, but he will be very surprised if it is not some place he already knows. The trick will be to pretend to Madame that it is new to him.

"Something for the head," is all she will say, twice so far. Her mood appears to match the dress she wears, it of the cheery tangerine hue.

The first time she said it he joked, "I could use a bit of that." The second time he merely smiled.

Thomas has to hand it to her. She has clearly gone to a lot of trouble on this surprise gift to him. It has been a half-hour march already and he still has no idea. Each time he glimpses some place ahead that he has heard about but not been in, he thinks that must be it. Coffee houses and private clubs, three different theatres, shops and more shops. Yet each time she keeps him walking on. For a fleeting moment he thought his gift might be a bird, the way Madame made them cross the street to admire all the brightly coloured birds in the cages carried on sticks over the shoulder of a craggy-faced man. But no, it was just to admire them all, especially the ones with the bright yellow chests.

"Sad, isn't it?" he said once he knew his gift was not a caged bird.

"What's that?"

"To be imprisoned the way they are."

Jeanne-Marie's eyes went wide. "But they have neither worry nor want."

"I suppose," he said, but that was not how he felt.

The great dome of St. Paul's now looms overhead. That must mean the surprise is not going to be in London at all, but farther on, in Westminster. That would make sense. La Beaumont knows he is less familiar with that part of the great megalopolis. He only hopes the gift is worth the time it is taking.

"Nearly there." The grin on her face is wide.

"Are you sure?" he replies with a wink. "I'm guessing it's another quarter hour, maybe a half."

"No," she says, the grin sliding away. "No, we are here."

Thomas stares at her. Surely this is a joke. They are at the door of Gallatin's bookshop.

"You don't mean here?" He gestures at the door. He tilts his head.

The look of anticipation and surprise are completely gone from La Beaumont's face. "You know it?" she says. "This shop?" She looks like she could cry. "And it displeases you?"

Thomas wishes he was not making her sad, but what choice does he have? He is stunned that the mystery destination is the shop owned by his old friend. "I am so sorry, Jeanne-Marie, but yes, I do know this place. The owner and his wife, they are, or used to be, friends. I had no idea this was the shop you were talking about."

Madame de Beaumont forces a lift to her disappointed lips. "I am sorry for the failure of my surprise. But I do like this bookshop better than all the rest, yes I do. And I wanted you to know it too." That comes with an extended shrug. "Which you already did. Oh well, I asked the lady here to hold two new books for you." Jeanne-Marie leans forward to give him a light kiss on the lips. "Happy unsurprising birthday, my love."

Thomas returns the kiss and peeks over Madame's shoulder. He wonders if Hélène or Gallatin might be looking out, watching his every move.

"Good morning, Madame de Beaumont, how good it is to—"

Hélène's words come to a halt as do her steps toward the entrance of the shop. Her eyes leap off Jeanne-Marie's face to he who is coming through the door behind her. Hélène's eyes dart back and forth between the two of them.

"Thomas?" Hélène recomposes her expression to that of the obliging shopkeeper. She starts again, her focus back on Jeanne-Marie. "It seems we have a friend in common, Madame. Good afternoon, Monsieur Tyrell. It is a pleasure to see you as well." She offers a slight curtsey.

"Madame Gallatin." Thomas touches his right hand to his hat and offers a tight bow. He has to admit the cut of Hélène's dress, stripes in three shades of blue, fits his old lover's form very well.

There is a noise in the back room. It must be Gallatin moving things about. Thomas recalls him often saying the shop was not big enough. Storage was practically non-existent.

"Yes, Madame Gallatin," says Jeanne-Marie, smiling as if she is about to share a joke, "it was only as we arrived before your shop door that Thomas explained to me that he knows you and your husband, that you are all old friends."

Hélène gives Thomas a searching look. As far as he knows he keeps his face blank.

"That we were, in childhood," Hélène says. "Back in France. A while ago, was it not, Thomas?" She raises her eyebrows at him in hopes he will agree.

Thomas leans toward Jeanne-Marie and makes a loud stage whisper. "Madame Gallatin leaves out a bit. It was me who introduced her to her husband. And who is the godfather to their child."

Hélène's expression shows relief. "It is true," she says, soft as wool.

"You are godfather?" Jeanne-Marie says with blinking eyes. "Thomas, I am pleased. That means you must watch out for the dear child as she grows up in her Catholic faith."

"It is a boy," Thomas says.

"No matter, the obligation is the same. This is good, Thomas, very good. You pretend to me ... he pretends to me, Madame Gallatin, that he does not practice his faith, that he has put it aside."

Hélène gives her head a disapproving shake.

Jeanne-Marie turns back to Thomas. "Yet I see now he has not been telling me the whole truth. Shame on you." There is now a hint of newfound admiration in her voice.

"I am shamed," Thomas says. He bows to hide the annoyance he is sure must be making an appearance on his face.

There is a thud in the back room, then a whimpering.

Hélène hurries toward the open door to that back room. "Tommy," she calls out. "Viens, mon petit." Her face is nothing but concern.

"He is here, Hélène?" Thomas asks. "The boy?"

Hélène does not reply, but disappears into the back room.

"His name is Tommy?" Madame de Beaumont asks.

Thomas nods.

"Of course, I see. The parents named him after you, his godfather." Jeanne-Marie looks as if she might cry.

Hélène swishes through the doorway. "He is not hurt." It looks to be more annoyance than relief on her face. "Come," she says sternly, beckoning the unseen boy to come out of the back room.

A lad peeks round the doorframe, large brown eyes and dark brown hair. Thomas has not seen him in six months. He looks much taller today, no longer a mere toddling child.

"All the way," says the impatient mother. "Quickly now. I want you to meet Madame de Beaumont. Your godfather, Monsieur Tyrell, is here as well."

Thomas gives Hélène a look. He does not want to be Monsieur Tyrell to this boy. For some reason, he wants the lad to know him as he really is, which is Thomas Pichon. He can only bite his lip at the London corner he has painted himself into.

Tommy takes a cautious step, into the doorframe, one hand hiding something behind his back. Thomas is impressed to see how well the boy's clothes, the breeches and chemise, have been tailored to his small size. The only thing missing is a tricorne upon his head.

"What did I say?" Hélène asks, a hand upon her hip.

The boy tilts his head, then seems to recall, because he nods. He takes the required steps to stand before Madame de Beaumont and offers a deep bow. Then with an impish grin he turns to Thomas and whips the hidden arm into view. It brandishes a wooden sword mere inches from the godfather's face.

Hélène is aghast. "Tommy, not so—"

Thomas does not flinch, but holds out a hand. "There, there, little man. May I?"

Tommy swings his head side to side but then changes his mind. With a pronounced nod he passes the sword by its handle to his godfather.

Thomas pretends to thrust and parry against an invisible opponent until he hears Hélène say to Jeanne-Marie, "The sword was a gift from Thomas to my son. At first, Tommy was too young. Now he takes it everywhere."

Thomas swings round to see what La Beaumont thinks of that. She must think the boy is sweet, because her eyes look wet as she presses a hand to her chest.

"Here, lad," Thomas says as he kneels down. The deep voice that comes out of him is a surprise. Is he trying to impress the boy or the two women looking on? Little Tommy, he decides. For he wants to be nice to Gallatin's child. His old friend is lucky, he thinks. He, Thomas, now thirty-seven, may well leave nothing behind in this world. It's not altogether too late, but the candle that is paternity is burning lower with each passing year. He has never given much thought to being a father – he could not see the point – but at this instant, with this boy in front of him, he can see how a child of one's own might make a man glad.

"Here," he says to petit Thomas, "you take your sword back. Someday you'll be a knight. Or a viscount perhaps."

Tommy grasps the toy and with a grin flails the air. "Roarrrr!" he shouts at a shelf filled with books. "Roar, I say," he says to the counter. "You had best flee." And then he spins and runs as fast as his little legs can carry him into the back room.

Thomas hears Jeanne-Marie sigh as the boy runs from sight, to which Hélène mutters, "We do think he is a dear child. Most of the time."

"He is, he truly is," says Madame de Beaumont. "Oh Thomas, will you come here?"

Thomas blinks at that, but he does as he is asked. He comes to stand beside Jeanne-Marie. She immediately clasps his hand.

"Madame Gallatin," she says with a broad smile, with a quick, unseeing glance Thomas's way, "you shall be the first to hear. This man ... Thomas and I...." She pauses to take in a shallow breath.

Thomas tilts his head. He is more than a little curious to hear what might come next. He notices Hélène's interest is similarly piqued. Her eyes are waiting for whatever pronouncement the customer in her shop is about to make.

"We are getting married!"

Jeanne-Marie looks as if she could burst. She raises Thomas's clutched hand and brings it to her lips. Thomas regrets it as soon as he does it, but he shows Hélène a shrug, then the slightest possible shake of his head. Luckily, Jeanne-Marie does not see.

"Really?" Hélène takes a moment to tame her startled face. "Why, that is news, good news. Congratulations, Madame de Beaumont. Yes, of course. And to you, Monsieur Tyrell. I will be sure to tell Jean. He will be pleased. As I am."

"Got you!" yells Tommy, rushing from the back room. He jabs his toy sword into Thomas's back.

"Not now," Thomas utters through tight lips. "Not now," he repeats, gentler, trying to present a contented face.

Two minutes become five, then longer still. Jeanne-Marie keeps waiting, but there is so far not a word from the tight-lipped man

123

walking beside her. It is all she can do to match his pace as they beat a retreat away from St. Paul's.

"Thomas, please," she says, taking hold of his wrist. "You have to talk. And we have to slow down."

He does slow his pace. But talk? No, he does not.

"I am sorry," she says, "you must believe that. It just slipped."

He halts. They are in front of a narrow passage that leads into a darkened impasse.

"Just slipped? You announced it."

"I know, but I was touched by the way you were playing with the boy and I felt a surge of emotion. I spoke from my heart. Even though I will not have children, I saw what a good father you would be. Which means a good husband. Thomas, you must believe that. It slipped."

Thomas hunches his shoulders. "I did not like the way you did it. It is a big step, Jeanne-Marie. I ... should ... should have been part of it. Not surprised the way I was."

"I know," she says as soothingly as she can, "and you will. Can we forget about what happened and speak civilly?"

"I shall do my best."

"That's a good start."

———

There is water.

No, not water that can be seen, but he can clearly hear its distant sound. It is water running and running fast. It has to be a river, a rapids or a falls. It is louder now, roaring.

Yet where is it, where is this roar? It is nowhere he can see. All that is before him are trees, a forest dark. Tall and slender they are, but they are growing by nature's whim, not in planted rows. On a branch there hangs a cage. The roar of the water dims and Thomas can hear the song of the tiny yellow bird. It is a call for help.

And he is in the air, taken to flight like he is the bird. He is flying through the dense, dark woods. Then the forest thins.

A pack of dogs, cousins to the wolf, are panting in his ear. They run hard, their footsteps drumming the ground. Coming near, coming for him. Thomas must be running too. Because the dogs have not leapt and taken him.

And suddenly the ground ends. It is water, roaring water beneath his feet. His legs churn the air. His hands go to clutch the long grass on the bank.

Then he pushes up and off.

A breath gasped, Thomas finds himself sitting upright in his bed, the bedclothes kicked to the floor.

He is up on his feet and over to the window. It is too dark to see the familiar rooflines and chimney pots, but he hardly cares. There are a few stars among the clouds and a half moon. It is enough to reassure himself that he is back in the world.

Then he is aware that he is chilled. His chemise is damp from the dream. It made him sweat, all that running through the woods.

Back to his bed he goes, to get under the covers. Head upon the bolster and warming up, he feels as awake as he ever has. It is as if his very skin is alive. Nonetheless, he forces his eyes closed. He wants to recall the dream. Step by step he brings it back. When he reaches the last scene he understands the message that the muse of dreams has sent him. The tiny yellow bird in the cage is the key.

The eyes come back open to stare into the gloom. So, what should he do about the warning he has been sent? The waking world is not as simple as a dream.

The marital state has to be seen from all sides. Yes, it is a comfort and a pleasure, but it is also a risk. Madame says Thomas needs control, and maybe he does. But if that is how Nature made him, should he not respect her choice? Or is he supposed to adapt and bend to Jeanne-Marie? He does not have the certain answer to either question.

What is fair to say is that he never wants to live without a woman as part of his life. They are, or rather can be, kinder, more succouring than men. Alas, they are more complicated as well, with layers and sentiments no man will ever completely fathom. Jeanne-Marie is a case in point. Hélène too. Élisabeth. Marguerite. Thomas purses his lips.

He kicks off the covers. He is sufficiently warmed up. He will put on his robe and his slippers and walk about his rooms. It is his way. It never fails to surprise him, how many possible escapes from a dilemma there can be. It is always wise to have more than one arrow in the quiver, because the first may miss the mark.

As he begins to pace he notices the darkness is less than it was. Day will soon be here.

Sure enough, a quarter hour later, the trunk pushed up against the wall is catching the first glow. It is the trunk that held everything he owned when he came to England, with Hélène, what seems like a lifetime ago. It could likely still contain all he would care to take away with him, should he grow weary of London Town.

Thomas comes to a halt in front of the window where the honeyed warmth is streaming in.

Is the trunk an arrow in his quiver? Of course it is.

Thomas recalls the phrase John Cleland used to spout. "Nothing ventured, nothing gained." Cleland meant laying wagers at some table, but Thomas thinks it is more wisely applied to life itself. He strides to his writing table and takes three fresh sheets from the drawer. Half of the first sheet must of necessity remain blank. It is a mark of respect for the position of the man to whom he is going to write. After that Thomas estimates it will take but two pages to broach as diplomatically as he can his cautious ambition, his fair arrow. To write such a letter does not mean this will necessarily be his course. It is simply to give himself an alternative just in case he should want one later on.

He picks up the stick of red sealing wax and rolls it between his hands while he considers how to begin. Should he call the addressee Monseigneur or use his title of Magistrate Judge? The latter, he decides. After that the first line will of course be politesse. It's what comes after the formality that counts. He has to ask not

for a favour but a consideration. It must not seem to be beseeching in any way. Ideally, it will not be a request at all, just an opportunity the judge might entertain, should he wish to bring the
previously much-valued Thomas back into the fold. Though he
must not be so bold as that.

Thomas gives the bottle of ink a good, long shake. As he does,
the words to his letter start to form.

Most Honoured Magistrate Judge,

*I hope and trust you will Remember me, for I showed capacity and
subservience to you for three years, six months. I am sending you this
Missive because I Recall with strong affection my time serving as your
Trusted senior first clerk. I held you then, as I hold you now in the
greatest Regard and Respect.*

Thomas lifts the quill and studies his opening words. Yes, it
is fawning, excessively so, yet so it must be. The man to whom
he writes demands deference before all else. And so such obse-
quiousness is requisite for another line or two. Thomas puts the
quill into its slot and lifts the freed hand to his brow. He cannot
help but wonder if the reason he has never risen as highly as he
should is precisely because he finds flattery so easy to compose. .
How much better to be one of those on the higher rungs who do
not deign for anyone.

Quill again in hand, Thomas knows he has to be careful with
what comes next. He cannot be seen to be a supplicant, though
that is what he is. The magistrate judge does not respect those
who ask for anything in unseemly ways. So the hint of a request,
an inquiry prompted by gentle curiosity must be slyly done. And
then at the end, as a casual afterthought, Thomas Pichon, for that
is who is writing this letter, will have to deftly explain that he is
on an information-gathering sojourn in Londres, staying with an
acquaintance by the name of Thomas Tyrell. That is to whom the
magistrate judge should reply, should he choose to reply. Luck-

ily, Thomas still has his old TP signet to sink in the molten red wax when it comes time to seal the letter and send it on its way to France.

———

Jeanne-Marie has waited six days to tell Monique de Vins the news. Yet when at last she gets the chance, on a bright sunny stroll through Green Park, she is disappointed with her friend's reaction.

"I see," Monique replies, inclining her head, the eyebrows arching up.

"I said, we are to wed," Jeanne-Marie tells her once more, in case she did not fully grasp the gist. Jeanne-Marie can feel her cheeks nearly crack at the width of her smile. "Thomas and I."

Again Mademoiselle de Vins's head dips. This time her lips come up with a careful smile. "Yes, it is truly wonderful. I am greatly pleased."

"It does not seem you are." Jeanne-Marie feels her cheeks droop and notices her arms and her legs are taut.

"No, of course I am." Monique extends a hand. She touches Jeanne-Marie lightly on the sleeve. "It's just that … well, I would have thought … No, no. Congratulations is what I mean." A quick clasp of hands then a pretend peck close to Jeanne-Marie's cheek.

Then, without a pause, Monique leans toward the adjacent garden bed to inhale a lilac blossom's rich scent.

"Lovely, is it not? Here." She pushes the violet cluster toward Jeanne-Marie, indicating that she too should dip close enough to take in its heavy bouquet.

Madame shakes her head. "I am marrying, Monique, not becoming a botanist."

"Of course you are, and that …" Monique's two hands explore the air "… is good, I suppose."

"You suppose?" Jeanne-Marie prays her face does not look as cross as she feels.

"Well, why do you bother?"

"Bother? Are you asking why I would marry Monsieur Tyrell?"

"Yes? That is it? Why?"

Jeanne-Marie cannot speak.

Monique holds up a hand, clearly wishing to explain. "You are a widow, my friend. Respectable and comfortable. You have everything. Why not leave well enough alone?"

Jeanne-Marie cannot recall ever hearing such views from her friend or seeing such a smug expression on what she used to think was a pretty face. "Because, Monique, because it is not right."

"Right? What is right? Or for that matter, what is wrong?"

"There must be a marriage for a woman to give herself to a man."

"Oh, my."

Jeanne-Marie sees Monique fighting the urge to laugh. "Is that not the way *you* see it, Mademoiselle de Vins?"

"Jeanne-Marie, it is 1737."

"Not in God's eyes, it is not. Right and wrong do not change. They are everlasting."

Monique halts to take both of Jeanne-Marie's hands in hers. "Do you really think God cares," she says, her voice hushed, "whether you are a Madame de Beaumont or a Madame Tyrell? Honestly." She gives Jeanne-Marie a sorrowful look.

Madame extricates her hands. "Clearly, you do not understand."

"I guess not."

————

Thomas needs to work out what is to be done. Sometimes he envies Jeanne-Marie's certainty about the marriage, mostly he does not. Wisely, he keeps his doubts to himself. To sort out the best course for him, he picks the Strand. He will wander as idly as he can. The movement and the noise of the crowd on the busy street will summon his inner Reason to speak.

A half hour later, maybe more, Thomas's invisible counsellor has not yet shown up. Truthfully, he cannot recall the last time any inner voice spoke to him at all. When he was a lad in Vire, yes, verses came all the time. Less often were the whispers in Paris. Since coming to England and becoming Tyrell, no muse seems to want to come near.

Is it his advancing age? Like the hint of the gentle paunch that has arrived. And the drowsiness that comes after only two glasses of wine. And the need to find just the right distance from his eyes to hold a pamphlet or book. How he wishes he had back some of his youth. It is enough to make him scuff his feet.

He takes a good deep breath. Can it really be that he would prefer to be unenlightened again, the way he once was? Yes, maybe he would. Innocence – a polite word for stupidity – has its rewards.

For instance, he can recall the comfort he once obtained by confessing his sins to an unseen listening priest on the other side of the screen. It made him feel better to have the imagined slate wiped clean. Though he no longer goes to any church, he would not mind having another fresh start. If only there was another way to have someone listen to him and give counsel in return. It certainly cannot be Jeanne-Marie. She would not smile upon him confessing the perplexity he feels about their impending marriage.

"Enough," Thomas mutters aloud. He severs the air before him with both hands.

There is a public house across the street. He reasons a tankard of strong English ale might clear his slate. No, he'll have an even stronger drink just to make sure. He'll ask for what Cleland calls a dog's nose, beer laced with gin.

"King's Head," reads the tavern sign, though the painted wooden boards show no head at all. There are only the two words painted in red with a golden crown dimly visible in the background. It occurs to Thomas that the owner is smart not to name or show which king he has in mind. An imagined king is always better than a real one. Like an imagined lover or wife, he supposes.

The gin-laced beer makes no difference. Whether he sips or quaffs, it sheds no light on whether Thomas should yield to what Jeanne-Marie wants, which is to pick a date, or to disappear back to France. As of yet there has been no reply from the magistrate judge. Thomas supposes it is too soon, unless the judge has cast the letter aside, having forgotten who Thomas is or was. And used the letter to light a fire in a grate.

He takes another sip. With each touch to his lips he likes the dog's nose less. The gin ruins the taste of what might have been a good ale.

Which brings him back to his unsolved dilemma. Does he marry Jeanne-Marie and spend the rest of his days tutoring thick-headed English boys, while Madame remains an author with more success than he never had? Or does he.... And that's it, isn't it? As things stand, he has no alternative.

Thomas looks round the King's Head. Except for the barkeep, he is the only man alone. All the other customers are tippling with their friends. He too once had some of those, but now, now he is a man apart. Well, so it is. Thomas raises the tankard and drains the last bitter drop.

"Another over there?" cries the small, thin keep from behind the counter across the way.

Thomas nearly says yes, to pretend he is enjoying his drink. But instead he shakes his head. "Maybe later," he shouts back.

"Certainly, sir."

Thomas pushes down on the table to get to his feet. He's tired of this place, of feeling weighed down. And he's annoyed by all the talk he has had to overhear. The three inkies at the next table are especially loud, nattering on about beards, bodkins and bottle-arses. Thomas knows the terms of the printing trade thanks to Gallatin, back when the two of them were closer than they are now, before his old friend enticed Hélène away.

Out on the Strand again, Thomas looks up at the sign next door. "Parfumerie," it reads. That makes him smile. Though the English boast they are first and best in everything, fashion and the perfume arts are two areas where they admit defeat. There is not an Englishman, or more importantly an Englishwoman, who would not say that in those areas the French excel. Thomas looks again at the sign. Beneath the word is the painting of a scarlet bottle with a curved form. It is clearly meant to be a woman's form. The glass stopper is slightly ajar, with wiggly lines indicating the escaping scent.

"More to see inside, sir. Would you like to step in?"

Thomas spins round and brings his gaze to a woman standing in the open doorway of the shop. She is dressed in finery fit for someone attending a ball. She is pretty and smiling at him. He inclines his head. He thinks maybe he's seen her somewhere before.

"As forgettable as that?" the woman says, switching to French. She makes a mock sad face.

"Mademoiselle de Vins?"

She curtseys low. "La même. Bonjour, Monsieur Tyrell."

Thomas bows and when he rises he too speaks in French. "I'm so sorry, Mademoiselle. This location … your dress and hair … I did not…. Please excuse me, will you?"

"Only if you come into my shop."

"The Parfumerie is yours?"

"Not yet." She sends Thomas a wink.

Thomas smiles, an encouragement for her to do whatever she must to make a living in this life. He does like this woman, a playful soul. Now that Thomas and Madame de Beaumont spend their time together at Madame's place, and not on strolls and promenades in the parks, he has not seen Mademoiselle de Vins in weeks.

"So Madame is letting you run free this afternoon?"

Thomas knows he blinks. Though the teasing comes with a smile, there is something else – it looks like mockery – in the woman's eyes. Is that what the world thinks, that Thomas is on a leash held by his fiancée?

"Oh, please forgive me," she says. "I meant it as a joke."

"I am amused."

"No, you are not, I can see. But I shall make it up to you. Come in and I'll show you around my shop."

Along with a beckoning gesture and a ready smile, Thomas likes the twinkle in her eyes. "How could I refuse?" he says with a half bow.

Inside the shop his nose fills with delight. Thomas forgets for a moment that his fiancée's friend, Mademoiselle de Vins, is by his side. His focus is only on drinking in the scent. It seems like a long time since he yielded to the pleasures of the moment he is in. Everything in his life has for too long become a routine, a habit.

"I could give you more, Monsieur Tyrell," she says.

"Excuse me?"

"More scents. I see you are enjoying the air of the shop, but that is merely a jumble, a blend of everything that's been opened recently. I could present you with some specific scents that I think you will especially like."

"I do not want to trouble you."

"It would be no trouble. You can see there is no one about."

"You're certain."

Mademoiselle smiles broadly as she waves at the empty shop, empty but for the two of them. "I think it's obvious."

"It is, isn't it?"

"Here. Come."

Thomas follows her over to the counter. She goes behind, he stays in front, but leaning in. He has never had anyone explain in any detail the different scents there are.

"We will do a few, enough for you to compare."

"Lucky me."

Mademoiselle's eyes seem to grow larger than he thought possible as she smiles at that.

She removes a glass stopper from a tiny bottle and leans toward Thomas, bringing it beneath his nose. He likes the flowery notes that tease as they pass by. He also likes the tiny expectant grin upon her lips. Then she takes the stopper and touches its tip to the inside of her left wrist. She smells its effect herself then holds the wrist out for Thomas to inhale.

"Notice the difference?" she asks.

"I do. Yet how is that possible? It is the same stopper, mere seconds apart."

"It is my skin. It adds to and combines with the perfume. Each woman is different, perhaps you have noticed?"

Thomas plays along, matching her coy smile. "I have."

"Let me present you with another. Take a deep breath or two. It will cleanse the nose's palate."

Thomas withholds his scepticism and does as he is told. And so begins his first lesson in the perfume arts. He had no idea of the craft and subtlety required. How oils are distilled from blossoms and how long it takes. And how the musky scents are obtained, from land and sea, sources it might be better to know nothing about. Where previously the floral scents were what Thomas preferred to freshen his own skin and clothes, and those of the women he was with, he can feel the appeal of the earthier notes. He especially likes what Mademoiselle says is called Aqua Mellis.

"Honey water?"

"Very good," she says. "We call it *King's* honey-water. That helps with sales."

"Of course. Who does not want to wear what the King wears?"

"Exactly. The truth, Monsieur Tyrell—"

"Thomas, please."

"Only if you call me Monqiue."

"I shall then, Monqiue. Please continue."

"The truth, Thomas, is that there is not a drop of honey in it, though it wafts like there is." For a second time, she lifts her wrist and brings it to his nose. He can see the veins in her wrist through her skin. And as she turns her arm slightly, he notices the tiny hairs on her forearm.

"That it does," he says.

"We compose it with two dozen ingredients and more than a dozen steps. Sandalwood, cinnamon, cloves, coriander and more. What binds it all and gives richness to that particular perfume is the spirit of musk and ambergris."

"Might I inhale the scent once more, Mademoiselle?"

"Monique. Of course you may, Thomas."

But this time she does not hold up her wrist. Instead, she walks around the counter and comes up close to him. Closer than any shop clerk or casual friend. He can feel the warmth coming off her neck. It is an appealing neck, made all the more attractive by the slender choker of pearls.

"Thomas?"

"Yes?"

"I have a confidence to share." She brushes her lips on his.

"What confidence is that?"

Monique brings him a second kiss, longer, fuller than the first. "I could give you an even muskier smell."

"I am not sure."

"Muskier than what any flask in this shop contains."

Thomas feels the air leave his chest. This kind of thing has its risks. He should not do anything that could be misconstrued. This woman is La Beaumont's closest friend. Or maybe not.

"It's getting late," he says. They are words, it occurs to him as he says them aloud, that he may one day be able to use in his defence.

"No, it's not," she whispers in his ear. "And I shall not tell, if that's all that holds you back."

Thomas looks up to the ceiling of the shop, and finds the answer he was hoping for. He would be a fool not to smile at fortune when fortune smiles on him. "Here?" he asks.

"No, I have to lock the shop. My rooms are not far away."

——

Thomas is no sooner through the door than Jeanne-Marie wonders if something is amiss. His smile is thin and he turns quickly round, as if studying how best to hang his justaucorps upon the peg. Then how to place his hat on top of the coat. What seems to be most important to him is that he keeps his back to her.

"Thomas," she asks softly, "is something wrong?"

He turns round right away. "No, why?" he replies with jumpy eyes. He makes to place a quick kiss upon her right cheek, but his lips do not touch her skin. They make a tiny noise in the air.

"Are you certain?" she asks. With both hands she takes hold of his chin. She peers into his dark brown eyes. They are pools, as always, but this evening they look to be especially wet.

"I did not sleep well last night," he says with a wistful smile.

Jeanne-Marie cannot recall ever seeing quite that expression on him before. He leans forward and kisses her lightly on the lips. He could be a butterfly.

Back to a safe distance he says, "It must be fatigue."

"Of course," she says, not wanting to say too much. Yet she is not certain that it is fatigue showing on his face. It could be something else.

————

Thomas fluffs the patch of dark curly hair then gives the area a light tap. "Do you know what this is called?" he asks.

"I have heard a few names." There's disappointment in her voice and in her eyes. "None I care to repeat."

"The Venus mound, with its humble smile," Thomas says. He asks with his eyes what she thinks of that.

"Really?" she says. "I think I like that. Tell me, are you a poet, Monsieur Tyrell?"

"Would that please you, Mademoiselle de Vins?"

"It would, if I am the muse."

"You are doing a good job so far."

"I am pleased to hear it. But do tell me more about my charms, if you please."

"Well, this mound of yours, camouflaged as it is, is worthy of Venus herself."

"Do you like it more than Jeanne-Marie's?"

"Shh." Thomas makes a stern face. "You know what we said."

"I do, but I am still curious."

"Then I suggest you take a bath with her. I am keeping my silent pledge."

"A veritable pretend gentleman. I am impressed. But tell me, do you think she suspects?"

"No."

"But then you'd never know, would you, being a man?"

"Are we so thick?"

"I'm afraid you are. But that's enough talk. Come here. I am ready for a little poetry, Thomas Tyrell."

―――

Looking back on how it began with Monique, Thomas reasons it was not wrong, at least not at the start. It was not planned on either side. Indiscretions and liaisons that are the result of scheming are by their very nature dishonest. They are sins, in the language of the Church. But something that happens by chance, that is different. It follows Nature's call. And bringing pleasure to each other, as he and Mademoiselle de Vins do once a week, is innocent in that sense. As long, of course, as the third does not find out. The third? Thomas glances skyward, beyond the top floors of the red brick buildings as he walks along. That is not a pretty way to refer to the woman who is, well maybe, going to be his wife.

―――

Mon cher Giovanni,

I am rushed these Days – and Nights as well, but that is quite another story, not one the Gentleman's Code allows me to share. I have just enough Time to provide you with the Details you asked for. Had I but more Time, I am sure I could have crafted a better, more pithy reply. Since I am pressed, I must send you a letter as it comes to me, written in what an English friend of mine calls a Jumbly Style.

Thomas puts the quill down and leans back. He stretches out his arms. For just a moment he closes his eyes, hands now behind his head. He really does not want to write this letter to Codignola, yet he must. His correspondence of the outgoing kind is back-

137

ing up. He understands that if he is to receive letters from others, which he dearly wants, he has to send his own out. It is a give and take, as is pretty much everything in life. The missives from other parts of Europe are practically the only things he looks forward to in the tedium of his hours in the fabric shop and trying to drive nails of French words and phrases into thick English planks.

Well, that is not quite true. He does look forward to those moments when he spends time with the women in his life. Though of late, only one brings more joy than grief. That is Nature's gift herself, the musky-smelling Mademoiselle de Vins. She is skittish and Thomas gladly plays along. He especially likes it when she rubs scents previously unknown to him on their bodies before they make love. It is a completely sensuous world, and even though she insists he always wear a French glove, it is a small price to pay.

La Beaumont, on the other hand, borders on cranky of late. She is so unsettled. It is as if there is something bothering her, yet she does not say it aloud. He figures it must have something to do with his prolonged delay in giving her a firm date for their wedding. He understands how that might grate on her, given that she was once deceived and exploited by her late husband. Thomas vows he will not do that to her. Luckily, his secret liaisons with Monique do no harm in that regard. As long as clandestine they remain.

Thomas comes back into his writing position. It occurs to him he will give Madame what she wants, a firm date. It will be three months off, no less than that. That will surely be enough time for him to have heard back from France. Should he receive an encouraging word from the magistrate judge, he will have time then to inform Jeanne-Marie that the marriage is off. She will understand. Or maybe she will want to move to Paris with him as his wife. The choice will be hers. Thomas would like to have her in his life for years to come, as long as she is back to her former playful self.

But none of this rumination is getting his correspondence done, is it now?

Thomas picks up his quill and gives it a dip.

The number of Presses and of Publications in this City is beyond belief, at least beyond belief from what I once knew in Paris. There must be 20,000 fresh publications put out each year, counting the Pamphlets as well as the Books. My Sources tell me that is double what it was twenty years ago. What's more, the number continues to grow. I would be most interested to learn what the situation is in Genoa.

You asked me, Giovanni, about the remark you heard from an Englishman making the Grand Tour. You stated he used the name of a particular London street to disparage the Entirety of all Writers. I have inquired about this and it seems there is indeed such a place as the name you heard, Grub-Street. It is said to come from an old English word. A grube was a drain or a ditch. Clearly, not a place one would choose to live. Unsightly with Smells.

Though the term was unknown to me until you wrote of it, I have since heard it twice in Conversations this week. It appears that it is the low-down association with penury that matters, not any particular address on any particular street. Grub-Street refers to those who toil in ignominy and without success.

We men are simple beasts, are we not? We are so easily swayed by Words, for Better or Worse. I Pity the poor Writers who are Maligned to be of the Grub-Street ilk, as I am sure you do too, Giovanni. They are doing their best at a Profession that is nowhere near as easy as it might appear.

It is not enough to put the letter in the post, but it is a good start. The Genoan also wanted Thomas's opinion on where the English draw the line between what is low and what is high literature. That to Thomas seems to be a continuation of the Grub-Street topic. He wishes he knew the answer, but as far as he can see, the line between the two is invisible, or constantly moving. In any case, Thomas will try to have a bit of fun making up something.

———

Jeanne-Marie continues to wonder what is troubling her hus-band-to-be. The occasional secretiveness. A near irritability when she asks what he has been busy with.

The explanation that comes quickest to mind is that Monsieur is having some difficulty adapting to the idea of being wed. As so many women like to observe, marriage is a commitment men are sometimes – or is it often – reluctant to make. Though like her, Thomas has been married before, so it should not be a great leap. Besides, he is different from other men, isn't he? Now, last night, a corner was turned. Last night they agreed on a date. It is a mere three months away. It is the first step in having Thomas commit to her for the rest of his life.

———

Six down and six to go. So much closer than it was, yet still so far away. Six long weeks in which to figure out exactly how much celebration they should put into the day. At least the first big decision is now made: the ceremony will take place in a Catholic church with a Catholic priest. Reluctantly, but eventually, Thom-as agreed.

He has definitely started to become more like his old self. The changes that were worrying Jeanne-Marie have disappeared. Gone is the furtiveness. Once again they are walking and talking as they used to do and sitting in her salon reading their separate books. And when the time comes, they take their bath and then they make love. Sunday is a day deliciously drawn out. Every-thing is as it was and should be.

Occasionally, he does have a new, odd scent. It must come from walking too far or too fast. It gives her pleasure to scrub it off with the sponge.

———

Thomas knows it is wrong to feel overly pleased with himself, but he has to smile. Monday morning to Saturday evening is as dull and disappointing as it ever was, what with his hours selling bolts of fabric or tutoring boys who have no interest in lessons at all. But from Saturday evening to late Sunday night, his life is as good as it gets. First, it's Monique with all her mysterious lotions and ways. Then La Beaumont, a sweet woman he likes — no probably loves. The fact that it's only four weeks until he and Jeanne-Marie are to wed adds an extra layer of pleasure to the arrangement. It is a feasting table that must be savoured before the foods can no longer be enjoyed. For once the ceremony has been performed, Thomas has vowed before his mirror, he will stop seeing Mademoiselle. He has not shared that with Monique, but he is confident she will understand. She would not want to cheat on her best friend after the marriage. But until then Thomas gets to savour the best of two worlds.

———

It is down to three weeks and there is still so much that remains to be discussed and decided. Where they see each other only once a week, Sunday already has too much packed into it. Something has to change, and Jeanne-Marie has decided what it is. She and Thomas will have to start getting together on Saturdays as well. As soon as he can leave the shop he will have to march to her place. There are important shared decisions they have to make.

"Thomas?" she says, as carefully as she can.

"Yes."

He does not even glance her way, which she supposes means he is especially relaxed. He is enjoying his evening chocolate while he reads a book about different diseases, their conditions and treatments. She does not understand some of his interests, but then they are not hers but his.

"I've been thinking …"

"Yes." He looks up and over to where she is pretending to read a book, but is unable to because her thoughts are elsewhere.

"I think it is time to decide who we want there. At our wedding, I mean."

An odd expression comes upon his face. She wonders if it is him fighting to not roll his eyes. She understands he does not take the same interest in the wedding details, but he has no choice about that.

"Yes," says Jeanne-Marie, more forcefully than before. "I know it is a second marriage for each of us, but it is still a celebration, is it not?"

"Of course it is."

Jeanne-Marie's heart lifts to see Thomas set down his chocolate, close his book and get up. He comes directly over to her and pulls the ottoman close to her chair. He sits and takes hold of her hands.

"Your interest in this pleases me, husband-to-be."

"That is good. Now, you tell me, Madame Tyrell-to-be, who do *you* want to attend?"

"Our friends. I would like them there and to sign the registry as witnesses."

"Do you have a list?"

"Not yet, but they are not numerous, are they? Neither of us has any family, but I have a small circle of friends, women you have not yet met."

"Invite them all," Thomas says. His eyes are as happy as his grin.

"All right, I shall. And as for you, there's John Cleland, I guess."

"No, he is off to India."

"Really?"

"It's true. Who else?"

"The bookshop couple and their boy, your godson."

Thomas's smile falters for an instant but then recovers itself. "Of course," he says. "I will speak with Jean."

"The only other person I can think of is Mademoiselle de Vins."

Thomas's face seems to stretch before Jeanne-Marie's eyes. Nonetheless, Madame continues on.

"Our friendship has grown a little chilly, but still, I think she— What is it, Thomas? Why that face? Why are you standing up?"

142

"I . . I am not sure about the perfume lady." His stride is quick, toward the window then toward the door. He is pacing fast. "You … you told me she was rude. Not happy to hear we are to wed."

"She was, but I'm sure she will be over that. Sit, please."

Thomas does as he is asked, but his previous good mood has passed. "Well, at least think about it, Jeanne-Marie. My strong opinion is that I think it would be best if Mademoiselle were *not* there." He is back on his feet.

"Thomas, I—"

"No." He holds up both hands. "She is your friend, but I … I…. That's enough. I've said my piece."

Jeanne-Marie is speechless as she watches Thomas head back to his chair and his book. She had no idea he felt so strongly about poor Monique. He is making it difficult for her to invite Mademoiselle to the ceremony, isn't he?

The air is crisp as Thomas strides back to his place. It is the right kind of evening to think straight.

Was he too forceful a few hours ago in objecting to Monique being invited to the wedding ceremony? Did he somehow tip his hand that he and perfumist might be involved?

No, Thomas thinks not. He made it about the strained friendship between the two women, nothing but that. He is safe, and should be for a while. But he still has to figure out how and when to tell Monique that their clandestine intimacy has to end. Where before he assumed she would take it in stride, now he is no longer so sure. No one likes to lose what they know and enjoy.

He flaps his arms to warm up. It's unseasonably cold for a spring night, is it not?

It is. Too cold for any answers to descend. Or is it rise up? Whatever direction they come from, he'll have to sort out what to do with Mademoiselle another time. He still has three weeks.

But his looming wife has asked to see him Saturdays too, and he has agreed. So he'll have to explain that to the perfumist as well and ask for a different evening of her week.

Thomas shakes his head as he sees his building ahead. A part of him will not be sorry to put an end to the current double life. It's getting more complicated than it's worth.

———

There she is, dear Monique. Jeanne-Marie had hoped to catch her old friend walking in Green Park, just the way the two of them used to do before Thomas came into her life. Because a conversation face to face is better than any letter sent through the post. And there, as Madame hoped, there she is.

Mademoiselle is crossing the small wooden bridge not thirty yards away. How odd that she looks to be walking with footsteps so very heavy. In fact, her usually erect posture is not there. She looks weighed down.

Jeanne-Marie purses her lips. What she has to say to her friend will not likely lift her mood. But there is nothing Jeanne-Marie can do about that. Her obligation has to be to the man who will be her husband in eight days' time. All Jeanne-Marie hopes is that her friend of several years will understand. She goes over yet again the little white lie she has rehearsed for days. The ceremony will be private and quick. There will be no one with Thomas and Jeanne-Marie but the priest, and the beadle and a deacon, she supposes, to sign as witnesses.

"Mademoiselle de Vins!" she calls out. "I am over here."

Monique looks up and finds her, but does not wave back. Nor does she smile. Nor does she hurry her steps. In fact, it looks like she is slowing down. Something is definitely wrong. Jeanne-Marie hurries to meet her sorrowful friend.

"Monique, are you all right?"

Mademoiselle nods. "I suppose I am." Her voice is monotone.

"No, I can see you are not. Tell me, friend, what is wrong?" Jeanne-Marie starts to give her an embrace. "Is there something I can do?"

Mademoiselle pushes her back. Then her eyes go wide as she laughs. It is not a friendly laugh. It is more like a raven's caw.

"Something you can do? *You,* you are the cause."

Jeanne-Marie blinks and blinks. "Me? What are you talking about?"

Monique stares at her, seeming to study Madame's eyes and face and then her entirety from head to foot.

"No, maybe you don't. Imagine that, you are the last to know."

"Know what? Please, Monique, tell me what is wrong?"

Again Jeanne-Marie tries to touch the sleeve of her friend's pale blue muslin dress. Monique does not intercept it, but she stares at the hand like it could be a snake. The hand recoils to the safety of Jeanne's own waist.

"Maybe you should ask him," blurts Monique. Gone is her pretty face. The chin is out, the eyes are a full dare.

"Him? Who is him?"

Mademoiselle shakes her head and sends her a smile, but it is not the smile of any friend. It is one of contempt. Then Monique turns and shows Madame her back. She begins to walk back the way she came.

"Monique!" pleads Jeanne-Marie.

The woman halts. Over her shoulder, with raised eyebrows that Jeanne-Marie can plainly see, she says, "I think you should wake up, my friend. You are wearing horns."

"Wearing horns?" mumbles Jeanne-Marie.

It is her chest that first figures it out. It tries to summon a great breath, but is denied. She feels the warmth flush from her face, a chill that spreads on down. Jeanne-Marie turns on her heels, her ears filled with a roaring sound.

———

Thomas cannot put a finger on what it is, but there is something wrong. Madame de Beaumont is not herself. She seems formal with him, even a little cold. It is like she is going through the motions of a play and not really feeling the part. It shows in her conversation, which is strained at best. Then there is what looks like tightness around her eyes and on her lips.

With only six days until their marriage ceremony on Friday, Thomas thought Jeanne-Marie would be in an even better mood than the pleased state she has been in leading up to where they now are. She does not know it, of course, but he gave Monique the news, which is how and why he is here in Madame's apartment on a Saturday. To say the least, Monique was not pleased, but that is a story he cannot share, water under the bridge as the saying goes. What matters now is only Jeanne-Marie, and something is bothering her. It must be nervousness concerning the step they are soon to take. Yes, that must be it.

And somehow or other, the mood she is in must be why she has insisted he be the first to get in the bath, instead of her as it has always been. About that, Thomas will not complain. He likes being in the wooden tub with the warmed water up to the middle of his chest when there is no skim, none at all. He will not lather too much with the soap and sponge, so it will not be too milky for Madame when it is her turn.

"What is it, my Beaumont?" he says. "You look like something is bothering you. Are you all right?"

"No, not really."

"And why is that?" Thomas reaches for the sponge. Without soap he starts scrubbing his chest.

"I know," she says, barely aloud.

Thomas turns her way. "You'll have to speak up. Did you say 'I know'?"

"I did."

"And what is it that you know? Look, the fire needs another log, I think. Would you?" He settles back, closing his eyes.

"Are you relaxed?" Thomas hears her ask.

Thomas smiles. "I am." Then he opens his eyes and sits upright. "The fire, Jeanne-Marie, it needs a log or two. To keep the air and water warm for you. Was there something you wanted to say?" He tilts his head at a quizzical angle. He shows her a face she can trust, a face she can tell whatever it is that is bothering her.

"A true heart," she says. "That was what I wanted."

Thomas squints at that. "Please do not play the sphinx. I am your husband after all."

Madame leans back and takes in a long breath. Thomas sees her shake her head as her lips curl. "Not yet," she says.

"No, but … Jeanne-Marie, are you ill?"

Thomas grabs hold of the tub's two sides and lifts himself to his feet. "Pass me the towel, would you please?" He does not know why, but he covers his groin with his hands. "I'll stoke the fire and you can get in. I'll help you out of your clothes."

Madame shakes her head.

"Here," he says, surprised to hear pleading in his voice, "the towel please. It is your turn. I insist."

Thomas sees her laugh. A snorting sound from her nose. If he did not know better, he'd say she is angry with him.

Thomas steps out of the tub, his wet feet and dripping body making large puddles on the wooden floor. He grabs the towel from off the chair and wraps it around his waist. "What is this?" he hears himself nearly shout.

Madame puts a hand on each hip, and gives him a look he has never seen on her face. It is not anger but some kind of pain. "I always knew you did not love me, Thomas, in the way that I love you. But I accepted it. I thought— well, I hoped— that in time you would show me as true a heart as I was giving to you. But you could not, could you?"

"Don't be foolish, Jeanne. Don't talk like—"

"No?"

"No, you are all upset. You need to get in the bath and—"

"Thomas?"

"I'm getting chilled, you know."

"Thomas, I spoke with Monique." She nearly spits the words.

Thomas feels his shoulders melt.

"Merdre," escapes from his lips.

———

Thomas wraps his arms as tightly as he can across his chest. It does not help. No matter how hard he pulls and flaps, he is still shivering. He cannot get home too soon. He wants to be wrapped in a blanket before a roaring fire. He hopes his numb hands will be able to spark the tinder with the fire steel and flint. Once the charred linen cloth comes alight, with its flames spreading to the kindling, only then will he be all right. Then he will heat a bowl of caudle to warm up his insides.

Alas, it is still a ways before he will be at his own door.

Is what just happened no one's fault but his? By that he does not mean to suggest Madame did any wrong, for she did not. La Beaumont is blameless, except for causing him a serious chill. No, he is asking if the culpability for this afternoon's *event* rests with him alone. Surely not. Monique the perfumist must shoulder a bit. Maybe half. Though that is beside the point. It is not an escape from guilt that Thomas seeks. He knows he hurt Jeanne-Marie and for that has to pay. But beyond that, he wants to know if in following Nature – a pretty name for lusting loins – was where he erred? It seems a paradox. Nature is supposed to be one's guide, yet look where it misled him. Fleeting delight over ... over a lasting marriage to a woman he ... a woman with a true heart. The words are Jeanne's and he likes them very much. Except that they make him wince.

All he has ever wanted is a woman in his life. Well, a position too, but that seems out of reach, so women are now his only dream. And not just any woman, but one with whom he shares a bond. And by bond he does not mean only the act. Calming fury that it is, the sexual union lasts but a short while. No, it's always been more than that he seeks. The right woman sees in him things he does not, and tells him so. She is a succour not just for his body but for his mind, his soul some priest might say. What he wants is just what Jeanne-Marie wants, but where is such a person found?

Is there some intrinsic failing or weakness in him? Is he capable of love in the way a woman wants?

Thomas glances at the clouds scuttling past a three-quarter freezing moon. It makes him think of a Greek play he once read. The drama hinged on the actions of the Goddess of Rhamnous, a darling Nemesis. That seems to be Thomas's lot as well. To be drawn to women – for there have been several – who are either his undoing or whom he eventually lets down on his own.

Was today his last opportunity? Surely not. But he cannot worry about what lies ahead, only about warming up. Thomas needs a blaze and a caudle first. The rest always looks after itself. *"I'm not done yet."*

VIII
Encore

London – April 1739

Thomas takes in a shallow breath the instant he sees the seal embedded in the hardened red wax. He knows it well. It is the seal of the magistrate judge from his old job in Paris. Thomas does not delay. He had all but given up hope of a reply, for it has been several months. To his desk he goes for his opener.

Oh, this is good. Not great, but adequate. The judge still remembers him and has offered a position. Not at the level Thomas once occupied, but two levels down. He would be a simple commis again, like he was years ago. That makes him bite his lip, but still, he has to be reasonable. It is better than anything London has offered him. He will just have to impress and begin the climb all over again. Thirty-nine is old, but it's not in the grave.

Still, it would be hasty to agree straight away. He should at least think it over. Measure twice and all that. True, judging by the grin he can feel on his face it seems the matter is already settled, but there might be some angle he is overlooking. He needs to take a bit of time to assess and reflect. Which means he needs to walk.

The letter goes in the right-hand pocket of his coat as he hurries to lock the door and clip down the stairs. He would not mind telling anyone in the building about the offer he has received, because they would like to know. They would want to be happy for him, whatever his final decision is, if they would only hear his clomp on the stairs and come out to ask what is going on.

But no one appears at any door, and a pity it is. They are in the dark as to how fortune's wheel has finally turned for their neighbour.

The first soul Thomas eventually meets is a long-faced man, a bricklayer by trade it appears. He crosses paths with Thomas as they both turn the corner onto Hedge Lane. The brickie gives Thomas a sour look, which makes the new Paris commis doff his hat. It is sad to see anyone in such a glum mood on a day like this.

London's streets are as busy as they always are, but there is no one Thomas sees who would not think it strange for him stop and chat, and hear him say, "Oh, by the way," as he pulls out the letter he has received.

So where to go and who to impress?

He has to shake his head. Coyness does not suit him much. He knows very well where he should go and whom he would dearly like to impress.

Thomas does not lift the brass knocker. He does not even climb the two stone steps. Instead, he stays out on the cobbles in front of No. 5. It has been months since he made his last trek to this address, and years since he called this building home. More years than he cares to count.

He steps back and cranes to admire the slender spire of nearby Christ Church. One of Hawksmoor's finer churches, many times he has heard it said. It is still fairly white from bottom to top, though sooner rather than later the coal smoke will smudge it like it does all else.

He does a scan of both sides of the street. Up to the tops of the Church Street buildings his eyes go. All is the same. At the top are the glass-windowed spaces where the Huguenot silk weavers ply their trade.

He sniffs the air, for it is sweet. Then he remembers, the Black Eagle Brewery is only a few blocks away. The sweet smell is hops. How much better than the tang of burning coal.

Away from No. 5 he starts to stroll, hands behind his back. Something tells him that coming here could be a mistake. These old friends do not want to see him nor hear his news. Not having knocked he could simply retreat. Back up to Red Lyon Street or farther on down to Brick Lane, and then circle back whence he came. He is not sure.

As he ponders, walking slower than he ever does, he can feel the cobbles beneath the soles of his shoes as he shuffles and scuffs. The slow pace makes him think of the letter he received a week ago from Madame de Beaumont. It came from Annecy, which she informs him is a small town in the mountains of France, near Switzerland. The setting, she asserts, pleases her a great deal, being beside a lake. She says the writing is going well and she is happy, except that she misses him. Thomas was pleased to hear it. But then came the ending.

All would be forgotten and forgiven, my dear Thomas Tyrell, if You were to come and stay. Annecy would be your home. Of course, you must come alone.

Thomas was tempted when the letter first arrived, but some instinct told him to delay writing back. Now, well, now, with the offer from the judge, he cannot imagine joining Madame in any mountain village, no matter how pretty it might be. Now he has in his pocket the offer of a position along the Seine, in the offices of a high-born noble who handles the justice of the kingdom of Louis XV. He will write back to Jeanne-Marie and inform her of his news, and he will do so kindly and without even so much as a hint of unbecoming pride.

Thomas's slow strides carry him back to No. 5. So Gallatin has painted his door black. Why ever would he do that? That brings a smile, for Thomas knows exactly who decides everything at this address. The mystery is how she does it. Whatever her secret, Hélène always gets what she wants. That is not to say she's sly, for that is an unkind word. More likely it's just that Hélène is cleverer than everyone else. Yes, that does make him sigh.

Does he really want to do this – tell Hélène and Gallatin his news and bid them adieu? For some reason he does. Buckle the buckle, as the saying goes. They were the two people who brought him to this city. He wants them to know that his stay is over. No longer bowed, he's going back to France. Thomas climbs the steps and takes the door knocker in hand.

———

The hard strikes on the door startle Hélène. She is in the basement, checking how well Pollyanna scoured the copper pots of the kitchen before she left at noon. Hélène holds a cloth dampened with vinegar and salt, to give the pans another few swipes. "Jean?" she calls up.

"Yes," she hears her husband reply. His footfalls thud from the salon toward the door.

"Thomas!" Jean Gallatin nearly shouts. "This is a surprise."

"Thomas? What can he want?"

Thomas's chest swells to see the broad smile on Gallatin's face. One never knows if old friends will still care for you when you rarely see them anymore.

"Thomas! This is a surprise."

"Hello, Jean. It is good, very good to see you again." Thomas adds a clasp to his friend's wrist as they shake hands. "It truly is."

"Come in, my friend, come in."

Thomas does as he is requested. Gallatin closes the door behind him and leans close. "Hélène will be pleased," he says in a low voice.

Over Jean's shoulder Thomas can see Hélène has already come up from the nearby basement stairs. She sends Thomas a wink.

"If we keep our voices down," whispers Gallatin, "we might—"

"Surprise me?" Hélène tilts her head back, eyebrows raised.

"Apparently not." Jean Gallatin looks at Thomas and shrugs.

"She's not easy to fool, is she? Unlike us men." Thomas nods at Gallatin and sends a knowing look to Hélène. The beige and brown stripes of her dress, with the bright floral stomacher, suit her nicely, Thomas thinks.

"What a delicious smell." Thomas makes a show of sniffing the air.

"Mulberry pie," says Hélène. "Would you like a slice?"

"No, no. Thank you."

There comes a silence, with all three taking turns to see who wants to speak next.

"Yes, well," says Thomas. "I have some news. Good news for once."

Hélène listens to them talk, two men who clearly like each other. It amazes her how they can banter about topics that hold little or no interest for her. Whether London is better than Paris; how the English differ from the French; the writers they admire and the ones they dismiss. On every point they seem to agree, and show it by repeating what the other has just said.

"No, there, you are wrong, I'm afraid," says Gallatin.

Hélène chooses to pay attention. The two men are both smiling the way they do when they are about to impart a more correct view of things.

"No, Jean, *you* have it backwards," Thomas is saying with a shake of his head. "It is the printers who make the money while the poor writers, the *sine qua non*, they starve."

Jean raises his right hand, the index finger pointing up. "But money is not the point. Writing is the nobler profession."

"Noble is hardly the word. Poor scribblers with lofty ambitions more like."

"Yes, but it's the aspiration that counts," Gallatin asserts.

"You're wrong there. Aspiration and ambition only double the sting of failure when there is no success."

"Oh, Thomas, you *will* succeed. Of that I have no doubt. It's only a matter of time."

Thomas half rolls his eyes. "Time marches on. Listen, let's change the subject, my friend. I'm curious as to what you think of the Tonson brothers' deluxe edition of *Don Quixote*. Good piece of work in your opinion?"

What surprises Hélène most is that each of these men would be so different were he with her alone. In either imagined combination the topic of conversation, the tone of voice and the language of eyes and limbs would not be what she hears and sees.

Hélène shifts in her seat and tightens the fabric of her dress across her knees. At this point, she would appreciate it if either or both would simply acknowledge that she is in the room. As it is, she might as well be on the other side of the Thames. Or in France.

"So, Thomas," Hélène ventures, "when exactly do you leave?"

"Hélène, if you please." Her husband's expression says he is disappointed in her.

"I am sorry, Madame." Thomas's face is equally grim. "Have I overstayed my time?" He makes as if to stand up.

"No, no," Hélène laughs. "I do not mean your visit with us. I mean when do you leave for Paris and the office of the judge?"

Thomas sits back. She sees his shoulders relax. "A fortnight. I have been given a date I must not miss."

"So this ... this is it?" Hélène is not sure her question should come with a smile or a frown. She chooses the frown. "Our au revoir?"

"No, not au revoir." Thomas gestures to include Gallatin but then swings his gaze back to Hélène. "It's adieu."

"Adieu," Hélène repeats, blinking fast. "Really adieu?"

Thomas shrugs. "Don't you think?"

"How slow of me." Gallatin is off his chair. He is coming to Thomas with arms outstretched. Thomas rises to welcome the embrace. "I had not realized the full nature of your news."

Thomas watches Hélène stay seated where she is. She has an odd, faraway expression. Sadness? He hopes it is.

"This is bittersweet then," Gallatin is saying.

Thomas finds a focus on his friend's mouth, then on his whole face. He steps back. "Yes, I suppose that is the word. But that does not alter the essence, which is that it is good for me. And let us remember that it is Paris I'm moving to, not across a distant sea. You two *could* come back to France, I suppose."

"You are right. Who knows?" says Jean Gallatin, though his sour lips say he has no intention of ever returning to France.

Thomas turns Hélène's way. She remains seated and apparently lost in thought. Whatever those thoughts are, they look to be beyond the banter in the room.

Hélène dares not at the moment look Thomas's way. Every once in a while over the past few years she has wondered if she should tell him what he seems not to have guessed. Or if he has, he has done a good job of keeping it to himself. A whispered word in his ear is all it need be.

Unless, of course, Thomas might then do the wrong thing. That is the risk. In which case, maybe a secret is best not revealed.

"We shall correspond," announces Gallatin. "Just like we used to do."

"Of course." Thomas presents a pleased face. He well remembers how they used to write to each other, but that was long ago. Much has happened since, including Gallatin enticing Hélène away from him and marrying her.

"Excuse me," Thomas says to Gallatin. He takes two soft steps in Hélène's direction. "Madame."

Her eyes seem not to be focussed anywhere. Thomas takes another step closer and again he speaks her name, "Hélène."

"Hélène," says Gallatin in a louder, sharper voice.

Hélène stirs and angles her head her husband's way. "Pardon me."

Gallatin points at Thomas, who is standing to her left.

"Madame … Hélène … I wonder if I might say goodbye to the boy before I leave."

"The boy?" Hélène stares at him, eyes wide then narrowing. She begins to blink.

"Petit Thomas. My godson." Thomas glances at Gallatin, wondering if Hélène is perhaps not well this day.

"Oh, of course." Hélène jumps to her feet. "You want to bid him farewell. I understand."

"I ... I thought I would ... should." Thomas shrugs. Is this not something a godfather is supposed to do?

"I'll go," Gallatin says. "Tommy likes to play in the attic. He has a few toys up there. You know the space, Thomas. You stayed there when you first came to the city. I'll be right back."

With Jean thumping the stairs, Thomas turns to Hélène. She gives him a slow, disapproving shake of the head.

"What is that for?" he asks.

"Nothing" she says. Her face and lips are as tight as he has ever seen.

"All right then," Thomas says, with a shrug. "Tell me about the boy. Is he doing well?" He gives her a tentative smile.

"He is."

Hélène shifts in her seat. If she is to tell him, there could be no better moment than this. A few words and it would be done.

"Robust health?"

"Most of the time."

"Smart?"

"He truly is," she replies with pride.

But then what's inside her chest compresses. It makes her close her eyes and shake her head.

"Hélène, what is wrong?"

She looks into his worried face. "Nothing," she says. "Something I ate."

"Are you certain?"

"I am."

Yes, it is better off the way it is. If this man has not guessed, he does not deserve or need to know. No good would come of it.

Then again – she is not likely ever going to see him again.

"Oh, Thomas. Please come here." Hélène grabs his forearms and pulls him close. She knows Gallatin will soon be coming down the stairs. "Please don't."

Thomas looks at her like she has lost her mind. He shakes off her grip. "Don't what?"

Gallatin's footfalls begin their descent. They are heavier and slower than on the way up.

"Don't leave London." Hélène can feel that her cheeks are flushed. She knows her eyes are showing a little wet. "Don't go back to France."

She has to move away from Thomas. Gallatin is getting close.

Thomas's friend is back down the stairs and coming into the salon. In his arms is a child much longer than Thomas recalls. He has grown so very much over the past number of months.

"Here he is," says Gallatin. "Our big lad."

Thomas bows to the boy. A light-hearted joke. It makes him chuckle to pretend that this ordinary child, waist high to himself, the son of his best friend, might be the Dauphin of France. "Good day, petit prince," Thomas says, coming up from his reverence.

Hélène's expression seems close to shock, but Gallatin at least is amused. Or perhaps just very pleased?

Hélène steps forward to take Tommy into her embrace. "There you are. How are you, my sweet?"

"Very well," the boy says, straightening up. He gives Thomas a quizzical look. A light comes into his eyes. "Monsieur," he says with a quick bow.

"It is good to see you," Thomas says. Unexpectedly, he feels an urge to make contact with the boy. A tousle of his hair or maybe a hug. Wherever does such a sensation come from? It must be seeing Hélène's outpouring of emotion with her son. Thomas clears his throat and reins himself in. "How much you have grown. Can you be only four? You are on your way to becoming a proper man." Thomas thrusts out his right hand.

Cautiously, the boy reaches out to touch Thomas's hand. It is flesh on flesh but there is no grip. No matter, Thomas gives it a firm shake.

Tommy tugs his hand out of Thomas's grip and tilts his head. "Are we making a bet?" he asks.

Thomas notices that Hélène beams at that, while her eyes brim with tears. What is going on with that woman? Meanwhile, Gallatin is covering his mouth with his hand, keeping in a laugh.

Thomas bends to the lad. "In a way we are." He glances at Gallatin then at Hélène then back to the boy. "We are betting, you and me, that we shall remember each other forevermore. For I am leaving London soon."

Thomas allows himself to give in. He pats Tommy's head and ruffles his hair. "How about that for a wager, young man?"

"If you say so." Tommy looks at his father and lifts his eyebrows.

"Yes, in a minute you can go," says Gallatin. "But first, first you must bid a proper goodbye to your godfather, Monsieur Pi— er, Monsieur Tyrell."

"No, you're right, Jean. It should be Pichon." Thomas bends to the boy. "Tommy, from now on, please call me Monsieur Pichon. Not Tyrell."

The boy bows at Thomas. "Monsieur Pichon. Au revoir." Then he spins and is out the door of the salon.

The only sound in the house is of the child climbing the stairs.

"Still very young," Gallatin explains.

"I could make him come back." Hélène is leaning toward Thomas. Her voice is deep, like something is stuck in her throat. "Jean? Would you?"

Gallatin moves toward the stairs.

"No, no." Thomas reaches out to catch Gallatin by the elbow. "Let him be. I'm sure he has better things to do than talk to me." He looks to Hélène for agreement, but that is not what he finds in her wet, dark eyes. He has no idea what he sees. Pity? Regret? Love for her son? Thomas hears his own deep intake of breath.

"Well, that is it. All done." Thomas bows but once. They can share it between the two of them. "Adieu, my friends, adieu." He strides into the hall, shoulders back, head erect.

"Thomas!" Gallatin is hurrying after him.

Thomas does not turn round, but he can tell that it's just two feet coming after him, not four. Hélène must have stayed where she was. He decides he will open the door and go down the steps, out onto the cobbles of the street, before he will turn round.

"We have to write," Jean Gallatin calls out, an upraised waving arm and an earnest face.

Thomas nods. He is pleased, he really is, that this man, this friend, has made a good life for himself. He not only has a wife but a son. Fortune smiles on him, in a way it has not yet favoured Thomas. That may change in Paris, or maybe not. All he can do is soldier on.

"Yes, of course," Thomas says loud enough for Gallatin to hear. Then he raises his right arm high. It's the Roman salute Jean used to sometimes use.

Gallatin makes the same salute, then looks as if he might cry.

"No, Jean, no," Thomas says. "We are friends. Distance will have no effect."

"You are right." Gallatin straightens up and puts his shoulders back. He spins and without looking again at Thomas steps inside and closes the door to his house.

At once Thomas hears a tapping sound. His eyes go to the ground floor windows, first to the one closer to the door then the one on the right. It's there he spies a shape. A hand. It stops tapping and presses against the glass. The hand blurs away, leaving a ghostly trace upon the pane. Then there comes a face. Hélène. She is sending Thomas a kiss.

Thomas blinks as he steps back. To catch a breath he has to turn toward the sky. The clouds are thickening overhead. It is as if an unseen hand were stirring the world.

Back to the window, Thomas sees Hélène is still there, the eyes even wider than before. She is beseeching him. But for what? To stay in London?

His shoulders hunch, but then he sees her wipe her eyes as she shakes a sorrowful head. Out on the cobbles an invisible hand takes hold of his chest. Thomas gasps. He has to manufacture a breath.

"Too late," Thomas mouths across the thick air.

"Too late," he repeats, this time aloud.

His eyes lower to the squared stones so he can stay on his feet. He fills his chest and forces his eyes back to the window. Yes, Hélène is still there. Two wet palms pressed against the panes.

Thomas returns the kiss she sent a moment ago, then spins. He is away.

IX
Travail

Paris – April 1740-March 1741

A sudden noise shakes his focus on the words. But before he looks up, Thomas has to make sure he finishes the line he is putting on the page. Three quarters of the document is safely copied over. An uncontrolled spill of ink at this point would mar or maybe even ruin what he has accomplished. He learned long ago that the secret to this tedious profession is concentration. Sloppy handwriting, a missed or repeated word, or a blob of ink are sure ways to stymie a scribe's career, and his career has already had more than enough delays.

Thomas puts the goose quill safely into the hole of the blue and white faience inkwell that rests at the top of his writing table. Only then does he turn to the sound coming from the window.

It is as he guessed. A splatter of raindrops on the panes and the drum of rain upon the slate tiles that lie out of sight on the roof overhead. Yet how odd. Out the narrow dormer window that is his sightline to the world while he is at work there is not a single cloud. It is an all blue sky, royal blue at that. And according to the stones of the buildings opposite, it's still a golden Paris day. Yet there it is nonetheless, a springtime cloudburst coming down. There must be a dark mass directly above the building.

What a marvel a sun-filled rain does make. Diamonds shimmer in the air.

"Pichon."

Thomas swivels to the voice. He finds his feet when he sees who it is. Mathieu Gaspard. Though the man is six years younger than Thomas, and dull and tiresome as a piece of wood, he is the supervisor of this part of the office.

"Monsieur," Thomas says.

He sets his expression so that it will betray nothing about what he really thinks of the recently promoted superior clerk.

"You do understand, do you?" Gaspard wiggles the fingers of his right hand at the documents on Thomas's tabletop, the original brevet and the as yet unfinished copy. "How urgently I need *it*? You can grasp that, can you?"

"I can and do." Thomas controls his lips. He offers Gaspard a stiff bow, as if his frame were made of oak.

"Well then."

"Right away, Monsieur."

"I hope so."

Another slight bend of oak before Thomas re-takes his seat. He will not let Gaspard see him rush. Instead, he puts on a display of assuming the writer's posture before he allows himself to reach for the quill. He verifies the two documents are aligned just right, and with a touch of his finger he locates exactly where it is he will pick up the copy-work. Only then does Thomas take the quill in hand. He first must examine its nib. Inspection passed, he grasps the plume, fingers where they need to be. As he dips the tip of the quill in the ink he can smell the audience of one leaning close to his shoulder. Cheese breath. Thomas exhales a silent jet, hoping to blow away at least some of the man's smell. He begins again to make a faithful copy of the brevet.

"More like it," Gaspard says before he walks away.

As the footfalls pad off, Thomas silently mouths, "Gaspillage." The nickname is not one he coined – it came from Arnaud, who occupies an even lower rung than Thomas does – but Thomas likes to use it now and then. It provides a fleeting satisfaction, the only way he has so far found to prick Gaspard's balloon, if only in Thomas's own imagination.

The copy of the brevet completed, Thomas puts down the quill and stands. He turns toward the end of the long room where the superior clerk is standing beside his high, brass-trimmed desk. Gaspard is in conversation with none other than the magistrate judge himself. Should Thomas hurry to deliver the wanted document, to show how efficient he is? No, better to wait. He does not want to demonstrate alacrity in working beneath Gaspillage. That would only serve to reinforce the mistaken idea the good judge might have that he has promoted the right man to be the superior clerk. Thomas will wait until the magistrate has sauntered somewhere else. Then he'll deliver his work to Gaspard. As for the judge, Thomas will have to find some other way to impress him, if and when he is able to speak with him alone.

"If and when," Thomas whispers aloud. A hand goes to his brow. At forty-one years, those are pitiful words. For what if there will be no if and when? What if the moment for him to impress and advance does not come?

————

A chill is in the air.

Though it is only the morning of the Saint-Michel, the penultimate day of September, it is cold. Winter's first breath, two months early. Oh, how Thomas would prefer if it were winter fading away rather than coming on. It is as if nature itself is taunting him with a fresh disappointment, pointing out how old he is getting with each passing benchmark on the year. The seasons chase each other like a dog chases its tail.

If someone were to ask Thomas to choose another day on the calendar he would prefer over a chilly Saint-Michel, he has his answer ready. That would be Easter, and not because of the story of a resurrection and a life eternal. No, it is because of what lies behind that wishful-thinking tale. It is the waxing, warming light and the signs of rebirth that come at that time of year. Easter brings a better mood than any feast day from late September on. Thomas shudders to accept that winter's onset has come so early this year, darkening and chilling the world. He tugs on the tricorne atop his bewigged head and turns up the collar on his great-coat as he continues his stroll along the cobbled walkway beside the Seine.

How familiar Paris has become to him again. It didn't take long after returning from London before it seemed like he'd never left on his English interlude. In fact, maybe that's what he should do. If someone ever asks if he has travelled beyond the borders of Louis XV's kingdom, he will affirm he never did. None but a few know the truth, and they're not around to countermand what he says.

Thomas likes the way Paris's spires and rooflines meet the clouds, especially the twin towers of Notre-Dame and the spire off on the right of Saint-Severin. Though he has turned against the Church, he still admires its architecture. Heavenly aspirations deserve silent applause. When he lowers his eyes and ears to absorb the crowded, malodorous and noisy streets of Paris, however, Thomas has to admit that the place has a few weaknesses. Still, the city is a living thing. There is always construction or repair, and the people one meets on the streets come from all levels and display every temperament. The loud seem to outnumber the quiet, but that's only because the quiet keep to themselves. Almost as numerous as the people, or so it seems because they cannot help but announce themselves, are all the horses clipping and clopping over the cobbled streets. In truth, the horses are few and far between when compared to the mice and rats. Silently, they skulk everywhere, with a legion of cats trying to keep them in check. As for the dogs and birds, they too are abundant. Paris is life itself, the best and worst side by side and astir.

The sound of a creaking cart catches him unawares. Thomas twists to see. There, coming along the Quai de Conti, is further proof the cold season is nigh. A cartload of firewood. Those who can afford to buy such bundles will keep warm over the weeks and months to come. Thomas gladly counts himself among that group. A wood fire may not be as strong as coal, which the English prefer, but its smoke is preferable. London's air had a stinging, sulphurous bite.

"Or so I have read, for I have never been there." Thomas's ever-ready lie makes him smile. It is easier than he ever would have guessed to edit one's life and thoughts into what one wants them to be.

Thomas gives the creaking cart a friendly slap on its closest wheel as it spins by. Yes, he does like having firewood in his rooms near the old church of Saint-Julien le Pauvre. Last winter's supply is nearly gone, so he'll soon have to purchase more. He hopes never to be reduced to huddling beneath a wool blanket when winter comes, with no fire in the grate. He thanks his fate for having the means to avoid that. There are many, not just in this city but everywhere, who are far from being so fortunate.

The only thing missing from Thomas's life, aside from the elusive higher rank and the hint of respect it might bring, is a woman with whom he could share more of his hours. He longs for it to balance some of the bluster, stupidity and facade of his own sex. He spends all his working days surrounded by men: judges, lawyers, clerks, scribes and copyists. They are a dull lot at best.

As for the nights … well, he mostly spends them in his rooms, if not reading then taking up his quill. Gone is the time of his life when he frequented cabarets and cafés, complaining about his lot in life with others of a similar bent. Now, he'd rather keep his disappointments to himself and not add anyone else's troubles to his inventory. Similarly vanished are his visits to courtesans and whores. He refuses to rut like a beast the way he once did.

His greatest pleasure these past few months is reading clever words in pamphlets and books and in the letters he receives. Or when he puts down what he thinks are some clever words of his own, sending them off to his correspondents. The network of enlightened minds he is in touch with across Europe is now up to eleven, with the addition of the Russian count in St. Petersburg and the young Swiss from Geneva who is working as a tutor in Lyon. Thomas will be writing the young Rousseau this evening about their mutual interest in the rustic, yet freer, peoples of the overseas world. Earlier in the week Thomas found a book on Accadie, which describes its fishery and its natural people. Some of what he read he wants to share with young Jean-Jacques.

From London there faithfully arrives a letter at least once a month, to which Thomas dutifully replies. Occasionally Jean Gallatin mentions a detail about his wife and child, but not often enough. The most recent informed Thomas that his godson and namesake had just turned six, but it said nothing about what the boy does and does not like. Thomas is curious. The last time he saw the boy there was something about him that reminded Thomas of himself at that age. Maybe it was how he preferred to be up in the attic by himself. Thomas wishes Hélène would add a paragraph or two about the boy, or maybe about herself, but she never does. More than a few times, Thomas has wondered what that scene at the window was about. Why didn't she just step out of the house and into the street? They could have talked, they could have—

But no. Instead, Thomas still does not know what it was the woman was trying to say. It had to be more than just goodbye and don't go.

Thomas sighs.

Every month or two Madame de Beaumont sends him a letter from Lake Annecy. He enjoys them a great deal, and he always replies. But it is a polite response, no promises does he make. It is inconceivable that he would ever move to a mountain village, no matter how fond he is of her or how often she tells him Annecy is the Venice of the Alps.

Thomas slows his stride and brings his gaze to the river. Advancing under two of the arches of the Pont Neuf are barges with eight-foot lengths of cordwood stacked high. It is not as if he needed another sign that the change of seasons is under way. Yet there it comes, and there in the green flowing water of the Seine is one more. The river today is covered with rising wisps as it yields its warmth to the overhanging air. Thomas cannot help but wonder, foolish as it is, if the Seine does not resent the winter coming to steal away its summer heat. Of course it does not, except in some poet's verse. He halts and takes hold of the stone rail.

Would that the missing muse, an old childhood friend, would visit him again. It would be a delightful change from the letter-writing muse, if there be such a thing.

It makes sense to him that all the muses are female. Of course they are, for they are in touch with the mysterious parts of life and the world of which no man can ever know. And yet, even as he acknowledges that, he has to chide himself that except for La Beaumont not one of his correspondents across the continent is a woman. Is that not odd? Women may not follow the body politic, nor the treaties or latest war the way a man might, yet they are shrewd, perceptive and witty about every other part of life. Should there not be at least one woman in the circle to whom he writes, aside from a woman he nearly married? He would dearly love to add the renowned Émilie du Châtelet to his list, had he her address. Though what would they talk about? She is the translator of Newton after all, and Thomas knows little of mathematics or its cousin physics. He'd likely only embarrass himself in any letter he might write. Still, the woman is said to be as beautiful as she is smart. Aim high is the rule, is it not?

As Thomas watches the heavily laden barges go by he feels a grin come to his face. The oarsmen of the small boats coming upriver have to change course when they are confronted by the barges. They must manoeuvre their narrow, pointy-ended boats to the river's far side. We all have to bow to someone else, Thomas muses.

"Sometimes even kings," he whispers to the Seine. If nothing else, his time in London, walking past the Banqueting House where Charles II lost his head, taught him that. A curious and inspiring example. Though it is unimaginable that such a turn of the wheel could happen in France. Louis XV may not be as beloved as he was when he was a boy and his life was in peril, but Thomas does not hear or read anyone talking about getting rid of him or the other notables of the realm. Rather, everyone, or Thomas at least, wishes he were in their place.

Behind Thomas there is a loud huff and puff and the sound of hurried foot-slaps. He turns to see two burly men in livery carrying a sedan chair. The curtains are drawn, but it's obvious that whoever is inside is especially heavy. The bottom of the box is barely above the cobbles and the porters are straining with all their might to keep things upright and moving forward. Thomas offers each man an understanding face. His kindness brings two appreciative nods in return as they grunt by.

Two women in sack back dresses descend from a coach farther up the street. Each casts a short cape round her shoulders and turns to walk his way. Thomas decides he should be in motion himself, toward them. He adopts an aristocrat's posture with his cane leading the way, shoulders firmly back.

As they near he can make out the patterns on their dresses. One wears a rose-coloured dress with a silver thread flower pattern as accents. The other has on a delicate mix of blue and white stripes. If Thomas is not mistaken, and he is not because he knows cloth, the blue dress is made of brocaded silk. The other woman has two remarkable pieces of lace dangling from her cuffs. Each presents a powder-whitened face with a beauty mark, topped off by a tiny white cap. Their shoes match the colour of their dresses. Above the sounds of the city Thomas can hear the fabric swish as they near.

He makes a respectful reverence. "Mesdames."

The woman in blue allows fleeting eye contact and a trace of a smile. The one in rose pretends she does not see or hear Thomas at all.

He watches the two-person parade as it moves slowly by. Though they wear short capes, the two beauties are walking as if it might be a warm summer day. They do not hurry or show any indication that it is cold. Thomas has to admire what they achieve. It is a stately appearance, no matter what.

It seems he should correct something he was congratulating himself about a few moments ago. His interest in the two women suggests that certain urges have not vanished from his life after all. They were merely dormant is all. He does not envy the life of a monk.

Yet while he waits for a new woman to make an entrance into his life, he has letters to read and write. It is a consolation of sorts. Still, how much better if he could have both.

———

Mon cher Rousseau,

I want to share with you a few Reflexions that come from a Book just read, for no other reason than I think they shall hold an Interest for you. It is a Book about a portion of the New World, and includes sections that touch on how Men and Women live together across the Ocean Sea.

But first—Is it not Marvellous when in a book shop you stumble on a Book that speaks to You, the You You are on that particular day? Of course it does not happen all the Time, but that is what happened to me this week. I was in a Left Bank shop looking at this and that when the keeper said, without me having said a thing, Sir, what about the New World? What about it? I replied. He pulled out a book by a Frenchman about Accadie, written by one Nicolas Denys. This, Sir, he affirmed, is an undiscovered gem. I knew not the Author's name nor much about that distant land. Do you know Accadie? It is, or rather was, France's colony across the Atlantic, at more or less the same latitude as France, and it extends out into the sea towards us in Europe. A highly contested Territory with the English it was and remains. We, the French, have a great interest there and have Established a Port and Strong-hold farther north called Louis-bourg on what used to be known as Cap Breton and now is rebaptised Isle Royale. It is said to be a Place that thrives.

And why should I recount to you this brief History lesson? Because, mon cher ami de plume, this book, written seventy years ago, is fascinating. It bears the unwieldy title of The Description and Natural History of the Coasts of North America, but it is a title that does not do it Justice. In fact, I ask you, why is it that so many Books bear the weight of dreadful titles? Do Authors and their Printers wish to scare off potential Readers? But I Digress.

Some parts of the Book you will pass over, I know you will. About its Fisheries and Natural History. Yet, when this Denys writes of the Sauvages, the original natural People of that part, I predict you will not lift your eyes from those pages. The author says the natural people are called Micmacs and he paints quite a portrait. To whet your Appetite, I copy here a short extract in the Author's words.

"They love their children much and are never afraid of having too many for they are their Wealth; the boys aiding their Father, going on the Hunt & helping in support of the Family, & the girls aiding their Mother; going for wood & water & finding the animal from the Hunt."

Does that not sound like a simpler life than what we know? I suggest it gives us a Window into how We, in the time of our ancient Ancestors, likely once also lived. Here is another portion of the book, wherein the Author Denys writes of the ancient customs of this ancient People.

"In Old Times a boy who wished to have a girl was Obliged to serve her Father for several Years according to an Agreement; going a-hunting to show that he was a good hunter, capable of supporting properly a wife & children ... For her part, the girl corded his snow-shoes, made his clothes, his moccasins & his stockings, as evidence that she was Clever in work ... The term being Expired, it was time to speak of the Marriage ... If one of the two wish'd not the Marriage, there was nothing further done; for they were never Compelled into it. But if all were in Agreement, a day was chosen for a Banquet."

Does that not suggest to you as it does to me, that we, the people of today, surround with altogether too much Pretence and Complication the fact of Marriage between Men and Women? Alas, we have lost the Simplicity of long-ago ways.

I would like nothing more than to observe the Micmacs with my own eyes, and speak with them, except that it requires a crossing of the dreadful Atlantic. That is something I do not envision. Happily, we have in Denys an Author who saves us the trip.

I must close, my dear Rousseau, but I believe you would not regret seeking out this Book. It gives us a striking contrast to the World we see before our eyes in our various European lands.

Thomas P.

———

Yearning is useless, is it not? That is Thomas's thought each time he sees Madame de la Rose come or go from the building where they each live. Thus far they have not exchanged a word, nothing more than a doffed hat on his part and a hint of a nod from her. Though he does think that a few moments ago, as they chanced to pass on the stairs, she gave him a passing look of mild curiosity. But then the sun was in its final hour of the day and it was painting the stairwell with a rosy glow. So her glance of interest might have been nothing more than an illusion he imagined.

Yet as he hangs his tricorne on its hook in his rooms, he thinks not. He wants to believe that there was an inviting warmth in her eyes today. In fact, he is inclined to think it was something of a dare.

All he knows about Madame de la Rose is what he learned from the concierge the first week he moved into the building and what he sees with his own eyes from time to time. He and the concierge were chatting just outside the main door, which faces the nearby church of Saint-Julien le Pauvre, when she emerged carrying her parasol. Without showing the slightest interest in looking either left or right, away she stepped as if she were in a salon, admirers on all sides.

"The tawny is from Martinique," whispered the concierge after she had passed. There was a disapproving curl to his lips.

"She is beautiful," Thomas recalls he said. And thought to himself, I would not use tawny but rather light chocolate to describe the delightful colour of her skin.

"You think so?" the keeper of the building asked, making a sour face.

"I do. Poised. Well-dressed. And just look at her. She is the definition of elegance." He was especially struck by the slender choker, a pale blue ribbon of silk she was wearing around her neck.

The concierge shook his head. "Well, she's not for the likes of you. She goes only with the highest ones. I don't know why she continues to live here, but she does. A mystery it is."

Since that day, Madame de la Rose has possessed an allure for Thomas, but with nothing to show for it. Until today. Now he has had a long look from her dark eyes to build on. It's a start.

———

At his usual table, its surface lit both by the nearby window and the flickering glow of a tallow candle that he has received permission from Gaspard to spark on this dark day, Thomas has to decide which particular project to turn to next. There is no shortage of documents he has been given to copy, and it does not help to be told that each is needed right away. This trade, nay this profession, can be done only one by one. Faithful matches are not willed, but produced by careful work.

He stifles a yawn as he sorts through the side-table assortment of originals Gaspard has given him. It really is a world of paper, is it not? Arrêts, brevets, commissions, confirmations of various kinds. Congés, contracts, declarations, dispatches, dispensations of all types. Edicts from the King on high. Letters as varied as the number of cheeses in the land. One to send someone to prison and one to set someone free. Letters to validate credentials or rehabilitate a marriage. Even letters to establish an admiralty court in a distant colony and another to give sole jurisdiction in that same place to a particular provincial branch of the Franciscans. Copies of all must be made and put away. And then there are the ordinances, issued by the different authorities. They are like the stars at night, so numerous. And what would life be like without passports, ratifications, remission notes, renewals of authority and after you're gone, testaments and wills?

It's enough to make Thomas wonder how the so-called un-civilized societies exist, those of the Indians he has read about in the Americas. The Micmacs of Accadie, for instance. No kings, no laws, no faith. The clerics and the high-born of Europe would have you believe that the newly discovered world is a chaotic hell on earth. Thomas knows from reading Nicolas Denys that is not the case.

He glances over at the framed map of France on the wall to his left. Then again, despite his ruminations about the desirability of a less ordered life, Thomas has to admit he does like certain things about the world in which he lives. He likes to see the red lines on the map coming from all directions and converging on Paris in the northeast. He recalls the first time he saw the map. With a single illustration it revealed a vital part of his life. For, as the legend explains, the red lines indicate the major routes of the kingdom that the coaches follow to carry the mail. Thomas has subsequently learned that in exceptional cases, couriers on horse-back are hired by representatives of the King to get documents from A to B quicker than usual.

"Wishing is not sufficient, surely you know that."

Thomas turns from the map. Gaspard has come up alongside Thomas's table. He is shaking his head disapprovingly.

"Excuse me," Thomas says, rising slowly from his chair. "I do not understand."

"Wishing does not get anything done. Is that not clear enough?"

Thomas tilts his head quizzically.

To which Gaspard glances at the pile of documents Thomas has on his tabletop. "There," he says, "is where your eyes need to be. Nothing goes out on the roads of the map until copies are made."

"Ah," Thomas says, keeping a straight face, "so that's how it works."

Gaspard gives him a scathing look.

Thomas reaches over to the side table for a document, any document at all. As he holds it up for Gaspard's approval he sees that his hand has selected a marriage rehabilitation.

"No, that's not it. We start at the top. Which means anything dealing with the King or a royal court. Honestly."

Thomas holds his tongue but manages to give Gaspillage a nod. It is the best he can do.

Is this why he came back to France, to toil under a dullard's thumb? To advance the interests of all those above him, right up to the so-called beloved king, who is neither so young nor so beloved anymore?

As Thomas's hands start to organize his tabletop to carry out the copying he has been told to do, there arises a single question in his mind. It is not for how many more hours on this day must he do this line of work. It is for how many more years must he keep on after that?

———

Madame de la Rose goes over to the console table and reaches down into the blue and white Chinese porcelain bowl she keeps there. Her fingers come up with a red ribbon, which she lets fall back in. Another dip brings a cluster of three – yellow, pink and grey. Back they go. It is the third exploration with her fingers that brings her what she wants. It is for the man she passed on the stairs the other day, the one who lives on the floor below and who has been giving her studied looks as she comes and goes ever since he moved in a few months ago. He has the look of someone she might like to converse with. Désirée will tie a ribbon of pale blue on the handle to his door. That ought to puzzle him when he returns from wherever it is he works all day long. Though she won't be there to see his reaction, she imagines he will be intrigued.

Then, if she pleases, she will tie another colour of ribbon on his handle another day. It will be what a scientist she once talked to in a salon would apparently call an experiment. In this case, the test is to see how long it takes before the man on the floor below connects the ribbons to her. If and when the fellow figures out what is going on, Madame de la Rose just might invite him to her rooms, where they could have a conversation they would likely both enjoy.

———

Thomas checks left then right, then cranes to look down the stairs he just climbed and up the ones that lead to the floor above. There is nothing and no one. There is only the blue ribbon, wound tightly on the handle to his door.

Someone is having fun. Thomas tugs the bow, and stuffs the ribbon into the pocket of his justaucorps. But who and why?

———

It has been a fortnight now, with ribbons coiled on the handle of his door every second or third day. It is always a new colour, and there is always the tiny bow. Clearly, it's a woman behind the game. To what end? Thomas thinks he knows the answer to that. But to select the wrong woman to playfully confront would be a serious mistake and likely end the game the real mystery woman is seeking to play. Thomas does not want that. And each day that there is no ribbon, only the cold look and touch of tarnished iron, he wonders if he has misplayed the game somehow.

———

More than twenty years have passed since Madame de la Rose was brought from Martinique to France. She was but seventeen and answered then only to Désirée. Though she was transported from Fort-Royal as someone's property, along with six others, all men and boys, she understood enough French to grasp that the arrival in France brought a change, in theory at least.

"There are no slaves in France," the official said in a clear, loud voice. That same official made her master – until then her owner – repeat the affirmation out loud. Which he did, though not half as loud.

Désirée could not detect any difference in her treatment once she and her master arrived in Paris – Monsieur de la Rose had never been a beast to her – but she never forgot the declaration that had been sworn. It altered how she viewed herself and what she did for Monsieur. Henceforth, the washing, cleaning and pleasuring was easier to take. She was no longer his slave but in her mind a *conjointe*.

So much has transpired since then, beginning with the death of Monsieur a dozen years ago. Désirée assumed his family name right away, even if the Church had not blessed them. Monsieur de la Rose had left her the entirety of his estate, and she figured she might as well be his widow in name as well as in deed. The estate did not include any fleet of merchant ships nor any châteaux, but there was the Paris apartment and his investments. Désirée has not wanted for food nor clothes nor heat since he passed.

Life as a widow has been better than good. Désirée has a servant, Aimée from Guadeloupe, whom she pays well and to whom she dispenses advice on how to survive in the world. Madame is able to purchase clothes and accessories when the need arises, and she attends as much entertainment and as many salons as she wants. She has a wide circle of acquaintances she knows well enough to grant or ask favours from time to time. Now and then, when she's in the mood, Desirée takes a lover, but never for long. She does not want to complicate her delightfully simple life.

————

Thomas feels the rise of his chest at the sight of the pale blue ribbon looped tightly round the handle to his door, and with its tiny bow. The very same colour with which the game began.

He does not unravel it, nor touch it at all. Instead, he climbs the stairs two at a time. He was thinking about the ribbons today at work, during the two-hour pause allowed for lunch. While walking along the Seine, Thomas pulled out the half dozen ribbons he keeps in his pocket in case some inkling about how to solve the mystery descends. It was while he was leaning against the stone rail overlooking the river that it dawned on him. There was something particular about that first blue ribbon. It had been a sufficient clue right from the start, but he had been too blind to recognize it for what it was. And now he has just seen further proof.

Thomas does not hesitate for a second. He thuds the woman's door with the side of his fist.

———

"Ah, so it is." Madame de la Rose steps back to open her door half-way, just slightly wider than the space where she stands. She is pleased to see eager expectation on the man's face, though there is no way she will let him know that. "Monsieur from downstairs, I believe. Is that right?"

"It is. Monsieur Pichon," he says, followed by a bow.

"And what is it that brings you to my door, Monsieur Pichon?"

"Madame," he says, thrusting his right hand into the pocket of his justaucorps. Out comes a clutch of silk ribbons, held in his hand like an offering to her. "I think these are yours."

"Are they now?"

"I think so."

"And what if they are?"

"Then I thought, I hoped, you would appreciate me bringing them back to you."

"Do you not think that presumptuous?"

She sees him relax, with a hint of a cocky smile appearing on his lips and in his eyes. Désirée does not mind. In fact, she likes what she sees.

"I was rather hoping," he says, "that this return of your ribbons might be … might be an opportunity for us to converse."

Désirée grants him a slight smile. "To converse. Is that what you would like, Monsieur, to converse with me?"

"Yes, Madame, to … to converse with you." He inclines his head.

"And the subject?" Désirée rolls her wrist.

"That, Madame, is entirely up to you. I shall be at your command." And with that he makes a second bow.

"Tell me, Monsieur, would you say anything to get me to open my door and let you in?"

"I think I would."

"And do you think such candour should be rewarded?"

"I do not presume," he says, holding out once again his ribbon-clutching hand to her.

Désirée laughs, and snatches her ribbons back. "Fortune smiles on you, Monsieur." She gives her door a gentle push to open it all the way.

———

Thomas likes that Madame keeps the custom going. When she wants him to pay her a visit to her upstairs rooms, she ties a short length of silk around the handle of his door. It seems to him the perfect means to a delightful end – simple and sensually feminine. His only wish would be that she give him the sign more than once a week. But he is not about to complain.

As always, they begin with conversation, an exchange that takes place in the salon while they are fully dressed. She insists on that, just as she never calls him anything other than Monsieur, to which he always replies, Madame. The opening never varies. She asks Thomas if anything of interest has occurred in his life since they last spoke. It is then his turn to ask the same of her. He understands she will not be rushed. Each step of the evening has its protocol. The time in bed must be preceded by what he thinks of as a slow warming up, in which it is her mind and not her body that is engaged.

It was not until the third evening, when they were in bed and the deed was done, that Madame put a hand on his shoulder and held his gaze. There was clearly something on her mind.

"Tell me, Monsieur, do you think me less than you?"

Thomas knows he leaned back. He imagines his face must have shown the shock he felt. "What is this?"

"You French, you have many terms for those of us who come from the Isles."

"Do we?"

"Do not be coy. You know you do. You make it a science, a pretend science, the calculation of the amount of French blood

180

that courses through our veins. No matter the percentage, we are always less, less than you."

"You mean a term like mulatto?"

"And griffonne. Quadroon. Octoroon. There are more."

"But these are not terms I use."

"No? Not even when you are back in your rooms, thinking of me, as your *dark* lover? Your tawny perhaps?"

"No, Madame. You are a beautiful woman. That is all. And it is more than enough." Thomas held up his hand. "I do so swear."

"And what do you swear upon? Tell me that. Upon a Roman Catholic God? Or maybe the King?"

"No, Madame. Upon my heart and head."

Thomas does not think he imagined seeing a hint of water upon her eyes when he said that.

Then Madame de la Rose told Thomas her story. How lucky she was to be the exception and not the rule. That to be considered pretty as she was on the plantation back in Martinique did not just help, it determined everything. It is what took her out of the fields and into a great house in Saint-Pierre, and then later from Martinique's administrative capital of Fort-Royal on a ship across the sea to France. Yes, it meant there were things she had to endure, like the two babies she gave life to at fourteen and fifteen and which were taken away from her back in Martinique. But she was able to get through it all. For that and for her face she is eternally thankful. It is why, she explained, she bestows what charity she can on others less fortunate than herself, whenever she gets the chance.

"Such as me," Thomas said, raising his eyebrows.

"I suppose," she said, scrambling to sit astride his waist. "Now, how about you give back a bit. I'd like one more before you go."

———

With Aimée having bid her au revoir and gone down the stairs to end her long day, Madame de la Rose and Thomas raise a glass of the sweet aperitif she wants him to try.

"Excellent," he says, glass upraised in a salute.

"Isn't it? It's called Pineau. It's from near La Rochelle."

"I like it." Thomas also likes how the flickering light dances upon the pale grey walls of the room, and upon the features of Madame de la Rose's beautiful face.

"Still the same, I suppose?" she asks after a long pause. "In the bureau, I mean." She puts her stemmed glass down and places a hand beneath her chin.

Thomas does not need to ask to what she refers. It is his situation at the magistrate judge's office, of which they lately talk every time they get together. Not wanting to have yet another pointless discussion he merely shakes his head. It is bad enough he has to endure a low-level job and Gaspillage. He should not have to talk about it as well. Instead, he takes another sip.

"Well, I do not like the sound of him, your overseer."

Thomas has to allow a smile at that reference to a plantation brute. "He is not quite that, Madame de la Rose. Young Gaspard rules me and others with his thumb, not a whip."

"Let me think on it for a while." She retrieves her glass and takes another taste. "I have friends, you know."

"I do know, Madame, but please do not trouble yourself on my account. Some things are meant to be endured."

"I thought you a *lapsed* member of the Church. Apparently not."

Thomas hunches his shoulders. Though he will not say so aloud, he does sometimes miss a couple of the sacraments. Confession and penance. There are times when he does something he regrets yet has to keep to himself. He occasionally wishes he could unburden himself by making a clean breast of it.

"Neither denial nor admission?" asks Madame de la Rose. She tips her glass to finish off her Pineau.

"No, Madame. I prefer to leave you the final word."

"As is right." She flexes her eyebrows. "Shall we then?"

Thomas rises to his feet. "With distinct pleasure, Madame."

It used to puzzle Thomas, how they could make love with consummate skill and passion every week, and yet continue to refer to each other with such polite formality. He had not once called her by her Christian name nor she by his. Then he realized that she wanted it like that. It must help her maintain detachment. He can understand that. So he does not complain. Madame de la Rose she remains, nothing less than that. She is at the moment not only the best thing in his life, but also the only good thing at all.

———

Heavens, that is strange. Désirée is coming slowly back into the world of thought after the rhythm of the act fades away, when suddenly a name pops into her head. Breteuil.

Why him? Yes, she has met the Marquis a few times. She even spent a couple of evenings getting to know Bretuil in the Biblical sense. He was a bore, but then maybe that is what he needs to be, since he is constantly around the King. The air at Versailles seems to bring out tediousness in all who inhabit the place. Certainly Breteuil was incapable of lively conversation and his trysts with her were a stiff-legged, wooden-handed attempt at amour. He was nothing in bed compared to the agreeable-smelling Monsieur Pichon. Oh, heavens – that's it.

"You!" says Désirée, pulling the bed cover up over her chest.

"Me?" Pichon says, more than a little startled. "What is it? Is there something wrong?"

"No," laughs Madame de la Rose. "But you shall be pleased. Thanks to your assistance—" she glances down at the sheet to where his loins are covered, "it seems the muse of love has given me a name."

"A name?" The man bites his upper lip. "A name for what?"

"Not what but who. A marquis no less," announces Madame de la Rose. She feels a smile bestride her entire face. "The Marquis de Bretuil."

Thomas blinks. "The Principal Secretary to the King? He who introduces all the ambassadors?"

"The same." Madame swings her legs and is out of bed. There seems to be somewhere she has to go or something she has to do.

Thomas watches as she puts her arms and her head into her linen chemise and pulls it on. As quick as that, her lovely form disappears.

"I don't understand," he says.

"No? You truly do not?"

He holds up his right hand and presents a solemn face.

"No matter. What does count is that I know Breteuil and he knows me."

"Lucky you, Madame. Am I correct in surmising it is time for me to go?"

She offers an apologetic face. "Yes, it is."

———

"Don't ask me," Gaspard instructs.

Thomas follows his supervisor to the door of the inner sanctum office. It is only the second time he has been called there since he came back to work here after his London interval. The other was when Thomas and the other clerks were summoned to learn who was to be the new superior clerk. And an instant later the magistrate judge asked Gaspard to step forward and stand at his side. The right hand of God, came into Thomas's head as he walked back to his table.

"Thank you for coming, Pichon." The judge turns to Gaspard and shows him a gentle wave of the hand. "Monsieur Gaspard, would you please close the door on your way to your desk?"

"But of course."

Thomas catches the accusatory glance from the fellow. He wishes he knew what it was that Gaspard thinks he has done.

The magistrate takes his seat behind his great desk with the enormous hand-carved legs. He gestures for Thomas to sit in one of the three bare wooden chairs lined up against the wall.

"So then," the judge begins, "I have to say it came as a surprise."

Frequent pauses are the measure of the man's speaking style. Thomas does not move or speak. He knows he is to wait.

"I did not realize you were … interested in.…" The magistrate checks something written on his desk. It looks like a letter, one with a bright red seal on its outside flap. "The hospital service of our armies." He gives Thomas a stern glance, which then disappears, replaced by indifference. "That is what I read here."

Thomas feels his eyebrows rise, but he feels he should still wait. If nothing else, his working life has taught him to never presume. Unless he is asked a specific question, he will not say a word. Still, whatever is it that the judge has on his desk? And how could it have anything to do with him? The hospital service certainly does not.

"Nor did I know," the judge continues after making one more perusal, before tossing the letter down to the surface of his desk, "that you were … connected."

"Connected?" Thomas repeats. He feels his shoulders rise. He brings them back down.

The magistrate squints slightly, as if to see whether Thomas is only pretending to play dumb.

"Yes, connected." The expression on the judge's face is now one of genuine surprise, verging on disbelief. "And as high as the Marquis de Breteuil," intones the great man. "Pichon, I had no idea. Well done. "

Thomas mouths the name of the marquis. It brings a slow smile of recognition and a long exhale. Thank you, Madame, he thinks, momentarily closing both eyes. Then, eyes back open, looking as relaxed as he can, he dares to say, "Yes, Monseigneur, the Marquis de Breteuil thinks well of me."

"So it seems."

The magistrate is off his seat and coming toward Thomas, who surges to his feet. The judge has the refolded letter in his hand and is holding it out for Thomas to take possession. The texture and weight of the paper in his hand feels like the best thing he has ever held.

"Congratulations, Pichon. Monsieur Pichon I should say. As you know, with the right connections in this world one can go far."

"Monseigneur," is all Thomas can say. He wants to open and read the letter for himself, yet he understands he has to resist. Until he is out of this man's sight.

"Is that not right?"

It seems the judge is asking Thomas something. "I'm sorry, Monseigneur."

"I say, connections can help us to rise, but just how high is up to us. This is your chance."

"Thank you." Thomas begins to slide backwards toward the door.

"Do not thank me. Thank whoever put the quill in Breteuil's hand."

Thomas nods that he will. Ribbon or not, once he gets back to his place he will bound up the building's steps, up to Madame de la Rose's and knock hard upon her door. If she is there and lets him in, he will press against her for as long as she can bear. He cannot recall anyone ever helping him like this before. The air inside his chest wants to explode.

The magistrate judge lifts his chin, a sign Thomas recognizes as the one the man uses to tell people it's time to go.

"Monseigneur," Thomas says with a deep bow.

But the judge has turned his back to Thomas and gone back to sit at his desk. His focus has now turned toward something fresh upon its surface.

As Thomas closes the door behind him without a hint of a click, what comes into his head is the view of Vire on its hilltop, as seen from the window of a bouncing coach. It is a coach rolling away froma life he could not imagine himself living and toward possibilities he could not yet imagine. He was so young back then. A mere boy. His entire life ahead of him, blank pages waiting to be written.

"That's right," he whispers just loud enough for his ears alone to hear. "And I'm not done yet."

He is but forty-one, with perhaps another twenty years to go. He can and will do whatever the letter in his hand requests. For apparently it gives him what he wishes, an escape from the magistrate's office, out from beneath Gaspillage's thumb. Where it leads matters not. All he asks for is an opportunity to shine. He is capable, he knows that.

X
Crossing

La Rochelle to Louisbourg – May to August 1751

"One rung after another," echoes in Thomas's head.

He knows the refrain smacks of self-satisfaction, but there is no harm in that. He has earned the right to a bit of pride. Besides, the words are what best goes along with the rhythm of the creaking sounds of the swaying coach. It comes to him like a chorus off the bending wood and straining leather. "One rung after another," the groaning coach is saying to him.

That his fellow passenger, has tumbled into sleep in the seat opposite, bewigged head lolling with the sway of the coach, adds to the appropriateness of the refrain. For the dozing man, the lanky comte de Raymond, Seigneur d'Oye, is the one who has lifted Thomas to the highest level yet. Thomas Pichon, born and raised in little Vire, is now nothing less than the right hand of a count, trusted confidant of a representative of the King. To be sure, it would be better to hold such a role and honour in France, in one of the naval ports or in a landward frontier town. Instead, Thomas is heading off to a distant colony. Across the turbulent ocean sea, nonetheless.

Thomas glances at the hedgerows the coach is bobbing between. The land here is similar to the bocage he knew as a boy in Normandy. It would be sweet as a cherry if word of his appointment would get back to Vire. Back to any and all who ever doubt-

189

ed him when he was growing up. His parents are dead, so they'll not know how wrong they were to try and force their son into the Church. He wishes there really was a life after death so people could recognize their many mistakes and faults, all the wrongs they've done. Thomas would like his parents to know how high he has climbed. Surely they would be pleased. And confess to him that they were wrong about him. And his sister too, wherever she might be. Yes, it would be satisfying if all of Vire was to hear what Thomas has accomplished with his wits.

Speaking of which, he must write to Gallatin before he sets sail, to let him know the latest twist and to tell him to send his letters henceforth to Thomas at Louisbourg. Gallatin will be pleased for Thomas, he will. As will Hélène, perhaps. Though a part of him wants her to feel regret, regret about the mistaken choice she once made. Thomas briefly closes his eyes. There really is no point to hanging on to bitterness, is there? If Reason tells us anything, it is that what is done cannot be changed.

Thomas feels his eyes leap open as he recalls their boy. The godson is not likely called little Tommy anymore. Thomas's namesake must be fifteen by now. No, that was last year, so he will be sixteen. Thomas supposes the young man will soon be going out on his own into the world. He would be like to hear how and what the fellow makes of himself. The letters Thomas exchanges with Gallatin do not really well informed about the lad. He would like to know more about how he is making his way in the world.

Thomas swings his gaze back to the sleeping Jean-Louis Raymond. He really does have a nose worthy of a Roman, an emperor even. Or is that assessment influenced by Thomas knowing what a glorious military career this man has already achieved? Service in some of France's finest regiments, those of the Troupes de Terre. Lieutenant de roi of Angoulême and recently promoted to the elevated rank of major general. And asked to take over the command of the colony of Isle Royale, so important to France's economic and strategic interests over the sea. And to do so with Thomas as his trusted secretary.

Thomas and the count have at least that much in common, the climb they have both made. The one sleeping comes from a noble family, and thus born rather high up on the ladder. Yet the comte did not stay where he was born. He went higher still. Ambition truly is the noblest virtue. Thomas's single advantage in life was and is his wits. Though long stymied, he has now had ten years of gradual rising. He takes the opportunities when they come, regardless of where they transport him on the map. He has already been – and is now en route to yet another – to some places he would never select. But then choices are not given to people like him. He has had to take – and accept – what he can get.

Thomas regrets that distant Louisbourg, capital of Isle Royale, for which he is heading now, requires him to go upon the sea. He hates the stomach-turning element as much as he hates anything. Twice he endured the Manche, and that was a short traverse. The upcoming crossing of the Atlantic Ocean, sailing from La Rochelle in a few short days, is said to typically take seven to eight weeks. Longer, which means worse, if the winds insist. Whatever it takes, Thomas asks only that he make it there alive. For it will be at Louisbourg, but recently returned to France by the treaty in 1748, that the comte de Raymond will be the commandant, with an indispensable scribe and organizer, none other than Thomas Pichon, at his side.

"One rung after another," comes again from the coach.

That's right. That is how it has been, and will be yet.

Thomas's climb started in Bohemia and Bavaria, where he brought a clear-eyed efficiency to the hospital service of the French armies to which he was attached. A decade ago that was. It did not hurt – quite the contrary, it made all the difference in the world – that his appointment letter bore the imprimatur of none other than the principal secretary to Louis XV. All were duly impressed. No one needed to know that Thomas owed his position to a woman born in Martinique who had influence over said aristocrat. Thomas never asked Madame de la Rose for details on how she wielded her power, for none of his business was it. The beautiful lady could have intimate relations with whoever she wanted, especially when the resulting oohs and ahs were to his benefit. He has not seen the dear soul since he left Paris, but he misses their conversations. And what came after the talk. Each year on her birthday, for ten years now, he sends her a small gift to express his thankfulness. She gave him the *sine qua non* of life's ladder climb, the first step. He will send her something before he sails, so she knows he has not forgotten what she did for him.

After Bavaria and Bohemia came an appointment as Forage Inspector in Upper Alsace. The title was dull, but it came with a huge responsibility and a higher salary. Success breeds success, that is how it works.

Through tact, hard work, discretion and a skill with words, Thomas has impressed those above him. More than that, those same men have all come to rely on him. His words become their words. He makes any document they put their names to better than if it were composed by their quills alone. They know it, and appreciate the talent he possesses.

Next came the challenge of organizing the French hospitals on the lower Rhine and in the Low Countries. There were a few hiccups in that effort, but none he needs to dwell upon. Or ever tell anyone about. Anything less than success is best put out of mind.

What is amusing about the past decade, though it's a joke he can never repeat to anyone, is that his appointments have been the real-life realization of a joke he once made. Way back when in London he told Gallatin that he had a cover story should anyone ask if he had ever left France. Instead of admitting he'd been to perfidious England he would say he was a *commis* with the French army in the Low Countries and the German States. How fortuitous is that! The truth came to mirror a story he once made up.

Thomas leans forward, to within an arm's reach of the count. Was that a snore? Or did the comte break wind while deeply asleep? No matter, the secrets of what goes on with Jean-Louis Raymond when he is resting are safe with Thomas Pichon. Keeping confidences comes easily to him. It fills his chest to know something about a great man that no one else will ever learn.

The weaknesses of the new commandant are minor. His eyebrows sometimes look like ears of wheat and could do with a trim. And he can be a little vainglorious by times, though that is to be expected of someone with his rank and authority. What matters is that when the comte de Raymond is awake and upright he is impressive. He holds himself like a prince, dominating any room or public square. Thomas merely wishes that he had but a smidgeon of the count's confidence. It seems, alas, this is not something those born in the lower orders can put on. It's not an auction-purchased coat or wig.

Oh, there's a hint of drool at the corner of the commandant's lips. That is unfortunate. As is the all-too-wide splay of his legs. It is as if the man's body is betraying the poor fellow while he sleeps. Luckily, Thomas knows better than to tidy what he sees. The comte will wake up soon enough and ably correct himself. Until then, the good secretary shall do the only thing he can. He will look away, back to his book, until the man he admires returns from the realm of sleep.

———

The last time Thomas stuck his head all the way out the window to suck in some fresh air, something different than the heavy, oily scent the comte de Raymond wears, the road was running between fieldstone walls. Before that, there was a forest, a palette of springtime greens and yellows. Now the route is cutting across open fields, with a flurry of black birds circling a solitary tree. Thomas cannot see the sun in the sky but it is obvious it is lower than it was. The shadows are lengthening and the barley and distant forest are a richer green than they were before. The earthen road has begun to glow like it's ablaze.

Seated again, retrieving his book, Thomas tries to read. However, as good as Montesquieu can be, Thomas has read enough pages for one day. Besides, he knows Raymond disapproves of all the philosophers. Yesterday Thomas was glancing through the young Denis Diderot's prospectus for a series of books touching on all subjects knowable, an encyclopaedia with engravings as well as texts.

"What do you have there?" asked the comte.

"It is for a new encyclopedia," Thomas replied. "The word comes from the Greek."

The curl on the commandant's lips was pronounced. "We know what an encyclopedia is, Pichon. But why on earth do we need more than we already have?"

"Let me read to you from what the authors write. They say—"

"What are their names, the authors?"

"They are the editors. There will be many authors. But the names of the principals are D'Alembert and Diderot. Two young Frenchmen." Thomas could see Raymond was not impressed, but he decided to continue on. "The editors write that the purpose of their *Encyclopédie* is, and I quote: *to collect knowledge disseminated around the globe; to set forth its general system to the men with whom we live, and transmit it—*"

"Enough of that," said the comte, turning to look out the window. "That Diderot spent time in a prison in Vincennes for what he wrote in some other book of his."

"But that was—"

Raymond's hand was up. "*We* do not need anything further from him."

And that was that. The only reading Raymond apparently wants to see Thomas doing is to be about the destination to which they are sailing so very soon.

Thomas glances at the count. As is often the case when the man is going through the documents from the box beside him on the seat, he is showing a scowl. Thomas takes it to mean that the new commandant disapproves of something – maybe everything – the governors of Isle Royale before him over the past nearly forty years have done. Confidence in his own instant assessments is the first rule of the comte. Thomas supposes that's the way it must be for all of those in command. To show any doubt about themselves and their judgement would undermine their position at the top of the pyramid. Thomas is eager to see how things will play out when Raymond steps ashore in the colony in a few weeks time, his loyal secretary at his side.

The secretary certainly hopes Raymond is right about when the coach will be arriving in La Rochelle. He said it would be around dusk, which cannot be far off. With such a long voyage ahead, Thomas would be smart to visit a lady of pleasure before they set sail. He imagines he will find a willing gentle companion somewhere under La Rochelle's renowned arcades. Likely wrapped in a cape or cloak to keep away the chill. She will be standing on the pavé of rounded beach stones, which Thomas has read have been brought back by the port city's merchant fleet as ballast from the New World. The evening's lover will have kind eyes, a soft voice and a curving form. And when she takes him to her room, there will be the scent and taste of salt on her skin, from the ocean air that swirls up and down that coast of France. His imaginings conjure a memory of a time with Hélène. Or was it Élisabeth or La Beaumont? Thomas cannot recall, but whoever it was they were near a sea and she was salty. Thomas liked it.

"Pichon, what are you about?"

Thomas snaps to meet the gaze of the comte de Raymond. "Monsieur le commandant?"

"Dreaming of somewhere else?"

"Of course not. This—"

"We are not finding it."

"Monsieur?"

"The bordereau. For last year. Certain it was—"

"Ah, the bordereau. There, right there." Thomas leans forward to grab hold of the lengthy document that has slipped off the top of the box and fallen behind the seat, out of the comte's sight.

"Thought so," Raymond says, shaking his head, beginning to run his index finger down a column looking for some detail.

Thomas slides fully back onto his seat and finds himself staring momentarily at the commandant. He understands they cannot be friends, for they are not equals. Yet could the one not be a little less chilly with the other? Thomas is an efficient secretary, a willing confidant. If not an outright thank you then at least the Seigneur d'Oye could offer an occasional appreciative nod. Or a gesture of the hand to show gratitude.

"Better things to do than explore idleness, we think."

The comte is speaking without looking up from the document in his hands. The tone of voice makes Thomas feel like an errant child.

"Of course," he says, reaching toward the box of documents.

Out comes the first sheath his right hand finds, and when Thomas turns its title page his way he feels his shoulders slump. It's the very list of colonists he looked at earlier in the day. The census that gives the names and other details about all the house-holds who returned to Isle Royale in 1749, after the place was re-turned to France by the peace signed at Aix-la-Chapelle. Thomas sighs. He'll have to give it another scan because he's not about to put it back and show the count he selected poorly the first time.

"Idleness does not serve anyone," purrs the comte. Still not so much as a glance Thomas's way.

The secretary pauses, then sits as upright as he can. "You are right."

"Hmph," grunts the count.

Yes, Thomas will have to find a way to excuse himself this evening from Jean-Louis Raymond. The secretary will not be de-terred, no matter what the commandant insists upon. He needs to clear his head. And everything else. He needs to unite with a salty woman. But he'd best keep that longing to himself. The count is so unfathomably serious and apparently does not need companionship of any sort. From neither women nor men. No, Raymond would almost certainly not grasp the virtues of night-time wandering under arcades.

———

The clumpity clump of the horses on a beaten earth road switches to the clatter of hooves and wheels on cobbles. Thomas turns to look out the window to his left. Sure enough, they have entered a town. Daylight is draining away but he can see stone buildings rising on both sides. He looks at the comte de Raymond, who in return gives him something like a smile.

"La Rochelle," he says. The commandant's expression suggests he too is relieved.

"Oh, I am glad. I am eager to see a bit of the town." Thomas feels he has to plant the seed right away.

"No time," says the comte with a shake of his head. "We leave tomorrow at first light. The *Heureux* is to have been readied at Rochefort this past week and been towed down the Charente this morning to the roadstead. All crew, provisions and passengers are aboard, save us. It was to sail up to just off the harbour of La Rochelle this afternoon. Tomorrow, its captain will welcome aboard Isle Royale's new commandant."

And its new secretary, Thomas thinks to himself. "Oh yes, I know," he says, "but I will have time for a quick look. You'll not even know I'm gone."

"You think so?" Raymond's head tilts quizzically. It looks like he is actually interested in what Thomas's answer will be.

"To be sure." Thomas makes sure his posture is erect, his voice firm. Yet with no hint of disrespect. "It will not take me long. I want to see the old towers. The great clock gate. The arcades as well."

"The arcades?" The comte's face is bewildered.

"Yes, I read they are worth seeing. Shops below, residences above."

Raymond narrows his gaze, unwavering, unblinking, firmly on Thomas's eyes. "No," he says at last.

Thomas hears himself snort. "No?" He forces a smile. The commandant surely jests. "What *no* is that, Monsieur?" Thomas is annoyed to hear his voice has come out an octave higher than usual.

"Are there different *nos*? We don't think so. *Noooo*," he says again, elongating the word.

Thomas holds out a beseeching left hand.

Raymond lifts his bushy eyebrows. "Pichon, you will *not* be leaving my side. Not to take a walk nor for anything else. We know where trouble lies."

"But I shall be quick, Monsieur, I shall."

"Not tonight you shall not."

"Perhaps you do not understand."

Raymond's lips turn down.

"You see, commandant, once the trunks and boxes are unloaded … organized … protected. Readied for our departure tomorrow. Then, only then, I'll hurry away. An hour. No, not even. You will not notice that I am gone." Thomas's upraised hands offer the final convincing touch.

"No."

"But this does not—"

"Secretary, you forget yourself. *We* tell *you* the what, the where and the when."

Thomas does not reply, not with words. For the words that come to mind would harm only himself. So he allows his silence, along with an inclination of his head, to show he acquiesces to the commandant's wishes.

"We are glad," says Raymond, "that you are wise. Tonight, once our meal is past, we are going over the Louisbourg military establishment. To arrive in the colony without being fully informed is a weakness we must avoid."

"But we do have a long sail ahead," Thomas observes with a soft voice. "Six weeks. Longer perhaps."

"Our habits define us, Pichon. Do you hear that?"

"I do."

"Tonight, you will bring us all there is on the different units. We begin with the regiments, the Artois and the Bourgogne. After that, the Marine troops. Lastly, if there is time, the artillery specialists. We will be reading late."

Thomas does not say a thing.

"Ah, there you go." Raymond is gesturing toward the window on Thomas's left. "There is the port you want to see. The sun is still on the tops of the towers. Have a look."

Thomas tilts forward. All he sees are boats and small ships and a forest of masts and rigging. Then beyond, through the jumble, yes, he does spy the towers of La Rochelle. He recognizes them from the engravings he has seen. They are even more striking in person, with the crests of their rounded forms seeming to glow in the setting sun.

"And if memory serves," continues the count, "just ahead we are about to pass through the old clock gate. Have an eye."

Thomas sits back against his seat. He will not look out of the coach again. His gaze is on his hands, clasped on his knees.

"Not so interested after all?" Raymond asks with a triumphant grin. "We are not surprised. It is only a small port. And a one-time refuge for the damned Protestants, a century and a half ago. Best not to linger and walk around this place, we say."

"So you do," Thomas dares to say. "And when are you not right?" The secretary believes he reveals no mockery, either on his face or in his voice. "Monsieur," he adds.

"Well said." The commandant gives Thomas a decisive nod.

The secretary leans forward, making sure he does not sigh. He begins straightening up the box of documents Raymond has been sorting through most of the day. Soldier on, Thomas says to himself. His fate, his destiny, is tied to this man. They are a kite. Well, more accurately he is the ribbon tied to the commandant's kite, but the important thing is the climb.

The rearranging of the documents box completed, Thomas presses his back against the seat just before the coach comes to a halt. The horses whinny as the driver scampers to the ground. Thomas watches the man hurry to pull down the step from which he and the commandant will descend.

"This must be it," Raymond says. "Our lodging for the night."

"Thank you," Thomas says before he can call it back. Luckily, his misplaced thanks draws no comment or raised eyebrow from the comte.

———

Thomas waits below, having stepped down from the coach carrying the box of documents in advance of the commandant's descent. The dutiful secretary feels his lower teeth pressing against his upper lip. Then it's his upper teeth biting his lower lip. What are his teeth trying to say?

How long it is going to be before he will again be with a woman. Not tonight nor for however long the dreadful ocean crossing is going to take, which could be as much as two months. And then the place he is going to, distant Louisbourg, he knows has a pronounced shortage of women. He has read the census forms. At best it is three men for every adult female. Of course, he will not be just another man in that place. He will be the commandant's right hand. Surely that will count. Still, the choices will be few. Thomas shudders to think he has finally climbed a few rungs, only to find he has to spend his nights alone. Life should not be an either-or.

Inside the shadow of the coach Thomas can see Raymond adjusting his hat atop his bewigged head. He understands that the commandant wants to exit as majestically as he can, fully attired, looking like a quasi-prince. Yet does the comte not see that he is taller than the doorway? He has to stoop no matter what. It would be better to keep the hat off until he is down to at least the first step.

Thomas glances round. What does it matter? There is no one to see what is going to happen, regardless if Raymond descends like a sultan or falls and breaks his neck. There is only Thomas and the driver of the coach standing in front of the inn. No, that's not quite right. Across the street, under the arcade, he spies a woman and her daughter pausing to watch. Each wears the customary floppy cap, each has a basket in hand.

The woman is tilting her head in a way Thomas for an instant thinks he recognizes. How funny it is that no matter where in the world one goes, one finds people who remind us of someone we knew somewhere else. Seeing this unknown woman across the way makes Thomas wince. But since he knows no one in La Rochelle, he will not give her a third glance. Yet he does correct his posture. Legs taut, stomach in and the box of documents high up on his chest. The commandant is right: Habits do define us. It is important to show who we are, even if the onlookers, the woman and her daughter, are nobody special in this world.

The commandant stoops to make his exit, hat in one hand, cane in the other. Down a step, he gets to thrust the hat onto his wig then to continue his descent. Feet on the ground, Raymond says not a word and makes no eye contact. He could be the Holy Roman Emperor, if one didn't know. For his admirers the count offers only a quick wave of his cane, not at Thomas and the driver but at the trunks and canvas-covered boxes as he strides by.

Thomas winks at the driver, who wearily raises his eyebrows. He, the driver after all, is the one who went up top and brought everything down to the ground. It seems his tasks are not yet complete. The secretary smiles. Does the man not know how it is with those on the rungs above? It is up to the lesser ones to take care of what must be done. It would not look right for the commandant to carry any load.

———

The water is astir, trembling hard.

Which makes Thomas shake his head. Is it not foolish to ascribe human qualities – in this case apprehension about the ocean voyage about to begin – to the natural world? Nonetheless, the surface of La Rochelle's protected inner harbour is showing tremors, it really is. Maybe all it means, he decides, is that the direction of the wind is twisting about and sometimes presses down from above. Perhaps that is what causes the harbour surface to shudder the way it does.

There is certainly no shortage of wind. It is swirling about, from time to time anointing everyone in the barge with a bit of spray. The sweepers, those pulling on the oars, have their caps pulled well down. The only two with tricornes, Thomas and the comte de Raymond, are struggling to keep them from blowing away.

Despite the gusts, the commandant sits rigidly erect. With one hand he clasps the blue cloak tightly round his thrust-back shoulders. With the other he presses the hat down firmly upon his wig.

Thomas sits facing Raymond, farther toward the front, but he has enough sense to bend down to reduce the cut of the wind. It means he does not have to keep his hand on his hat every single minute. He gives the lead sweeper a glare for saying it would take only five minutes to transport them to the *Heureux*. It must be twice that already and they are still not past the two towers. And once they pass those landmarks, the lighter will be only at what Thomas judges to be halfway to the where the king's ship waits, tethered to its anchors.

Thomas wonders if it would spread the weight in the barge better if he were to move from where he is to sit instead alongside the commandant. No, the comte would not want that. He wants any bench he is on exclusively to himself. Should Thomas try and join him, Raymond would elbow him back to where he is.

"Stiffen up."

Thomas lifts his eyes to meet those of the commandant. He asks with a hand tapping his chest if Raymond is speaking to him.

"Don't embarrass yourself."

So Thomas straightens up, which means a hand has to go permanently to keep his hat in place. He tries to keep resentment off his face, but it is not easy with more wind and spray stinging him. Yet, he reasons the comte could be right. First impressions are all-important. While it matters little what the sweepers might think of a doubled-over passenger, it will be different when the lighter comes close to the waiting King's ship. For the eyes of that ship's captain and other officers, and whatever passengers there be, Thomas Pichon, secretary of the commandant of Isle Royale, should present as upright an appearance as possible. No matter how strong the wind blows.

———

It does not surprise Thomas that there is a planned sequence, a pecking order, governing how he and the comte and their possessions are to go aboard the *Heureux*. Of course, there has to be order and control. The comte has spent a lifetime in the army. The sequence, not surprisingly, will be from bottom to top. Up first will go the trunks and canvas-wrapped boxes. Then, penulti-mately, Thomas. The comte, as is fitting for the rank of his office, will be the last to go up.

A man the size of a boy descends the rope ladder. He is dressed for a midsummer's day with only his faded red breeches and a rolled-up grey woven shirt. He wears neither jacket nor coat. It makes Thomas shiver just to look at him. The sailor's skin looks like leather, only with goose flesh up and down his sinewy arms. He has to be at least ten years past fifty, Thomas thinks, which is what the regulations state is the age limit for sailors in the navy. Maybe his skin and face are what a life at sea does to a man, and he's really much younger than he looks.

The sailor does not say a word. By himself he is able to hoist the first trunk sufficiently to tie a rope around it in secure loops. It is as if the trunk were nothing more than a sack of bread rations the way he handles it.

Up Thomas's trunk goes and the sailor turns next to the trunk of the comte and then to the canvas-wrapped boxes. Thomas wants to tell the little man how impressed he is with his work, but the little fellow does not even glance his way. Then suddenly he does.

"You first?" he asks.

Thomas looks at the comte, just in case he might have changed his mind.

"Of course," says Raymond. "The commandant is saved for last."

The sailor steadies Thomas as he stands to begin climbing the rope ladder. Though he does not much like the sag of the rope rungs, Thomas is relieved to be out of the lighter and heading for dry land. Well, not land, but a ship that will be by far the largest vessel he has ever been on. Surely its size will make for smoother sailing than was the case with any of the small boats he has previ-ously been in. Just the overhead webs of ropes and lines running to and from the three masts and the booms and the spars is aston-ishing. The cordage is of every possible thickness and length. It is as if a million giant spiders have been at work.

Thomas hears a mêlée of voices as he nears the top of the lad-der. Chatter and occasionally shouts. Of course. He read yester-day that the crew of the *Heureux* stands at two hundred fifty, plus the half dozen passengers they are taking along. Hard to believe that a handful of officers is sufficient to rein everyone in. The magic of command, he supposes. He is not so inclined, alas. For better or worse, his inclination has always been to shy away from groups rather than to try and wield influence.

Thomas inhales the deepening smell of the ship as he nears the ladder's top. It is strong and it is good. A mix of oakum, canvas, tar and pitch. He can feel his nostrils flare and twitch. But then he also picks up something else. It is the stink of men who do not cover their natural smell with any flowery water. Well, Thomas will approve of that as well. Why should these men, agreed by all to be the hardiest yet most detestable species of entire mankind, care about the pretences of civil society on land? They should not. Theirs is a different world, and he and Raymond and the other passengers will be in their tough hands to get safely across the Atlantic. Let these men smell and behave any way they will.

A hand reaches though the opening in the rail. It belongs to a young sailor with a cloth cap atop a grinning face. Thomas accepts the help. The man's yank, though, is too hard. Thomas nearly misses his foothold on the deck. His right leg buckles but he regains his balance just in time. He gives the sailor responsible a sharp look.

"Watch your step." The sailor dares to widen his grin.

Thomas wonders if there is an officer nearby to give the fellow a reprimand, but the only officers he sees are not looking his way. Dressed in their dark blue breeches and jackets, they are locked in a conversation on the other side of a coil of thick rope. It dawns on Thomas that it is only these officers who are wearing any sign of a uniform. The sailors, scurrying here and there, are dressed in all different colours and styles, as best as they can afford. Back to the clutch of officers, Thomas decides the oldest, a stern-faced man in his late thirties, must be the captain. The other two, both younger, are showing deference for his every word.

"Here he comes!" shouts the sailor at the rail, the one who yanked Thomas a moment ago. He has dropped the grin and removed his cloth cap. "The governor!"

"In lines," calls out one of the officers, ending that small group's conversation.

A dozen sailors, those closest to the opening in the rail, scramble to form two short lines. They make a ragged combination but they do draw to attention. The rest of the sailors – at least fifty Thomas can see keeping busy on the far side of the deck and toward the bow and stern – carry on as if there was no command at all. They continue to jabber, lift, carry, pull, tie and whatever else it is they are about. The officers show no displeasure at the continual clatter they make. In fact, two of the youngest head off, as directed by the captain, to opposite ends of the ship. Only the captain and the youngest officer, no more than a lad, come to stand in front of the small honour guard. The way they hold themselves reminds Thomas of the noble hosts of a salon. The captain pulls out a mouchoir to deal with something troubling his nose.

Thomas can feel a slight roll to the ship. Though he knows it is still at anchor, he feels a gentle sway. Would it not be wonderful if the rolling did not get any more pronounced than it is right now? The *Heureux* would live up to its name.

"Gouverneur!" the sailor at the rail sings out. He adds an awkward bow then extends a hand.

The comte ignores the proffered hand and continues the climb by his own means. Then he makes his own, unaided, stumbling passage through the opening on to the deck. Two feet firmly planted, the commandant presents the quiet smile of a kindly prince.

"Monsieur le Capitaine," Raymond says, saluting as he strides toward the captain of the ship. The bow is minimal, but it is the only reverence Thomas has ever seen the comte give.

"Monsieur le Gouverneur." The ship captain returns the salute and precisely the same bow that he has been sent.

"Ah, it is Commandant not Governor," Raymond corrects. "We will be the first, the first military officer Louisbourg will have. Our predecessors were merely—"

Thomas leans forward. How will the comte get out of this? He knows Raymond was about to say "naval officers," for it is the truth. Yet with "merely" attached it is a criticism of the very service in which the ship captain serves.

"Good men they were," Raymond says. "Our task will be to be better, if we can."

"Understood." The captain produces a sly smile then turns away. He makes a gesture to someone out of Thomas's sightline. At once Thomas and everyone else notice a flag running up on the small topmast overhead. Then a cannon fires somewhere off to the right. More of a pop than a blast, it must be a small calibre signal gun. Next, Thomas notes a few sailors are turning a wheel. It is generating a cranking, hoisting noise. It must be an anchor starting to come up. Thomas feels his eyes go wide. Can his voyage to the New World, his new life, be under way?

The captain of the *Heureux* looks satisfied and swings back to face the comte de Raymond. The latter's expression is that of someone very impressed.

"Yes," says the captain, "we are off. The wind is in our favour and the pilot says we should not waste it. So we will not. We take advantage. The midshipman here will show you to your cabin. Commandant, you are under the quarterdeck, close to me."

Raymond smiles and clicks his heels as he offers an inclination of his head.

"Well then," says the captain, dusting his hands, "I'm afraid you will have to excuse me. I must be busy about. As a commandant yourself, you understand."

"We do. Excellent and well done." Raymond puts a hand on each hip. His eyes are filled with more wonder than Thomas has ever seen.

The captain nods and strides away, toward the bow. Thomas notices that the two lines of the sailors' temporary honour guard have already dispersed.

The secretary steps alongside the commandant. "And me, Monseigneur? My cabin, it is also with yours? The quarterdeck, the captain said."

"Not now," Raymond says over his shoulder, strutting away with the young midshipman. The young naval officer is pointing toward the stern of the ship.

"Not now?"

———

Third time lucky. Thomas finally finds a sailor who knows where his trunk has gone and where he is to be lodged. It is not, to his warm-faced embarrassment, anywhere near the raised quarter-deck in the stern, to which Raymond has retired with his trunk and all the boxes of documents.

The gaunt-faced sailor looks like he has to hide a laugh. "No, you go below."

"Below? How far below?"

"As deep as it goes. The Sainte-Barbe."

That makes Thomas squint. Saint-Barbe is the patron of engineers and artillerymen and all who work with explosives. Is it a place as well?

"Where we keep the gunpowder," the sailor offers.

"A magazine?"

"That's right."

"And I am to sleep among racks and barrels." His hands go up.

"That," the sailor shrugs, "or in a hanging grave. With the lot of us."

Hammocks. Which Thomas knows are shared. The shift determines who the hammock belongs to, for four hours, then it's the next man's turn.

"Are there beds in the Sainte-Barbe?" he asks.

Again the sailor shrugs. "Not been down that far before."

Thomas brings a hand to the bridge of his nose. He has nothing to say.

"Ready then?" the sailor asks.

"Apparently," he mumbles back.

———

It is not easy to keep up with the little man as he darts in and around the constantly moving crew. The sailors are pulling ropes and lines, and tying things down. They don't choose to give way.

"Watch your back!"

Thomas ducks, but for no good reason. What he was being warned about was not something from on high but a rolled-up spare canvas sail being carried waist high by two sailors in a rush. The sailor in the lead gives Thomas a firm push. Pressed against the rail, he cranes up. All three masts, but especially the main, tower so very high. He imagines they would almost pierce the roof of the largest church he has ever been in, Notre-Dame in Paris. It would be close. And the ropes on the ship are as thick as arms and legs. The pulleys and deadeyes are as big as his head.

"Secretary!"

Thomas searches for where his sailor guide's voice is coming from. He looks around.

"No, 'ere. Down 'ere!"

Thomas finds the gaunt face ten feet away peering up. He is apparently standing down in a narrow stairwell that goes beneath the deck.

"Coming," Thomas says.

As he turns round to go down the narrow stairs, Thomas feels the ship lurch. Not side to side, but forward and with some speed. He looks up to the masts. Yes, a first sail is already catching the wind. And there are a dozen men, standing on a skinny line at a second mast, working to loosen the brails to free another. He supposes that once safely out to sea, all sails will be in play. He has read that with the right winds, a vessel this size can advance fifty leagues a day. Though that's exceptional, and sailing westerly it is unlikely to continue. The more usual daily distance is half that.

A chart Thomas was looking at the other day stated it was 711 leagues from La Rochelle to Louisbourg. The calculation is easy to make, if the sea allowed for averages. But it does not. There will be contrary winds and a current to go against. Still, that captain said the winds are favourable today and that's all that counts. Every extra league the *Heureux* can squeeze out of the first day's winds will shorten the trip.

———

With each downward step the air becomes more foul, then fouler still. The scent of rope, wood, wind and salt, which was the smell of the world above, disappears. By the time Thomas is at the bottom of the stairs, in light that has gone increasingly dim, he is covering his nose and mouth. It's a heavy, putrid reek that he can taste in his throat. Just as bad, the ceiling is too low for him to stand fully upright.

"First time, is it?" his guide asks out of the darkness to the left.

Thomas nods. Then he removes his hand from his face. "What's wrong?" he asks. "The stink," he explains.

"You'll get used to it."

"Will I?"

"Yeah. It's how the nose works."

"And why is there no light? A lantern or two."

"Can't," the sailor says, seeming to find mirth in Thomas's bewilderment. "Risk of fire. The eyes, like the nose, gets used to that as well."

Thomas takes two cautious steps to his left and peers into the slightly lifting darkness. There is a room, or maybe it's just an open space. At most, the ceiling is five feet. Suspended from the beams are a few dozen hammocks. Thomas can see some men are asleep.

"This is the first of our between-decks," his guiding sailor says. "My swing is here. When it's my time, that is."

"Let's go," Thomas says. Surely, his room in the Sainte-Barbe will be better than where the sailors have to sleep.

Two more sets of narrow steps, the daylight getting dimmer and the air worse the farther down he and the sailor go. In one spot there is a biting smell of vinegar, which Thomas figures is someone's attempt to cleanse away a particular stench. It passes through his mind that it might not be a bad idea to soak the entire below decks of the ship in vinegar. And then open up all the darkness and stinking spots to light and fresh air. As if ... as if a real ship could have its layers lifted off the way some models can.

As predicted by the sailor, Thomas's eyes do adjust to the lack of light. Though it is a dark gloom, he is able to make out where he is going. His nose, however, is as it was, still twitching and recoiling from what it takes in. Thomas realizes that rotting wood is only part of why the *Heureux* reeks down below. There is also the smell 250 men give off when in their hammocks and which does not go away when they leave the dark. Here and there is the sharp biting smell of piss. Whether from a man or an animal he cannot say.

Between-decks is where the living food is kept. There are cages of fowl, the birds shrieking and flapping their wings as he and the sailor go by. Thomas supposes their eggs, and later their flesh, will be consumed before the ship reaches Louisbourg. And then there are the improvised pens. He has counted more than a dozen pigs, a near equal number of sheep, a few cattle and even a horse. Poor thing, that horse, tied in all four directions by ropes. The sailor told him the droppings are cleaned up regularly. And cast overboard, Thomas supposes. Well, not often enough. He has shit of some kind on the bottom of his left shoe and he can smell it travelling with him wherever he goes.

"'Ere you are," says the sailor, raising his voice. "Your quarters."

"The Sainte-Barbe?" Thomas calls out.

"It is."

Thomas stares at the man to see if this is a joke. There is such a loud, creaking, grinding sound. "What is that?" he asks, pantomiming by touching his ears.

Thomas thinks he sees a hint of a smile. "Rudder tiller," says the sailor. "Passes here. At the stern, we are."

Thomas briefly closes his eyes. His eyes, his nose and now his ears. What next will he be required to alter in this world?

He squints to discern what his quarters for the next two months are like. There is not a square foot to spare, barely any open space at all. The walls are mostly racks filled with barrels. Gunpowder and artillery stores, he presumes. Beside where he and the sailor are stooped, unable to stand completely upright because of the low ceiling, are five trunks, stacked as three and two. He recognizes his on top of the stack of three. To the left a small area is partitioned off, no more than five feet by three. The work must have been done recently judging by the newness of the boards. The canvas hanging at its entrance must be to serve as a makeshift door. Where the artillery rack ends there are two tiers of bunks. Because of the low ceiling, the space between the bunks is barely more than the thickness of a man. At least each sleeping area appears to have a straw tick mattress that is new. Still, Thomas cannot recall the last time he was reduced to sleeping on a paillasse. He was a boy, not the secretary of an important colony. Thomas shakes his head.

"Who is with me here?" he asks above the grinding sound.

The sailor gestures to the bunk set-up on the right. "Couple of Récollets."

Thomas nods. He sees a book that looks to be the thickness of a Bible on the upper mattress, along with a brown homespun cloak hanging from a hook. Beneath the lower bunk he spies a leather box he deduces contains rosary beads, holy water, oils and crucifixes. There is also a pair of well-worn leather shoes and a pair of wooden and leather sandals.

The sailor swings his pointing arm over to the other bunk. There are at least eight books in two neat stacks under the bed and a tricorne with what looks like gold trim hanging from a hook. "That's a major, and—"

"A major?" Thomas cannot believe he has heard right.

"It is."

"Down here?"

"Surlaville is the name, I think." The sailor scratches his chin. "Somethin' like that."

"Really?" It had slipped Thomas's mind that the comte's protégé in all things military, Michel Le Courtois de Surlaville, was coming on the *Heureux* as well. And like Thomas, he will apparently be travelling in the bowels of the ship, not up in the quarterdeck with his great admirer, the commandant. This is rich. For Thomas will be in the bunk above Surlaville. There is satisfaction in that.

"And I bet it is Surlaville who has two trunks," Thomas says.

"I do not understand."

Thomas points at the trunks. "There are five, but only four of us. I doubt the religious need very much, so I figured the extra one must belong to the major."

"Ah, no. No, the fifth is hers."

"Hers?" Thomas smiles. The creaking of the rudder tiller is loud, but did the sailor just make a joke? "You said hers."

"He means me."

Thomas turns to the new voice. A woman, young and pretty, and dressed like someone of good rank, is standing within the doorway to the partitioned off area. She is holding the canvas curtain slightly ajar.

"Oh my God," Thomas mouths. "A woman," he says above the grinding sound.

"So I am."

And with upraised eyebrows and a cheeky grin, the woman lets the canvas curtain fall closed.

————

Inside the privacy of her tiny wood and canvas space, Marie-Louise Chassin de Thierry enjoys the moment. Why is it that men find a woman's presence on their ships both a surprise and an annoyance? Are not women often carved in wood as the figureheads on ships this size? Marie-Louise hunches her shoulders at that.

More seriously, are women not necessary to have a world at all? That is beyond discussing. And she knows, from observation and not her own experience, thank God, that sailors are keen for women when they arrive in port. Right after they have become stupid and courageous through drink. So it is. A real live woman aboard a ship, however, that is another thing.

Yes, the world at sea is a man's realm. A stinking realm, though her nose seems to have adapted somewhat over the past twenty-four hours. She no longer notices all the foul smells as she travels around the ship, not the way she did when she first came aboard. There's good in that, she supposes. Except that her clothes will be absorbing the fetid reek that in Rochefort assaulted her nose.

As amusing as it was to surprise this fourth man with whom she shares this dark and noisy place, Marie-Louise does not want any more than what is necessary to do with him or the rest of them. She will see them all at the Captain's table, she has been told. And at those meals she will be cautiously pleasant, no more than that. She does not want to encourage any man to get the wrong idea. Even the priests, she knows from tales she's heard, sometimes do the carnal act. As for the civilian who has just arrived, and the military man yesterday, she will have to be especially distant with them. Life will be hard enough for the next six to eight weeks, with the inevitable discomforts and sicknesses. She does not need either of those two thinking she would allow them to take liberties with her.

"No," Marie-Louise whispers firmly to the canvas curtain. She has quite enough complications in her life as it is.

———

Thomas does what is necessary in the bucket in the Saint-Barbe, then washes his hands in chilled, murky water in the copper basin. Next he checks as best he can in the small mirror's reflection that his clothes and wig are as they should be. He wants to look his best for the rendezvous he is to have up on deck at four o'clock.

As he begins to make his way through the passageway toward the first set of stairs, Thomas's thoughts go over what has lately been on his mind.

He can hardly believe his luck, and by extension that of everyone else aboard. Two weeks out to sea and the winds have so far produced a most agreeable ocean upon which the ship gently rolls as it advances. He found his sea legs right away, which has meant his stomach has not been troubled. Nor has he seen anyone else get sick, though the two Récollets did look a little green the first day or two. But as far as Thomas knows, the missionaries did not bless the bucket or the sea with any heaves. So far so good and fingers crossed that the friendly ocean continues as it has been.

The reason for the good fortune is that the ship has been favoured mostly by easterlies ever since it left La Rochelle. There is the occasional direction switch, which causes the sails to flap, but those switches have not lasted long nor come with much upset. The crew simply makes the necessary adjustments, tacking to keep the sails filled.

According to the pilot, with whom Thomas spoke briefly two days ago, the ship at that time was 397 leagues from France. Not 400 but precisely 397. It stunned Thomas that the man could be so accurate, or pretend to be, since the only reference points are the sun, moon and stars, and the endless undulation of breaking waves. The astrolabe, of course, gives a fair reckoning of latitude. Thomas understands that. When the pilot says they are at 47 degrees 5 minutes, Thomas knows pretty well what that means. But as to how far west the *Heureux* had travelled, Thomas quietly questioned the precision of the pilot's number. Was not longitude a conundrum for all mariners, and the object of an enormous reward posted decades ago by the British government?

The pilot's lips soured at that, but he quickly mumbled something about using a backstaff and a new quadrant and said he paid attention to the numbers coming from the rope with knots tied in it that was pulled through the ocean as they sailed along. And then he turned and strode off.

Thomas has no idea if the man really knows what he is talking about or blustering. But he prefers to think the pilot is more or less accurate. That would mean that the *Heureux* is indeed more or less halfway to Isle Royale. Thomas can feel the smile spreading to his cheeks. Yes, it would be wonderful if the ship were to reach Louisbourg in something like four instead of the usual eight weeks.

He starts to climb the second set of stairs, after waiting for two sailors coming off-duty to pass. He knows now that he shouldn't have, but he could not help speaking up at the Captain's table last night, based on what the pilot had told him. He wondered aloud, looking at the captain, if any King's ship had ever completed the voyage to Louisbourg as quickly as they were on pace to do. The captain looked at him like he was a child, then visibly exhaled. He did not reply. And the comte, seated beside the captain as he is every meal, gave his bushy eyebrows a disappointed raise for all to see, followed by a sad shake of his head.

It was only then that Thomas realized his mistake. By asking about good fortune, he might have jeopardized its continuance.

Surlaville, seated as always on Thomas's left, felt obliged to score a point. He leaned sideways as if he were going to whisper, but then in his usual voice said, "It can be four weeks west to east, Pichon, but never east to west. You should know that. The winds *will* switch around, they just do. Mark my words."

Thomas chose not to reply. He will have to deal regularly with Surlaville once they are both at Louisbourg. Better the major thinks Thomas is not his match. That way he may surprise his military colleague one day. When it counts.

But, for the record, yes, he did know about prevailing winds and currents and the usual sail times in both directions. His question essentially was: How long can an exceptional situation last? For if it is good fortune to have had mostly easterlies for two weeks, why not for longer still? However, instead of saying that to major de place Surlaville, Thomas inclined the other way.

"Tell me, Mademoiselle, is the chicken to your satisfaction?"

"It is," she said, with a brief glance his way.

Thomas kept the conversation alive. "Very savoury the way the cook has used the rosemary and thyme, is it not?"

Mademoiselle Chassin de Thierry's mouth was full, so she could only nod.

"Hard to believe," he continued, to give her time, "that we are able to eat like this. Here we are, out in the middle of the Atlantic, yet we enjoy a meal as good as any on land. While—" and for the confidence he was about to share, Thomas leaned a little further and lowered his voice. "While those in whose hands we are, the lowly sailors, get only hard biscuit, much diluted wine and salt pork and beef. It is unbalanced, I think."

"But is that not the way of the world, Monsieur Pichon? Not only on this ship, but everywhere. The few benefit from what the many do."

The accuracy and economy of her words took Thomas by surprise. It must have shown on his face.

"You think my observation apt, do you?"

"Most apt. Tell me," Thomas said, keeping his eyes on hers as she kept hers on his. "How does one so young as you acquire such profound insight into the true nature of this world?"

"Ah, you aim to flatter. Please do not."

"I mean no harm. Truly, it is just—"

"I read, Monsieur Pichon, I read. And when I do not read, I keep my eyes and ears open to catch what goes on."

"Your method serves you well, Mademoiselle, very well."

"You are kind. It is, after all—" said Mademoiselle breaking off a small piece of bread to absorb the flavours of the sauce on her plate. "My wits, after all, are all I have."

Thomas did not counter that she was being falsely modest, for she has both youth and a pretty face. She had already warned him about flattery. So he simply smiled and broke off a piece of his own bread so he too would not let any of the savoury drippings on his plate go to waste.

The climb completed, all the way up onto the deck, Thomas checks the sky and the wind. A thick mat of grey, with a light wind still coming from the east, from Europe. It seems Thomas

Pichon is no jinx after all. Fortune continues to smile on him and the ship.

Deeply he inhales through his nose, sending the old air out through the mouth. Yes, he tastes the salt in the air. So much better than the foul, trapped air everyone has to take in down below. Equally, how much better to hear the creak of wood and the pull of ropes than the constant grind of the rudder tiller in the Saint-Barbe.

Thomas pulls out his watch. It is nearly a quarter hour past four. He expects she is already waiting for him somewhere by rail.

———

"Monsieur Secretary," she'd said, touching him lightly on the sleeve as they both came to their feet when the meal was done. All the others in the room were on their way out of the wardroom, their backs to the two of them.

It seemed to please the man to hear her use his title.

"Would it be possible for us to talk sometime? Quietly, I mean, Monsieur Secretary."

His eyes went very wide for an instant, but then he presented his more usual face. "But of course, Mademoiselle Chassin de Thierry. We could—" He gestured at the chairs from which they had just arisen. "Right here and now if you wish."

"No, no. Tomorrow."

"Tomorrow. I see. Of course. Well, I have two hours with the comte in the morning, going over more of Isle Royale's documents. You understand. There is much to prepare for. That session begins each day at ten. Then we usually go over things for another hour after the midday meal. Which means I should be free by mid-afternoon."

"Free?" she repeated with a wry smile, which she instantly regretted, because she had no joke. She switched back to serious. "Four o'clock?"

"Four? Yes, all right. And down … down in the Sainte-Barbe, Mademoiselle?" His question came with a frown.

"I would prefer up on deck, Monsieur, unless the weather does not permit."

"So be it. Tomorrow at four on the deck, Mademoiselle."

——

Marie-Louise knows she was bold to reach out and grab his sleeve the way she did, to hold him back as the rest of the table was exiting. But she has grown to like and even trust her tablemate. He does not appear to be anything other than what he presents himself as, a kindly man. True, that is merely the surface, but it is a good surface in his case. And she is a fair judge of others, she is convinced. Surlaville, for instance, she does not much like. He reminds her of her late father. No sense of humour and no outward sign of compassion. Thomas Pichon is different. He is more what the English call a gentleman. More importantly, he occupies a role that puts him closer to the new governor at Louisbourg than anyone. Surely, the King and those around him would not select someone unworthy for such a position. He should be able to be trusted with what she is going to confide.

She glances along the rail to her left, past three sailors who are having their meal seated on the deck. Sardines, it looks like, along with the always-present hard tack and a mug to drink. She swivels to the right, where other sailors are coiling ropes under the watchful eye of a midshipman who looks like he could be ten years old. One of the men is an African, she supposes, though he could be from the Isles. Or for that matter from Louisbourg. Her own family often has a slave. Then again, why does she assume a person with dark skin is enslaved? He could and should be free. She has read the philosophes. She notices the African sits as he coils with a posture that is very erect.

Marie-Louise sighs. No sign of the secretary either way, and it is past four. The bells sounded a while ago. Did the comte detain him longer than usual? That would be her luck. She presses her teeth against her lower lip. Or did Thomas Pichon simply forget? Or, worst of all, decide it was not worth his time?

She tightens her grip on the rail. It feels like the sea is getting a little rougher. Yes, the waves definitely have a different look. They are not rolling as they were but appear to be driving at the ship, breaking at a faster pace. And is it her imagination, or is the wind not blowing now from a different direction than it has been for the past two weeks? It feels different. Impossible to tell, however, without a compass. The ocean does not wear a sign that tells east from west or north from south.

Marie-Louise sharpens her focus on the most distant clouds, along the horizon. It looks to her like they are thickening and darkening. If they are moving this way, it means some difficult weather is coming on. That makes her briefly close her eyes. If it gets rough, with strong winds and hard rain, she and the four men she shares the passenger quarters with will have to stay below. God forbid. How much closer and more fetid the Sainte-Barbe will smell if they cannot escape to clear their heads.

She fills her lungs with fresh sea air. While she can.

Thomas sees her clutching the rail, not far from where the sailors are setting off, carrying two immense coils of rope. It surprises him to see her head cast down the way it is. He did not think her to be one of those prone to discouragement. She always presents herself in public with an erectness he admires. Not just her bearing, but her lively eyes and conversation, any time they have had an exchange. Thomas has had far too much nattering with the men on this ship about the weather, the crew and the tasks ahead in Louisbourg. An unhampered talk with a woman, even a young one such as she, will be a welcome relief.

He wonders if that solitary position of hers, as the lone woman on the *Heureux*, is what makes her ask for a rendezvous. There must be times she feels awkward, even vulnerable. He is guessing she has a confidence she wants to impart. Perhaps a sailor has put his hands on her. Or one of his fellow passengers, down in the chamber the five of them share below. He would not be entirely surprised. There are those who lust after the barely nubile. Could it be that Surlaville or one of the priests is such a man? Thomas curls his lips. That is not how nature is supposed to work. Mademoiselle Chassin de Thierry is young enough to be a daughter, for God's sake. She should be left alone.

"Ah, there you are, Mademoiselle," he says from six feet away, to let her know he is coming near.

Mademoiselle Chassin de Thierry turns his way. She straightens and shows an expression of relief. She pushes off from the rail and turns all the way round to offer a curtsey.

"I apologize," Thomas says with the requisite bow. "I know I am late."

"No, Monsieur. You are here."

"That I am."

It appears she does not know what to say next. If she had something prepared, it has flown away. It is up to him, apparently, to put her at ease, for whatever conversation it is that she wants to have. He will not press. Instead, he gestures to the tossing sea.

"So it has happened," he says. "A strong westerly at last. I chanced upon the captain this morning on my way to see the comte. He said, and I quote, 'We will be in for it now.' The way he said it, I am sure he blames me."

"Because you asked how quickly a crossing could be made?" Marie-Louise's face is back to being composed.

Thomas shrugs. "I broke a rule it seems, albeit one I did not know existed."

"Oh well," she says, giving him a sympathetic shrug of her own. "Speaking of which." There is a tremor on her lips, a hesitation.

"A rule?" he asks, puzzled.

"Yes. Do you have a few moments?"

"Is that not why I am here?"

"Yes, of course."

Marie-Louise takes her time to find the words she has been rehearsing the last day and a half. She begins where she must, with her family situation. And that starts with her father, of course, born more than half a century ago, a son of the billeting officer for the King's household at Versailles.

"Really?" Monsieur Secretary says.

"Yes, it is true. My grandfather on my paternal side was at the court of Louis XIV."

"A close confidant of the king?" Monsieur Pichon asks with a trace of curled lips.

"No, but—"

"But still, a lineage that is better than most."

"Yes, I suppose. My father was put into the military while still a lad. First to Isle Royale – Louisbourg – then to Louisiana then back to Louisbourg. Distinguished himself at the siege of 1745. For which he was made a chevalier of the Order of Saint-Louis."

"You must be proud."

"I am finding it difficult to tell you my story, Monsieur Pichon. You keep interrupting."

The secretary pretends to lock his lips with an invisible key.

"My mother is the daughter of a Rousseau de Souvigny, who, at the time of her marriage to my father, was an even more senior officer in the Louisbourg garrison than my father was."

"Your family on both sides is military through and through."

Marie-Louise lets him see her grimace. "That is just it."

"What is it?" the secretary asks.

"Are you married, Monsieur Secretary?"

Marie-Louise watches him lean back and sees his eyes go wary. She did not think it was a prying question. If it is, what secrets does this man have?

"I was," Thomas Pichon says, glancing around.

"I'm sorry," she says, placing a hand upon his sleeve. "I should not have asked you that. It does not matter."

"I would not think so." His eyes have narrowed. "Why, Mademoiselle, am I here?"

Marie-Louise has to get it out fast. "Monsieur Secretary, my father died a year ago."

"I am sorry to—"

"And my mother, fearing penury on the small pension she receives, is forcing me to marry. Against my wishes."

She can see she has rekindled the secretary's interest with that. Though the expression on his face is hard to read.

"She wants me to wed an ancient military officer in the garrison at Louisbourg," Marie-Louise continues, lifting her voice so she can be heard above the squeal of some sailor's violin farther along on the deck. "I thought you, a man of influence, might be able to help me. To prevent an injustice."

———

Thomas hopes he keeps his tinge of disappointment to himself. He had imagined this young woman had been threatened by someone on the ship with lusty loins. Thomas was to be her confidante, her assisting knight. He would make the complaint on her behalf. Perhaps begin the investigation. Eventually see that a punishment was meted out.

But no, it is nothing of the kind. He has been summoned to learn that Mademoiselle is but the latest daughter to be forced into a marriage she does not want. Does she not realize her predicament is old as time itself? In her case, she is well past twelve, the age at which the Church sanctions marrying off a girl with the parents' consent. Does she not know that boys also suffer under their parents' control? It is how it is, which makes it hard for him to feign as much sympathy as she clearly wants.

"Well," she says, holding out two waiting hands, "will you? Help me?"

"I'm not a priest," he says with a small shrug.

Mademoiselle frowns. "What does that mean?"

"Marriages fall under the Church."

"Oh, surely you know better than that."

Thomas shows her raised eyebrows.

"You have influence," she says. "Or should have. You are the man closest to the governor."

Thomas hunches his shoulders with modesty. His right hand comes to his chin.

With the education she has received, of which she is so clearly proud, has she not learned that parents control their children until the females reach twenty-five and the males thirty? They may not be slaves, but they are pawns in the matrimonial game. Unless they take themselves clear off the board, the way he did as a boy, getting away from what his parents had planned for him. "Let me think," Thomas says.

"I have grown up in a military family, Monsieur Secretary. I know all officers require the commandant's permission to marry. You could speak to the comte de Raymond. You could make him understand."

"And what is that?"

"That the man my mother insists I marry I have no affection for. None. He is dull, very dull—"

"Oh, Mademoiselle, if dullness were an impediment, few would ever wed."

"This is not a joke. The man is ancient, more than twice my age."

Thomas is able to rein in the smile that wants to appear. His one and only wife was considerably more than twice his age, and neither he nor she complained. Not about that. The union was to their mutual advantage. Does this smart young woman not realize how foolish she sounds? Our lives, and the marriages that come along, are not novels to be imagined.

"Please excuse me, Mademoiselle." Thomas covers his mouth to hide a smile. Then he takes away the covering hand. "I do admire your youth."

The young woman places a hand on a hip. Anger colours her face. "What of my youth?"

"How old are you?"

"Nineteen."

"And the man whom your mother wishes to be your groom, the military officer?"

"At least forty-five. Nearly in the grave."

Thomas fears he will mock her openly if she does not stop. Does she not know that he just passed fifty-one? He looks out to sea. The darkening sky is coming closer all the time. It is a heavy sea and the swells are lengthening. Maybe the captain is right: Maybe this change of wind and weather really is his fault.

"I could," he says, when he turns back to Mademoiselle Chassin de Thierry, "I could ask the comte."

Her face is alight. "Would you?"

"I would."

"Today?"

Thomas studies her face. Hope and fear rise and fall in her eyes. How sadly sweet it is to see such an expectation of happiness. Such naïveté. Is she not life itself?

Which to Thomas's surprise brings to mind the godson who carries his name and lives in London. He has not seen petit Thomas in years and is unlikely to ever see him again, which makes the sudden thought of him more than a little strange. He would have thought his interest and affection for the boy would have dimmed with time and distance, yet it seems not. Why is that?

"Are you all right?" Mademoiselle Chassin de Thierry asks.

Thomas tries to focus on her face but then shakes that focus away. He takes firm hold of the rail.

That time in the Cross Bath ... with Hélène ... it was not to fuck but to conceive. The boy, her son, petit Tommy, he is Thomas's, not Gallatin's.

"Monsieur Secretary? What is it?"

Thomas holds up a hand to shut out the voice.

Oh, he has been dull and thick. For that also explains why Hélène acted the way she did the day he left. She was trying to tell him the truth. Oh God. Thomas closes his eyes and gives his head a shake.

"You still there?"

Thomas feels a touch upon his sleeve. He blinks back open to see a young woman standing before him on the deck. There is concern upon her face.

"I am sorry, my dear," he says. "I … I lost myself." And yet he cannot help but beam. A son. Far away and out of sight, but his nonetheless. And with Hélène.

"You were seized," the woman announces triumphantly. "I have an aunt who does the same thing."

"No. No, I was not." Thomas shakes his head and gives Mademoiselle a smile. "Something occurred to me is all. Listen— Where were we?"

"You promised to intervene with the comte."

"To *speak* with him, which is different. Yes, I shall, but not to-day. Our sessions are over and I would not raise it at the captain's table."

"Of course not."

"But when the time is right, I will pick my spot."

Marie-Louise Chassin de Thierry looks as if she might burst. But then a serious expression returns. "Montalembert," she says.

"Excuse me?"

"You need to know the officer's name. The one from whom the comte will be withholding his permission to wed. It is Pierre Montalembert de Cers."

"Montalembert. A pretty name. I shall remember that."

"Thank you, Monsieur Secretary. You are a good man."

And a father, Thomas smiles back secretly.

———

The next week is as turbulent upon the waves as the first two were not. The winds come only from the west and they come very hard. Most days are gales, bringing a rain that stings. No one needs to ask the pilot what the change in the weather means. It means the ship is doing well not to lose ground. Not to be blown back to Europe. The tacks north and south are long and they're hard. The deck is wet all the time, slippery as ice. Thomas has heard of a half dozen sailors who have been injured, slipping on wet wood or tumbling from the rigging above.

As for the passengers, they are warned to stay below, except for coming to the quarterdeck for meals, or in Thomas's and

Surlaville's cases, to meet with the comte de Raymond. When the passengers do go up on deck they seek handholds wherever they can. Ropes, crates, the pump near the mast, and of course the rails. When it is especially bad, the passengers choose to stay where they are. Bad as the air already is, it gets worse. The seawater that comes aboard finds its way below-decks and spreads the animal droppings wherever it goes.

Despite the foul stench, it is an easy choice to stay below. Better to pinch one's nose or sprinkle ample sweet-smelling water on one's clothes than to go up top and risk one's life. Besides, with the *Heureux* tossing the way it is, no one has any desire to go to the wardroom for meals. Neither Thomas nor Surlaville has yet vomited, but Mademoiselle and the two Récollets have each spent time at the bucket, a bucket that does not get emptied but once a day.

The first time Marie-Louise is sick, Thomas keeps his distance. But the second time he cannot. He simply has to cover her with a blanket, to stop her shivering. Then he rubs her back as well. He can see Surlaville disapproves, but the Récollets do not. Maybe they are too ill themselves to care.

Mademoiselle thanks Thomas each time he helps her back into her small room. And each time she worries that she has ruined yet more of her clothes. No, Thomas always assures her, they will come clean, though he doubts some ever will. Only once so far has she asked him if he has yet spoken to the comte. Thomas shook his head and she let it drop. She appears to understand that the weather is making for a delay.

The week after is marginally better. Yet the contrary winds are still strong. The wood and ropes of the ship still creak and moan. The ocean becomes a surface of deep troughs, into which the *Heureux* plunges then fights its way back up. Though at least the rain is not as hard, nor as frequent. One day – Thomas has lost complete track of the days of the week – the sun actually comes out. All the passengers are up on deck when he comes out of his two-hour morning session with the commandant. Surlaville is waiting to go right in, and the two Récollets have some colour in their cheeks as they strut around, hands clasped in front of them. Mademoiselle Chassin de Thierry is following close behind the missionaries.

"Any news?" she whispers as she passes by. Thomas sees expectation is huge in her eyes.

"No, not yet."

Mademoiselle gives him a sharp look. He nods that he understands her concern. "Soon," he mouths, which brings a disappointed pout from her in return.

He does not want to tell her that he did in fact broach the subject with the comte de Raymond that very morning. It was, or so it seemed, a propitious moment. The commandant was going on about the poor quality of the Louisbourg garrison. How its officers were the ones to blame. They needed stiffening, a rigour they clearly lacked. Which the comte and the new major de place Surlaville were going to instill and show by their own example. So Thomas spoke up, offering that he had heard one of those Louisbourg officers needed to be taught a particular lesson.

"A lesson? What officer is that?" Raymond's brow was deeply knit.

"Montalembert. I hear he wants to marry a girl less than half his age."

"Who doesn't?" the commandant said, with an actual laugh. It was like a caw from a crow. "Where did you hear that, Pichon?"

"I'm not sure, Commandant. It must be in one of the reports."

"We don't recall. But in any case, there's no need to meddle with that. There are enough more important matters to take up our time. Here," he said, handing Thomas a new sheath of papers, "let's go over the troop roles again. We need to grasp the degree to which desertion is a problem."

Thomas cannot see how he will ever bring the subject of Montalembert up again. It is a lost cause. The problem is, how can he break that to Mademoiselle?

———

Nearly six weeks now the ship has been at sea. Where exactly they are in terms of longitude Thomas knows no one can tell with certainty. But he was encouraged to hear from Raymond that the captain thinks they are nearing the Grand Banks. Apparently some sea birds were spotted late yesterday. And the sails of two or three distant ships. Fishing boats is the guess. When Thomas goes to the rail to verify the rumours, he spies nothing but rolling troughs of grey. But then he is not at the top of any of the masts, nor does he have a telescope.

He does, however, agree the weather has changed. He overheard a sailor this morning describe the breeze as fresh. That is certainly how it feels. "Light air and variable" was how a midshipman put it in another conversation. That too sounds good to Thomas. He doubts he will ever fully grasp all the nuances of the language the men at sea use to describe their world. But then he has no need. He is a man of the land, of the quill. He wants nothing more than to see the end of this voyage.

"Sails!" comes the shout from high up above.

Thomas finds the sailor in the crow's nest and follows where his arm points. Sure enough he does see something this time. A sail. No, two. And there is a flock of gulls wheeling over the ocean in between here and there. The *Heureux* truly must be on the edge of the banks.

———

"Weakness," mutters Marie-Louise as she comes out on the deck into the sun. To her surprise, it is a pleasant breeze. She notices a couple of sailors have lines over the side, and there are already a few fish flopping in the wicker basket at their feet. So it is true, she says to herself. There is the proof. They really are on the banks. Fresh fish will be a great change for everyone, especially the poor sailors who have dined on their hardtack and salted meats for nearly seven weeks.

The lightening of her mood, however, does not last long. She is too deeply frustrated. Monsieur Pichon promised he would intervene with his superior to have her would-be aged husband's permission to marry her declined. Yet he has not. It is always "soon." Well, she is running out of soon. Soon will soon be too late. The ship will be in port. No date for the wedding has been set, as far as she knows, but the opportunity to convince Raymond of its sheer folly is slipping away.

"Weakness," she whispers to herself yet again. That must be what it is. Despite his assurances, the secretary must be too afraid of jeopardizing his own position by pleading her case. If it is to be done – and because it is her life, it is to be done – apparently she will have to do it herself. It makes her shake her head.

There is a great boom, which shakes the ship. She sees the puff of smoke rise up from the port side. The sea birds who were on the water are alarmed and take flight.

"What is it?" she asks the closest sailor, he with the skin of an African.

"A bit of fun," he says. "Time for the baptisms."

"The what?"

"That's right." The sailor is grinning like he has just been made a knight. "Even you."

————

Thomas is found up as close to the bow as he can get. He is found by a sailor wearing a grotesque mask and an unruly wig that lwas once the floppy head of a mop. He also has a staff in one hand. The fellow pantomimes an invitation, but Thomas knows it is no invitation. It is an order he cannot refuse.

He had hoped he might be able to go unobserved. He would prefer to miss the ceremony. But no, the ship is too small to hide away. He will have to play along. A few days ago the comte warned him and Surlaville, the two of them together at the same time, that when they reached the Grand Banks there would be a custom they would have to endure. According to the commandant, something similar happens at other "crossing points" around the globe, like the Equator, the Tropics and the Dardanelles. When it is someone's first time across, he has to sit upon a pole balanced over a barrel filled with seawater. He has to give a few coins to the crew, or else they dump him into the barrel.

"You too, Commandant?" Thomas asked before he realized what he was saying.

It drew a look, well, two looks. One from Raymond and another from Surlaville. Thomas shrugged an apology. No, the comte would not be placed upon a pole above a barrel.

"Because you want to hide," says the young face beneath the mop-top, "you go first."

"No need to push," Thomas says.

———

Marie-Louise is at the end of the line of four, right behind Surlaville. In front of him are the two Récollets. There are at least five dozen sailors crowding close, close enough that the scent of the crowd is filling her nostrils. The smell of wine, undiluted, thickens the air. However much drink has been consumed, it is making the sailors bold. They are not shy about giving the passengers an occasional shove or tug.

Her father told her about times like this. Not the *this* of a mock baptism at sea, but the *this* of those on the lower rungs getting a chance to kick the ladder over once in a while. It is a vent that is best allowed, though only once in a long while.

No doubt her father was right, but that does not mean it has to be her out on the wobbly pole the way the secretary is now. She does not want to look as bewildered as Thomas Pichon does. That pole could turn on her, and she has on her last decent dress.

"Is there a way for me to avoid that?" she asks the sailor closest to her. His face looks kindly enough, though she can see by his eyes that he too has had quite a lot to drink.

"Indeed there is."

"Does it involve me giving you a coin?"

"You guessed it." The sailor holds out his hand.

"But I don't have any with me."

"Pity."

"That's right. Pity, lady," chimes in another sailor listening in. "No tribute? Into the font."

Marie-Louise searches for someone to help. "Major de place Surlaville," she says, reaching to tap his shoulder.

———

Thomas does not understand. He slipped one of the sailors a coin before two others strong-armed him out onto the pole. The soles of his shoes are now well into the water of the barrel and he has his two hands firmly clasped around the pole. He can feel its stickiness. Spruce or some other type of gum. The traces of where he is sitting will be all over the seat of his pants. From time to time, as the ship sways, he feels the water in the barrel lap onto his socks.

The only thing he can think of is that the coin he gave was kept by that sailor for himself. The others do not know about it.

"Might I pay a tribute," Thomas says in a loud voice, "to avoid this rough baptism?"

That draws huzzas from the sailors pressing close. "Indeed" and "Pay up," he hears. He lifts his right hand off the pole, adjusting his balance point. One shoe goes in the water up to his ankle. Steady again, he wiggles two fingers into the right pocket of his breeches. They find two coins. Out they slowly come.

"Here you go." He tosses his payment in the air, quickly grabbing hold of the pole again.

"Paid up," a voice calls out.

Thomas slides over to the barrel's edge. Four strong arms lift him up and then down onto the deck.

———

It is when Surlaville says for the second time that he requires neither the coin back nor any further thanks – it is a question of honour to help a lady such as herself – that Marie-Louise realizes this might just be the opportunity she has been waiting for. If the secretary has been too overawed to ask the commandant on her behalf, perhaps this senior military officer will serve that purpose instead.

"Monsieur major de place," she says the instant they are away from the throng around the barrel, who are in high spirits now that the first Récollet is out above the water.

"Yes, Mademoiselle."

"I have a favour to ask."

"It would be my pleasure."

Marie-Louise takes a breath. "There is an officer in the Louisbourg garrison whom my mother has—"

Surlaville raises a hand. "Ah, I am sorry. Is this about a marriage that is arranged? Involving one Montalembert?"

Marie-Louise leans back. Her eyes go wide.

"Secretary Pichon spoke to me about this a couple of weeks ago, after the commandant gave his opinion. No, it is not a matter I or anyone else will involve ourselves in."

Marie-Louise is speechless.

"If there is nothing else." Surlaville waits, rising on the balls of his feet. "Good day, Mademoiselle."

Marie-Louise can only stand and watch the major stride away.

———

There comes a stillness to the sound and motion of the ship that rouses Thomas from his bunk. He hasn't been able to sleep for at least an hour, so the change in the motion – no swaying or rocking now at all – is odd. As is the absence of the grinding of the rudder tiller. Since he is already awake, he might as well go up top and see what is going on.

Down from his bunk he climbs, carefully avoiding stepping where he imagines in the darkness Surlaville's shoulder or leg might be on the bunk below. Safely on the floor, in the dim light he glimpses the missionaries nearby. One has a gaping mouth, the other is curled like a child.

He sees the door to Mademoiselle's small space is pulled tightly shut. Of course it is, but he wonders if she might be awake.

Thomas knows that she found out that she is not going to get any help from anyone on this ship to alter her fate, a marriage to a man she detests but who brings advantages to the family. At least she gave Thomas a half-hearted thanks for trying to help.

"Though it does mean," she concluded, "that my life is over."

"Hardly," he replied, but she would not let him say any more.

Since then she has chosen mostly silence in her dealings, including with him when they are side-by-side at the captain's table. Thomas would like to get through to her before they reach port, if she will let them have a conversation. He would tell her to concentrate on what is positive. That her lot in life remains well above so many others'. That she is fortunate to be marrying someone with a good rank. And, perhaps, he might even tell her that marriage is simply an arrangement the Church insists upon. It is not a physical cloister that actually locks her in. Yes, it may be complicated, but she should still be able to have a true lover if that is what she wants. If she doubts him, he could tell her about certain times in his own life. Those times were not perfect, but they were better than bad. Such a talk, however, is not for right now. Now he has to go up on deck to see what is going on to make the ship so still.

He advances through the dark, arms reaching out blindly in front of him to lead the way. At last he finds the first of the narrow staircases that lead out of the hold.

At the top Thomas pushes up the hatch that gives on to the deck. In the east he sees a hint of lightening of the sky. Dawn must not be far off. The deck itself is aglow from the floor boards up. There are a half dozen lanterns and a great many sailors milling about. A few are running, others are lifting and moving things around like Thomas has not seen before. Some are tying down cases, bales and the large coils of rope. Up in the rigging he can make out rows of men starting to take down the sails. What is going on? Everyone's face is fierce, as if in anger. Is the ship under attack?

"What is it?" Thomas asks.

No one answers because no one hears. There is a hum of hurried talk and the shouts of the officers above the drone. No one has taken any notice of him. So Thomas grabs a sailor rushing by.

"What is it?"

The man shakes his head and pushes past. Then he halts and waves vaguely above the rail. "Look! Just look!" The sailor hurries away.

Thomas does as he is told. He goes to the rail and leans out. But there is nothing, nothing he can see. It is simply the end of night. The sky is lightening along the horizon to the east. He sees no enemy ship, no ship at all. Nor any iceberg, which he knows is sometimes a threat. It is only the start of the peep of day.

He swings his gaze back to the swirl of activity all over the deck. There has to be something he missed. Once more he peers out over the water, scanning the horizon, far right to far left.

"Oh."

Looking directly ahead, through the web of masts and rigging to where the bow of the ship points, he sees what the sailor must have been waving at. There is a ridge, an almost purple dark that is different from the rest of the night sky. It reminds Thomas of a bank of fog, only it is apparent it is no idle cloud of mist. It is moving, it is coming fast toward the ship. And below it, he can see now, the surface of the water is trembling. It is some kind of great wind, a dark wind as foreboding as any Thomas has ever seen.

"Here! Over here."

Thomas turns round, toward the centre of the ship. There is a man, in nightclothes, waving like a windmill. The face beneath the cap, the voice as well, they are vaguely familiar.

"Now, Pichon, now! We need a hand."

To hear his name makes Thomas take two steps in the man's direction.

"Monsieur le Commandant," Thomas says. He has never before seen the comte in a state of undress.

"Come. Hurry now."

"What do you want?" Thomas yells.

"Just come."

"But there's a wind, a storm." Thomas points to where the dark ridge is churning toward the ship. He cannot believe how much closer it now is. It is nearly upon them. He feels his body want to crouch.

"Now, Pichon! We need to pack the papers and maps. They must be—"

A force of wind, such as Thomas has never felt before sends him to his knees, then flattens him spread-eagle on the deck trying to grasp the smooth boards that have no grip. The ship lurches, tipping like God himself is playing with it. Raymond is lifted up off the deck and seems to fly. His cap is gone and his nightshirt rides up to his waist. But then the airborne comte is sent against the pump beside the mast. His eyes close as he slumps to the deck. He is sprawled where he falls, dead to the chaos all round.

Thomas feels the entire ship shake and quiver. The wind is swirling in no way he has ever seen or felt before. It is coming from all compass points at the same time. The masts and booms, the ropes and lines, everything is crying out. He hears cracks coming from wood somewhere. Then there are shouts. Thomas glances up. God forbid, there are still men aloft. They are hanging on for dear life. How will they ever get down?

The roar of the storm fills his ears. It is impossible to think.

From sloping steeply up the deck is now sloping down. The sprawled, unmoving commandant comes back into Thomas's sightline. He starts to claw at the planking, staying out of the wind, pulling himself forward to where the comte lies. There must be something he can do. Cradle the man until he comes round. Or, if he is expiring, comfort him as best he can. Could that be? Raymond, to whom Thomas's career is attached, could he perish just like that?

Thomas momentarily closes his eyes. This is not the time for such a thought. He has to go to the commandant. Though not a man he has much affection for, he is a man nonetheless. Thomas goes back to his crawl, like a salamander.

The ship tosses again, up the other way, and then tips farther still. Thomas cannot maintain his hold if it keeps up. He rubs and presses his fingers to the boards. Another moment and he will slide down, into the rail or over top and out to sea. The waves are a seething cauldron, but of cold not boiling water. He would not last a minute.

"*Pater Noster*," comes off Thomas's lips, "*qui es in caelis—*"

The ship suddenly rights itself, then begins a slow tilt the other way. Thomas stops the prayer that has come up from somewhere deep within him. He has not said the words since he was a boy, but they cannot hurt. Words are all he has against the onslaught of wind and toss of waves.

Suddenly, sheets of rain descend. They look like curtains and feel like nails. Thomas stares numbly at the water dancing on the decking. Though the rain is chilled his hands feel hot. Thomas lifts each hand in turn. He has splinters in most fingers, so hard was he grasping to stay where he was on the deck.

He hears a shout, then another. Up he looks. One of the sailors is flying through the air. He is off into the night, out where the sea awaits. The others still aloft look like bugs in a web. All that is keeping them in place are arms or legs crimped over spars or tangled in lines and cords. Thomas watches one struggle to right himself, but when he does, he comes loose. His arms and legs whir as he plummets. His body bounces like baggage on the deck. There he lies, not six feet from where the commandant is either unconscious or dead.

Thomas exhales deeply. "*Pater Noster*," he mutters through clenched teeth. It really has become every man for himself.

His eyes go wide. Every man? What of the woman, the only one aboard this ship? Thomas does not want Mademoiselle to be trapped below. If she has to die, along with him and everyone else, she should at least be out of that damned hold. She is the only one on this ship he truly cares about.

———

It is not easy going down. The waves breaking on the deck, along with the driving rain, are making a freshet down the stairs. The sailors who were sleeping in their hammocks push past him on their desperate way up. No one questions him about the forbidden lantern he picked off a hook up top and is taking belowdecks.

The animals that are still left are crying out in alarm. Their eyes are wild. It is the noise, the tilting of the ship and the water rushing into their cages and pens. The horse's eyes are especially strange. Thomas fears he will either break his rope bonds or break his legs as he kicks against the wooden wall. Thomas hurries past. It would only make it worse to untie the beast. There is nowhere he could go. He would only hurt himself more than he is doing now.

"Wrong way, Pichon." It is Surlaville on his way up, thrusting a boy sailor back.

"Mademoiselle," Thomas says, "and the others. Still below?"

"Too late," says Surlaville. "Save yourself."

Thomas shakes his head. The major squeezes by, a look of contempt on his face.

"Oh," Thomas calls out to the back of the major's legs. "The commandant, he may be dead."

"What!"

"By the pump. At the main mast," Thomas yells, then swings round to continue down.

The water is sloshing ankle-high in the Sainte-Barbe.

"Oh, thank God, Secretary." It is one of the Récollets, the one with the especially gaunt face. He steps toward the flickering light Thomas has brought. "Help me, you must help me get him out of here."

Thomas holds the lantern up and out. The religious who spoke to him retreats to a bunk. He starts to yank on something – a brown-clothed arm. Thomas cannot see a head or face, but it is the other Récollet.

"No!" he hears the unseen face shout. "Punishment comes from God. If this is it, I want to perish here, in my bed."

"Secretary, *you* must speak to him. Help me get him out of this place."

"Not now." Thomas turns his back to the two religious and goes to the door of the partitioned area.

"Mademoiselle," he says, knocking loudly. He grabs hold of the latch. "I am coming in."

The lantern casts its amber glow. He can see her form curled beneath a blanket. Upon the bolster, as the light shifts, is her head. Her blond hair is covered by a maid's cap.

"Marie-Louise," he says softly as he bends down. It is the first time he has spoken her Christian names. Her eyes are open. They are the colour of plums in the lantern light. There are tracks of tears on her cheeks.

Thomas sees her lips move but there are no words he can hear. The Récollets are shouting too loudly on the other side of the wooden wall. And then there's the roar of the winds attacking the ship. "You have to speak up."

"I don't know what to do," she says.

"Yes, I know it is hard. But Marie-Louise, if I might, I am going to put my arms around you. Is that all right?"

She nods.

"I'm going to carry you up on deck. Do you understand?"

"I only have a nightdress on," she says.

"That's all right," he says. "I'll take one of your blankets to wrap around."

"Am I going to die?"

Thomas looks into her troubled eyes. "I hope not."

"I don't mind," Thomas thinks he hears Marie-Louise say as he lowers her inside the large coil of rope up on deck closest to the top of the stairs.

"You don't mind what?"

"Dying."

"Shush, you're a child."

Thomas adjusts her cap. The rain has already soaked her blanket. Her nightdress and skin will be next. But what can he do to help her? There is no shelter. There is nothing to do but to try and outlast the storm. Then they'll start from there.

"Stay here," he says. "I'll be back."

He goes down on all fours as he sees a great wave coming toward the ship. The vessel bends and dips as spray cascades like a waterfall. The ship rolls front and back, left and right. When it bobs back up to near level Thomas rises to see if Marie-Louise is still where she was. She is. She is wet as if she has been for a swim. But there is a fresh expression on her face. It's like she is waking up.

Thomas covers his ears. He has to shut out the wail of the wind so he can think.

Marie-Louise is for the moment safe, as safe as anyone can be in this nightmare. He should likely check on the comte. He could crawl there, he could, before the next wave rocks the ship. He just has to do it holding on, holding on to something secure.

Thomas reaches to grab a stick floating by in the skim of seawater washing over the deck. It's a broken-off fragment of something he does not recognize. If the storm persists, the entire ship will be reduced to that. Flotsam for the sea to play with. He tosses the stick away. Instead, he takes hold of a rope. He can see it is attached to the mainmast thirty feet away. He'll be able to pull himself along, back to where he last saw the commandant.

Halfway to the mast Thomas stops to look up. There are no longer any sailors caught in the rope web. He doubts any got down alive, not in this shrieking wind and not with this toss of ship. But then, maybe they are the lucky ones. Perhaps it is better to be dashed upon the deck or blown out to the waves than to suffer on and on. When his time comes, he hopes it will be quick.

The remains of a smashed crate sweep by. Thomas looks round. He has to be on the look-out for the brace of barrels he saw earlier careening up and down the deck. To be struck by them would mean being crushed.

He sees something coming from the stern but cannot make out what it is. Then he knows. It's a body, face to the deck. He thinks he recognizes the red pants as those of the little fellow, Onions, the cook's helper. The lifeless body shoots across the boards, arms outstretched.

Not far ahead now is the base of the mainmast. Thomas sees the comte is very much alive. He is on his bare knees in his soaked nightshirt. He has his back to Thomas, concentrating on something in front of him.

"Commandant!" yells Thomas from a body length away. The wind is picking up again. He pulls himself closer using the rope. "Comte!"

"Who is there?" Raymond says over his shoulder, unwilling or unable to turn round.

"Pichon!"

"Come."

Thomas pulls himself the final few feet. He keeps one hand on the rope but with the other taps Raymond on the back. "I'm here. What— Oh Seigneur."

He sees what it is, no, who it is. The commandant is attending to Surlaville. The major is stretched out, trembling as though freezing cold. There is a long sliver of snapped wood – perhaps from a shattered spar – protruding from his thigh. The major's eyes are open, but they are staring unblinking at the sky. Around the wooden spear, Surlaville's blue breeches are stained a purplish red.

"What can we do?" Thomas looks to the comte.

Raymond shakes his head.

"Should we not pull it out?"

Raymond gives Thomas a blank look.

"I think we should." And with that Thomas takes hold of the wooden shaft. "Here goes."

Out comes the spear, but at once the seep of blood from the wound becomes a gush. Surlaville's cry is louder than the wind. Then his whole body twitches and his eyes snap shut.

"You killed him," says Raymond.

Thomas kicks off his shoes and unfastens his breeches. He stumbles to step out of his wet pants. They are stuck to his legs.

Surlaville's blood is coming fast.

Thomas's hands are numb and resist, but he is able to peel off his breeches then spread them as long as they can go. They become a bandage he wraps twice around the gushing thigh. The flow of blood appears to stop.

"Misjudged you," Raymond says.

Thomas keeps the pressure on his makeshift tourniquet as he glances at the commandant. Yes, that appears to have been a compliment.

"The surgeon will do better," Thomas says, "unless *he's* dead." That makes him smile. Thomas Pichon is *not* dead, not yet. Though who knows how much longer these winds and waves will go on and how much more damage they will inflict.

He must get back to Marie-Louise. See if she is still there, and if so, how she fares.

———

The wind is light. Pleasant. There are long swells coming from the westward. It is the aftermath, two days after the storm.

Thomas watches as a small boat from a brig comes close enough for one of its number to shout up an offer of assistance. The man, the brig's first officer he explains, says his own vessel is a merchant ship coming from Québec heading for Bordeaux.

Thomas cranes up to look yet again at the havoc over his head. Yes, he can see that even at a fair distance a passing ship would notice that the top of the mizzenmast of the *Heureux* has snapped off.

The first officer comes aboard, up the rope ladder and then over the side. The captain of the *Heureux*, with his arm in a sling, is there to meet him, and tell him that sixteen men were lost and another twenty-one injured, himself included. Thomas is standing close enough to hear. He admires the stone-faced matter-of-fact way the two men talk. They are all about what happens next. It is something he would like to learn.

The officer commiserates with a nod, no more than that. He counters, apologetically, that his ship was fortunate. While the storm was sweeping across the Grand Banks, the brig was still in the St. Lawrence River. Nothing more than a few tangled lines and bruises. Then: "Can we help?"

"A couple of barrels of water and one of hard tack would do that," the captain of the *Heureux* says.

"They are yours," the first officer replies with a salute. "I'll send them over once I am back aboard."

"That should do it. The pilot says he knows where we are. With what canvas we still have we should be able to sail into Louisbourg tomorrow."

———

The land is a line, a blue line stretched long and thin. It hovers between two other blues. Pale sky above, dark sea below. Each pitch of the ship brings the line a little closer. An approaching coast begins to take shape.

The clouds are swirls of cream.

A fully defined coast comes into view, finally green, no longer blue. It looks to be an endless forest rising out of jagged rocks. It is more wilderness than Thomas has ever seen. An endless cover, a woodland vast. No wonder people call it a New World. It is both the promise of a fresh beginning and the threat of the unknown.

Thomas returns to the rail. The last session prior to entering Louisbourg harbour is over. Once again, as he has since the storm, the commandant insisted both Thomas and Surlaville meet with him at the same time. "Our dear cousins," the comte has taken to calling them. Thomas is certain the camaraderie will pass, but he welcomes the generosity of spirit while it lasts. It is so much better than Raymond's usual way of being in the world.

How much closer to the shoreline the ship is now than it was an hour and a half ago when he went into the comte's damaged room in the quarterdeck. Damaged, yes, but not ruined as is the

stinking Sainte-Barbe. There is still ankle-deep seawater coursing around. The passengers have been sleeping in hammocks
between-decks with the sailors since the storm. To be out in the
sun, with its warmth on his back, feels good.

"There it is," Thomas breathes aloud.

On the right as the ship undulates onward he recognizes the
landmarks of Louisbourg that he has seen depicted on many
maps over the past few months. No more than half a league away
is the stone lighthouse on its rocky shore. That means the entrance to the harbour is coming fast. There has been a light there
for thirty years, the only such aid to navigation in all of New
France. Thomas is glad to see it. Once the *Heureux* is safely past
the lighthouse, through the narrow channel between it and the
Island Battery, they will finally be within the anchorage. Fifty
days at sea it has been.

Farther away, Thomas can make out the two spires that dis-
tinguish the *intra muros* of the fortified town. If it were a port in
France the ship were sailing to, or indeed anywhere in the usual
Catholic world, such spires would belong to churches. But not
this place. In curious Louisbourg what pricks the sky are steeples
of two King's buildings, a barracks and a hospital. In fact, from
what Thomas has read, the town has no church at all, only a few
chapels. Furthermore, its residents refuse to pay the tithe. And
will not accept secular priests, only regulars. Thomas is more than
a little intrigued. Can this overseas colony be a place where Reason finally rules? He will soon find out.

A hand presses on Thomas's back. He turns round.

"I thought you would be up here, Monsieur Secretary."

There are flickers of light in Marie-Louise's eyes. Thomas is
pleased to see it. He tenders a formal bow. "Mademoiselle."

They agreed in a short, snatched conversation yesterday close
to their hammocks that it would be inappropriate to continue to
use their Christian names in public conversation.

"The place of your birth, is it not?"

"You know it is."

Thomas holds her gaze. Silently he asks how she is feeling, now that she is so soon to be ashore, on the cusp of a marriage she wishes to avoid.

Mademoiselle shrugs and looks away, toward the lighthouse as the ship angles past. Thomas notices for the first time how little canvas the ship has aloft. Of course, the *Heureux* must creep into the harbour so it can come to anchor without striking any of the many ships and boats already moored there.

"Life is not easy," Thomas says at last, "but it can be done."

"I suppose."

Thomas looks round then decides he does not care who might see. He reaches around Marie-Louise and gives her a quick hug.

"And what of you, Monsieur Pichon? How will you fare in such a small place, so far from the world you know?"

It is Thomas's turn to shrug. She is right, what will he do besides toil with his quill for a vain commandant? More importantly, how long will he have to spend in this overseas colony before he receives his next reward, a rung higher back in France?

"Tell me, Mademoiselle, are there women of my great age in your town?"

Marie-Louise's eyebrows rise. "At your age do men still—" She puts a hand across her mouth.

Thomas exhales and shakes his head. "I am not done yet, my dear."

A few notes
and acknowledgements

The three individuals to whom this book is dedicated deserve a few additional words. Mary Topshee comes first, as she has done since 1970. I could dedicate all of my books to *ma conjointe*, but that would be a bit much. Editor Kate Kennedy is pretty close to my north star when it comes to finding my way through the fictional world I aim to create for Thomas Pichon and friends. Mike Hunter, editor-in-chief of Cape Breton University Press, has believed in the Thomas Pichon project since the manuscript for the first novel landed on his desk back in 2011. Together, we have now put out three novels in four years, leaving only one to go to complete the quartet.

In the interval between the publication of *The Maze* and the finalization of this third novel I gave a number of "History & Fiction" presentations at universities, libraries, museums and community halls around the Maritimes. The subject was primarily the Thomas Pichon project and my transition from historian to novelist. Those talks and the questions and comments from the people who attended helped me clarify what it is that I am aiming to do with these novels. I want to thank the following for their part in organizing those events or for other contributions to advancing the project: Meaghan Beaton, Susan Borgersen, Mark Delaney, Paul Doerr, Wendy Elliott, Margaret Herdman, Beth Keech, Jenna Lahey, Anne Marie Lane Jonah, Jordan LeBlanc, Jackie Logan, Elke Love, Elinor Maher, Elizabeth Mancke, Susan Marchand-Terrio, Maura McKeogh, Dana Mount, Stephanie

Pettigrew, Peter Twohig, Kat Wright Sandy Balcom and Ken Donovan. I fear that list leaves some people out, and for that I apologize.

One of the things I told the audiences at these talks was that although my central character is inspired by an actual historical figure, my Thomas is a fictional character living in a fictional world. Some of what has happened in the first three novels has been guided by what I know to have happened to the historical figure, but a great deal more is simply me exploring a period and the themes that manifest themselves in all historical periods: ambition, longing and betrayal. For instance, I have no idea whether or not the real Thomas Pichon ever went to Bath during the years he lived in England or whether he ever had to deal with highwaymen. No matter, I thought it would be interesting to take my characters on that road trip to open this book, back before the spa town had acquired all of the architectural features it now possesses.

Though most of the women who come into Thomas's life as lovers in these novels are inventions, a few are not. Marguerite, a character in the first two novels, was based on what little is known of that much older wife of the historical Thomas Pichon. Similarly in *Crossings*, both Madame de Beaumont and Mademoiselle de Vins were real people whose relationships with the real Thomas Pichon were fairly close to what I present, though I set those events more than twenty years earlier than they occurred in history.

Finally, I'd like to acknowledge some of the authors whose writings on London, Bath, Paris and the French bureaucracy were helpful to me in researching and writing this book: Barry Cunliffe, James Sharpe, John C. Rule and Ben S. Trotter. Gilles Proulx, a former Parks Canada historian, deserves an extra special mention because I relied heavily on his *Between France and New France* for the final chapter. Merci, Gilles.

Previous Books by A.J.B. Johnston

NOVELS

The Maze, A Thomas Pichon Novel. Sydney: Cape Breton University Press, 2014.

Thomas, A Secret Life. Sydney: Cape Breton University Press, 2012.

HISTORY

Grand Pré, Landscape for the World. Halifax: Nimbus Publishing, 2015.

Louisbourg, Past, Present, Future. Halifax: Nimbus Publishing, 2013.

N'in Na L'nu: The Mi'kmaq of Prince Edward Island. Charlottetown: Acorn Books, 2013.

Endgame 1758. The Promise, The Glory and The Despair of Louisbourg's Final Decade. Lincoln, Nebraska and Sydney, NS: University of Nebraska Press and Cape Breton Univeristy Press, 2007.

1758 : La finale. Promesses, Splendeur et Désolation dans la dernière décennie de Louisbourg. Québec : Presses de l'Université Laval, 2011.

Storied Shores: St. Peter's, Isle Madame and Chapel Island in the 17th and 18th Centuries. Sydney: Cape Breton University Press, 2004.

Grand-Pré, Heart of Acadie. Halifax: Nimbus Publishing, 2004. Co-authored with W. P. Kerr. French edition: *Grand-Pré, Coeur de l'Acadie.* Halifax: Nimbus Publishing, 2004. traduit par Sylvain Filion.

Control & Order: The Evolution of French Colonial Louisbourg, 1713-1758. East Lansing: Michigan State University Press, 2001.

Life and Religion at Louisbourg, 1713-1758. Montreal & Kingston: McGill-Queen's University Press, 1996. [Previously *Religion in Life at Louisbourg, 1713-1758*, 1984] French edition: *La religion dans la vie à Louisbourg (1713-1758).* Ottawa: Environnement Canada, 1988.

Tracks Across the Landscape: A Commemorative History of the S&L Railway. Sydney: UCCB Press, 1995. Co-Authored with Brian Campbell.

Louisbourg, An 18th-Century Town. Halifax: Nimbus Publishing, 2004 [1991]. Co- authored with Kenneth Donovan, B.A. Balcom and Alex Storm.

Louisbourg: The Phoenix Fortress. Halifax: Nimbus Publishing, 1997 [1990]. Photographs by Chris Reardon. French edition: *Louisbourg, Reflets d'une époque.* Traduit par Robert Pichette. Halifax: Nimbus Publishing, 1997.

From the Hearth: Recipes from the World of 18th-Century Louisbourg. Sydney: Cape Breton University Press, 1986. Co-authored with Hope Dunton.

The Summer of 1744, A Portrait of Life in 18th-Century Louisbourg. Ottawa: Parks Canada, 2002 [1983] / *L'Été de 1744: La vie quotidienne à Louisbourg au XVIIIe siècle.* Ottawa: Parcs Canada, 202 [1983].

Defending Halifax: Ordnance, 1825-1906. Ottawa: Parks Canada, 1981 / *La défense de Halifax: artillerie, 1825-1906.* Ottawa: Parcs Canada, 1981.

About the Author

A. J. B. Johnston has published fourteen books and hundreds of articles over a thirty-plus years career studying and writing about 18th-century French colonial history in Acadia. In recognition of his prolific career as a historian and writer, John was invested by France with the title

Photo by Mary Topshee

Chevalier of the Ordre des Palmes Académiques (Order of Academic Palms). Johnston has now turned his hand to fiction.

Long inspired to explore the world of Thomas Pichon (1700-1781), in his first novel, *Thomas, A Secret Life* (CBU Press, 2012), Johnston applied his considerable sense of 18th-century French history to imagine young Pichon's early life in Normandy and Paris. For *The Maze* and *Crossings*, he did extensive research on 18th-century London and Bath.

Twitter: @AJBJohnston Facebook: A J B Johnston, Writer

http://www.ajbjohnston.com